Dark Starlight

Archaic Races Book 1

Hannah West

ISBN: 1986055582
ISBN-13: 978-1986055581

DEDICATION

In memory of Grandma Julie.

Hot sadness pressing down,
Cracking fragile skin,
Dark,
Sunlight seeps in.

Summer days,
Teatime haze,
Wild grass and pretty weeds,
Framing fields and skirting trees.

Happy sigh.

ACKNOWLEDGMENTS

Thank you, Mark for believing in me.
Thank you, Imran Siddiq for another amazing book cover.
He's got this weird ability to reach inside my brain and
pluck out exactly what I want.
A massive thank you to Anne Loshuk, Nichola Miles and
Gemma Ballard and Lauren West for being my beta
readers. It's a dirty job and I'm eternally grateful.
And an enormous thank you to my readers. You're the
reason I keep writing, and I'll love you forever.

PROLOGUE

Doctor Minting pulls a chunk of papers from a black folder and spreads them out on top of his desk. His eyebrows pinch together with each piece of paper he puts down. I'm too short to see what's on them, so I sit tall in my seat beside Mummy to see if I can find out what's making him frown. My eyebrows shoot up when I see my pictures.

'These are some of the most concerning articles,' Doctor Minting says.

Mummy leans forward to get a closer look. She studies my pictures, some in paint and others in crayon.

'I don't see what's concerning about them,' she admits.

Doctor Minting plucks a pen from the front pocket of his jacket and uses it to point at one of the pictures.

'Black is a common indicator of a disturbed child,' he says tracing his pen over the black paint on my picture. 'And Primrose uses it in every creative project depicting herself.'

Mummy and Doctor Minting look at me and I stare back. I feel like I've done something wrong but I'm not sure what. Mummy knows about my darkness, though she's just like everyone else in that she can't see it like I can. She calls it my imaginary friend.

'See how she uses black to halo herself in each picture?' Doctor Minting says. 'It's why Primrose's school suggested this consultation. Mental health is very important and we're introducing a scheme to recognise symptoms early on. Has Primrose demonstrated any concerning behaviour?'

Mummy's gaze slides to me then back to Doctor Minting. 'What do you consider concerning?'

'Well, does she tell you what the black represents in the pictures?'

'It's her imaginary friend,' Mummy says.

'This doesn't concern you?' the doctor asks.

'Why would my five-year-old daughter having an imaginary friend concern me?'

Doctor Minting's eyebrows pinch closer together. 'Her imaginary friend is a dark presence around her.'

'Well, when you put it like that, it does sound...odd,' Mummy murmurs and slides another glance my way. 'Primrose, why don't you go play with the toys in the corner,' she suggests.

I push from the seat beside her and go sit at the little table in the corner. There's a box of toys and I fish through it until I find two dolls. I pretend the boy one is Drew and the girl one is me, and we're going to the park. Behind me I hear Mummy and Doctor Minting talking. I pretend I can't hear them, though I'm listening to every word they say. Grown-ups are stupid like that. They think because I'm sitting in the corner with toys that I can't hear them.

'Is Primrose's father around?' Doctor Minting asks.

I hold my breath at his question, knowing the subject of my daddy is a forbidden topic at home. He hurt

Mummy really bad before I was born and she doesn't like to talk about him even to me.

'No,' Mummy answers, tone sharp.

'Does Primrose ever exhibit signs of aggression?' the doctor says.

'No,' Mummy answers again. 'Why, have the school said something?'

'No, no, nothing like that,' the doctor answers. 'They're simply concerned about the images she produces during creative play.'

'I can't believe she's being made to endure this,' Mummy hisses. 'Primrose is a happy, thoughtful little girl. She's never been aggressive towards other children and loves going to school. The fact she uses black in her artwork isn't grounds to start finger-pointing, Doctor Minting.'

'I'm not here to point fingers, Ms-'

'Then what are you here for?' Mummy demands.

I've never heard Mummy so angry, and I turn to look her way. She's standing, hands pressed to the top of the desk as she leans closer to the doctor. I've never seen her act this way, and I feel like it's because Doctor Minting mentioned Daddy. Mummy always gets upset when people mention him, but never this bad.

'I just want to make sure there's nothing untoward with your daughter's health,' he answers. 'Like I said, her use of black in paintings is-'

'Untoward?' Mummy cuts in.

'Yes,' Doctor Minting answers.

'I think it's creative,' she counters.

Doctor Minting blinks, like he didn't expect Mummy to say that.

'Ms-'

'No,' Mummy says and looks over at me. 'Primrose, it's time to go.'

I put the dolls back in the box and push from the little table. Mummy takes my hand when I reach her side and guides me to the exit. She turns as she opens the door and looks at Doctor Minting.

'Thank you for your time, Doctor,' she growls then leads me out.

Mummy buckles me into my car seat then sits behind the wheel and stares out the windshield. She's breathing deep and I hear her sniff.

'Mummy, are you okay?'

She sniffs again and wipes her face, before turning to look at me. Her eyes are red and her makeup smeared. Dark smoke rises from my skin in response and wraps me in a comforting hug. It always hugs me when Mummy is sad. I look at it shimmering like a glittery shadow around my skin, and remember the pictures Doctor Minting laid out on his desk. We had to see him because I draw the darkness around me in pictures, even though others can't see it.

'I'm okay, sweetheart,' Mummy says.

'Are you sad because of me?'

'No, baby,' she says. 'Why would you ask that?'

'Black is my favourite colour and Doctor Minting said that is a bad thing.'

Mummy shakes her head. 'It isn't a bad thing, Primrose. You can like whatever colour you want, okay?'

I bite my lip then ask, 'Why did he ask about Daddy?'

Sad lines crease Mummy's face and her eyes fill with tears. She blinks a few times then paints a pretend smile on her face. I hate that smile. Mummy hides behind it when she doesn't want to tell the truth.

'He shouldn't have asked about your dad, Primrose,' she murmurs.

'So, you're upset about him asking about Daddy and not because I'm not normal?'

'You *are* normal,' she says, sounding a little angry.

'But, my darkness-'

'It's not real, Primrose,' Mum snaps.

My eyes go wide and I press into my seat. Mummy sighs, shoulders sagging. I bite my bottom lip and try not to look at the darkness flaring around me in response to her anger. It's like a dark, glittery cloud that curls around my body. Sometimes it reaches out to touch people and sometimes I can't see it because it sinks beneath my skin, but it's always there. Mummy says it isn't real, but I feel it, so how can it be pretend?

'I'm sorry, Primrose,' she breathes.

'Okay,' I whisper.

But it's not okay.

I turn my face to look out of the window. I hear Mummy sigh before starting the car and pulling out into traffic. Mummy doesn't believe me when I tell her my darkness is real, and I think it's because it scares her. I think it scares my teacher at school too, which it why we had to come to see Doctor Minting. Nobody ever believes that my darkness is real and it's never been a problem, but maybe I should stop telling people about it. If I don't talk about it and I don't paint it in my pictures, Mummy won't get angry and won't be sad.

CHAPTER 1

A raindrop splashes the top of the coffin, followed by another and another. They come faster and faster, until water is sluicing into the grave below. I feel like those raindrops, lost in the cold earth beneath my feet. The vicar's voice drones on, reciting lines meant to bring comfort but serve as a reminder for what I've lost. I step from beneath the umbrella I'm sharing with Aunt Katherine. Rain drenches me in seconds, plastering blonde hair to my scalp and trailing mascara down my cheeks.

I place the rose I've been clutching beside the wreath atop the coffin. Blood smears my palm from the thorny stem, and I blink at the crimson staining my skin. I smooth my hand along the polished wood, thinking of Mum inside it. The ache in my middle inches wider, feeding the dark cloud around me.

A slender hand takes mine from the coffin and I meet Aunt Katherine's gaze. Her cornflower blue eyes, the same shade as Mum's, are bloodshot from crying. Mascara paints her face in bold stripes and her bottom lip quivers. I glance at our joined hands, where my darkness forms a complex pattern, as it weaves its way up Katherine's arm. It opens a doorway to her emotions and my darkness glitters in response. It leaches pain and grief from her,

1

tinged with the love she feels for me. I meet her gaze to find her tears drying and she musters a smile. My darkness has eased her pain and for that I'm grateful.

'Come on, Prim,' Katherine murmurs, tugging me back under her umbrella.

I let her take me to where Uncle David waits with the crowd of mourners. David and Katherine stand me between them, guarding me like sentinels. I release Aunt Katherine's hand and stare at the coffin. The vicar speaks of committing Mum's body to the ground and the coffin lowers. It's hard to breathe and darkness pulses around in prickling flames. Midnight tendrils reach out to the lowering coffin, caressing the polished wood.

'Bye, Mum,' I whisper.

The ebony tendrils slip from the coffin and curl across the grass to me. Darkness fills me up, my flesh stinging against the writhing midnight beneath my skin. I glance down at my arm, expecting the skin to split and shadow to leak out. My darkness feels too much, like it's grown too big for my being. It has been a part of me for as long as I can remember and it's never done this.

Shadow creeps across my vision, the skin around my eyes tingling. The sobbing people around me grow distorted, like I'm underwater, and my heart speeds up. I suck in a breath and step from between my aunt and uncle. Sweat beads on my brow, mingling with the rain on my skin, and I curl my hands into fists. Something is clawing at my insides, like the entity in my middle wants out.

'Prim?' Aunt Katherine calls, concern painting her tone.

I slide the heels from my feet. 'I need to go.'

I turn from the grave and start running. Katherine and David shout my name but I don't stop. The darkness inside me drums an unrelenting rhythm. My skin grows tight, stretching thin, and I push on faster. My bare feet press into sodden earth, as I dodge between graves and find the path leading out from the graveyard.

I break free from the churchyard and sprint down the main road of the village. There's nobody to stop me, everyone still standing by Mum's grave. I burst through the front gate and skirt the side of my cottage, taking the garden path through the archway cut into the hedgerow at the bottom. The rain slows as I enter the meadow pattering to a stop by the time I reach the middle. My dress is drenched and sticks to my body, wild grass and flowers whipping at my bare legs.

I slow to a stop then drop to my knees in the mud, wildflowers brushing my shoulders. Something snaps in my middle, sending a ripple of pain out from my centre. Shadow blasts from me in an agonising wave and I scream in pain. It forms a tornado around me, funnelling upward, trapping me against the mud. I cry out and curl up in the centre of the vortex, body aching.

Minutes pass and the pain lessens, bringing fear in its wake. I don't know what to do. The darkness is a part of me, but I've never been able to control it. It just does what it wants, sometimes reacting in response to my emotions. It has never acted like this, and I don't know how to calm it down.

The midnight tornado grows stronger, rising taller, until all I can see is a circular patch of sky. It goes still and eerily quiet, and I push to my feet. I stare at the sky, blue from where the rain has receded. My hair whips around the stinging skin of my face and my heart pounds against my ribcage. The disc of sky is getting smaller, the funnel closing above. My world goes black and all I can hear is the pounding of my heart. I count ten beats before the darkness slams into me. It forces me to the ground and I lie on my front, pressed against the earth, struggling to breathe. My lungs sting with the need to take a breath, while my head swims with desperation. I close my eyes when I start to feel dizzy, then there's nothing.

Another squirrel climbs the tree swirling up the trunk so fast it makes me smirk.

'Primrose, what on Earth is so funny?' Miss Mantel demands.

I cringe and look to the front of the classroom. She's scowling at me, hands perched on her narrow hips. Fierce grey eyes glare at me over the top of her bifocals. The woman is the bane of my senior education and I dread the next two years in her class.

'Nothing, Miss,' I murmur.

'Then you won't mind continuing from where Trevor left off,' she says.

I glance at the book in my hands and swallow. I was too busy watching the squirrel outside to listen, and don't know where Trevor stopped reading.

'Were you even listening?' Miss Mantel demands, moving until she's standing beside where I'm sitting at my desk.

'I-'

She snatches the book from my hands before I can answer. 'You're not even on the right page, Primrose!' she snarls and I cringe into my seat, skin prickling. 'You-'

Darkness explodes from me in inky ribbons and wraps around Miss Mantel's arm. She sucks in a breath, the book slipping from her fingers, as her eyes go wide. A wave of her frustration hits me, followed quickly by confusion, as she stares down at the book on the floor.

'Miss Mantel?' Isla asks from Miss Mantel's other side.

I meet Isla's gaze and shrug like I don't know what's happening, while disguising my panic. In my head I'm chanting for my darkness to retreat. Please don't do what you did to the man on the beach. Miss Mantel might be prickly, but she doesn't deserve his fate.

The darkness doesn't retreat like I want. It never does. Instead it continues to take heavy pulls of Miss Mantel's emotion, until all I feel from her is a haze of calm and confusion. The inky ribbons uncurl from her arm and join the dark aura now framing my body. Nobody reacts to it, so I pretend it's not there and continue to *stare at the teacher with the rest of the class. I'm good at pretending like this.*

Miss Mantel blinks a few times then bends and retrieves my book from the floor. 'Page thirty-nine, Primrose,' she says in a calm voice and goes back to the front of the class.

I stare after her in surprise for a second, along with my classmates, before thumbing to page thirty-nine and reading from the top. I don't register any of the words I'm speaking, too wrapped up in what just happened. Did my darkness just influence her emotion? I've always been able to feel what others are feeling, as long as my darkness is touching them, but controlling what they're feeling? I refrain from snorting at the notion. I don't control anything. My darkness does whatever the hell it wants and I don't get a say. It's a part of me, and although it isn't sentient in it's own right, it seems to react on instinct, based around my wellbeing. Like with Miss Mantel just then. I was stressed because she was angry and it responded.

Like with the man on the beach that day.

I shudder and block thoughts of that day from my mind, relieved for now Miss Mantel didn't suffer the same fate.

I blink in daylight and cough as I sit up, looking around in confusion. The dark funnel is gone, along with the immense pressure on my chest. I feel bruised all over and dirt cakes my skin. I ignore my shaking legs to push to my feet to look around. The flowers and grass surrounding me are shrivelled and black. I turn a slow circle, to find I'm standing in the centre of a blackened disk in the meadow, dead plant life crunching beneath my feet. The diameter is at least ten metres across and I feel my mouth hanging open.

My soles tingle when I crunch my way from the circle of dead plants. I look behind me, stopping in my tracks when I see the inky footprints I'm leaving in the live grass of the meadow. I lift a foot and bend to see my sole. It's caked in mud but isn't black. I press the same foot to a patch of fresh grass and feel the tingles surge through my sole again. There's a perfect imprint of my foot burned

5

into the grass when I lift it away. I bend to stroke a finger over the footprint. It's dry and crispy, like the flowers inside the circle.

Dead.

It occurs to me that I should feel something, but there's nothing. I just feel hollow inside – numb. I stand still, looking around the familiar sight of the meadow, wondering what to do next. I finger my mud-incrusted dress then start walking, making my way home. I duck back through the hedgerow and follow the path to the backdoor of my cottage. I left my bag in Aunt Katherine's kitchen, for me to pick up on the way to the wake, so I fish the spare key from under the windowsill and let myself in. I trail mud into the cottage but don't burn footprints into the flooring, which is good. I suppose if I could feel anything it would be relief.

I stare at my reflection in the bathroom mirror. My dress is ruined and mud cakes my hair and skin. But it's not what holds my attention. My eyes have always been black, irises almost as dark as the pupils, but now the whites have been swallowed by midnight too. My eyes are like the lightless space between stars, and I stare at them in fascination.

The darkness inside me feels bigger, like it's taking up more space in the universe. It feels immense now; it's power drenching my being, condensing into the wild entity that lives in my middle.

'Prim?'

I turn at the sound of Katherine's voice and shut the bathroom door, sliding the lock into place. I pull off my ruined clothes and turn on the shower. When I turn back to the mirror my eyes have returned to normal. Feeling creeps into my flesh, the numbness fading. I step into the shower before my emotions can return fully, letting the hot water turn my pale skin pink. I take time washing the mud from my hair then switch off the water and grab a towel from the rail.

Maybe it's because I've been different all my life, I can compartmentalise what has happened to me so well. I've learned not to react to the strange things that happen until I'm alone long enough to think them through. Whatever happened in the meadow didn't kill me or anyone else. My eyes turning black is new, but isn't any weirder than the shadow clouding my frame for as long as I can remember. That's not to say I don't feel sick with worry. The image of the dead flowers is clawing at my brain with frantic fingers but I won't - can't - freak out yet. Not until I'm alone long enough to figure it out.

'Primrose,' Katherine sighs as I step from the bathroom wrapped in a towel.

She only uses my full name when she's worried or angry, and her expression is definitely worried. Guilt weaves through me. I lost my mum but Aunt Katherine just buried her sister.

'I'm sorry,' I murmur.

'Don't apologise, Prim,' she says, closing the distance between us to wrap me in a hug. 'It's okay,' she tells me, rubbing my back. 'Everything is going to be okay.'

I rest my head on her shoulder and breathe her familiar scent. The skin on my face tingles where it touches her bare neck, and the taste of her emotion floods my mouth. I pull away so fast I almost get whiplash and stare at her in shock.

'I don't want to get your dress wet,' I blurt at her confused expression.

'Oh, Prim, I'd take a soggy dress to hug you any day,' she tells me.

I force a smile and step around her. 'I should get dressed for the wake.'

'I'll wait downstairs,' she answers. 'The rain has stopped, so we can walk to the village hall together.'

I want to tell Katherine to leave me alone, that bringing up moving in with her and Uncle David every five minutes is driving me crazy. Mum might be gone but this is still my home. Mum left me the cottage in her will and I'm staying put. I bite my tongue to stop from venting, knowing my short temper will cause more damage than good. I remind myself Katherine pesters me because she cares.

CHAPTER 2

I take my coffee outside and sit in the starlight, hugging my cup against the chill as I stare toward the meadow. Out there, behind the hedgerow, is a perfect circle of dead flowers. I remember the crunch of them beneath my feet and ponder what it means. I sip my coffee to thaw the cold dread in my middle. The tingling sensation I get from walking on the grass is the same sensation I got when I hugged Katherine after my shower. I could sense her emotion so strong I could taste it, and it scares me to think of what would've happened if I hadn't let go of her. I think of the dead, crispy flowers and bile snakes up my throat.

I spent the time at Mum's wake trying not to touch anybody, which isn't easy in a village of concerned neighbours. People here are close-knit and extra nosey. To them, I'm a sister, daughter, niece or grandchild, even if we're not related by blood. The community has mothered me to within an inch of my life since Mum died, and it's suffocating despite the thoughtfulness. The constant uninvited hugging at the wake has left me with the taste of sorrow on my tongue and the bitterness of pity at the back of my throat.

As soon as I made it home I took another shower, trying to wash the layers of other people's grief from my skin. I tried to sleep after, but every time I close my eyes all I can see is Mum's coffin lowering into the ground. My eyes are raw from crying and lack of sleep, and my skin prickles with the strength of the darkness inside me. I'm a hot mess with no idea how to fix it.

Awareness prickles down my spine and the hairs on my nape stand up. I look up from the coffee cup in my hands and search the garden. I've never been afraid of the dark because it's a part of me, but I can *feel* someone out there, watching. It's like nothing I've felt before, and I can't see them, but I *know* they're there. I push from my perch on the patio wall and move to where the *feeling* takes me. The sensation of someone being there grows more intense the closer I get to the hedgerow.

I stop just before the archway leading to the meadow. 'I know you're there,' I shout.

Sensation washes over my skin, like a physical caress. I suck in a breath at the foreign feeling and back up a step. The darkness inside me fizzes to life when something presses against it. It feels similar to when Mrs Jacob's cat rubs up against my leg in greeting, except it's not a physical touch. Whatever it is just brushed against my darkness, a part of me that isn't physical, and I'm too shocked to move. My darkness presses back, brushing against the entity in response.

'Knock it off,' I hiss when whatever it is curls around me in an intimate caress.

A deep chuckle sounds from beyond the hedgerow and amethyst light shines through the densely packed leaves. 'You no longer wish to play, Anya?' the voice rumbles.

Holy crap.

I stare at the light through the hedgerow, wondering if this moment is real or if I've finally lost it. It's so long since I slept, and the grief of losing mum could've finally pushed me over the edge. I pinch my arm and frown at the little hurt, before looking back to the light in the hedgerow. Something about it invites me in. I can't explain what it is exactly, just that an unseen part of me wants – needs – to get closer. It's in direct contrast to my brain, which has little red flags of danger waving around in warning.

'Who are you?' I ask, fighting the need to inch closer.

'I'm yours,' the light answers.

'My what?' I ask, losing the battle and creeping closer.

Bah, it's just so enticing. I want to touch it, smell it – taste it. Blaring sirens have joined the little red flags in my brain. I shouldn't get any closer, but I want it more than my next breath.

Another deep chuckle accompanies the sharp pounding that's starting behind my temples. I'm split between the instinct to run and to move closer, and it's making me sweat. My stress level is DEFCON 1 and this guy is teasing me? My infamously short temper flares and I grit my teeth to hold back a retort, angry at the fact I'm still creeping closer. The wildness in my middle is gripped with desperation to meet the owner of the light behind the hedgerow and I can't deny it. Despite my apprehension, I'm sure I want to. All my life I've been an outsider; different from everyone around me, and I'm curious to learn more about the owner of this purple light. I've wished for so long for someone to understand me – to see the secret parts of me.

'I'm your equilibrium,' the light murmurs. 'It's a pleasure to finally find you, Anya.'

I frown at his answer. He speaks as if he knows me when I know nothing of him. There's a familiarity in his tone I don't like and it's keeping me cautious. It's curtailing my desperation for someone to know all of me, by injecting logic into the situation. My darkness can do some pretty freaky things and this guy is calling me his equilibrium – his symmetry? He seems to know more than I do on the subject of my otherness and I don't want to end up like the man on the beach.

I take a deep breath and back up a step. 'I think you're mistaken,' I answer. 'My name isn't Anya and I have no idea what you're talking about.'

The leaves are still too dense to see through the hedgerow and it makes me nervous that I can't see him. I take another step back and straighten my spine, trying not to show my underlying fear.

'Why don't you come through the archway, so I can see you,' I say.

A rumble of amusement sounds through the leaves. 'You're a delightful surprise, Anya.'

That invisible caress curls around me again then, sinks beneath my skin to stroke the entity in my middle. I inhale a sharp breath and back away, indignation flaring through me. Did he–? Did he really just cop a feel? I feel violated in a way I can't describe and I stumble back a few more steps.

'Hey,' I snarl ready to march to the other side of the hedgerow and beat the crap out of him.

'Prim?' Aunt Katherine says from the cottage, snapping my attention to the back door. She's silhouetted in the doorway, light spilling out from the kitchen behind her. 'Are you out here? I can't see you.'

I glance back to the hedgerow but the amethyst light is gone, taking the sensation with it. I huff, a little disappointed but still annoyed and freaked out enough to be glad he's gone. He's bloody lucky he left when he did because I'm fuming.

'I'm here,' I call to Katherine and make my way back to the cottage.

The back of my neck prickles as I reach where Katherine is standing. The hot weight of *his* gaze presses against my back, igniting fresh anger inside me, but I dare not look back. Having Katherine here clouds any curiosity I have about him with fear. I don't know who *he* is and I can't put Katherine in danger.

'What were you doing out there?' Katherine asks when we're back in the kitchen.

I put my coffee cup on the side by the sink and turn to face her. She gives my pyjamas an assessing look then meets my gaze with worried eyes. I can see the speech coming before she even opens her mouth.

'I'm not moving in with you and David,' I say before she has chance to suggest it again.

'Primrose-' she starts but I cut her off.

'I want my key back.'

I go to her keys on the table and start to unwind the key she has to my cottage from the bunch. The encounter in the garden has me freaking out. The last thing I need is for Katherine to come barging in unannounced on something she won't understand. If she gets hurt I'll never forgive myself. Katherine comes over and tries to wrestle her keys from me, but it's too late. I've taken my key back and hold it tight to my chest.

'Primrose Finley,' she snaps, 'give me that key.'

'It's *my* key to *my* home,' I answer then take a breath at the hurt in her expression. 'It's not I don't love you, Katherine,' I say. 'But I'm a grown woman and I need time to grieve.'

'You can still greave if I have a key,' she argues.

'Not properly,' I counter. 'Not without worrying you'll find me upset.' I take a breath choosing my words carefully. 'I know you love me but I'm twenty-two. *I* cared for mum in this cottage through her illness. Things happened inside these four walls you know nothing about. Mum and I planned her funeral together. I helped her pick out a coffin and flowers. We spoke of the songs she wanted playing. I cooked her meals and helped her in the shower. I brushed her teeth when she was too weak to lift her hands. I've proven I'm capable. Mum's life insurance means I don't need money, and I know where you are if I need to talk.' I take a deep breath and wipe tears from my face. 'I'm not telling you this to be cruel,' I sniff. 'I just need my space, and you love me so much you can't help but invade it.'

'I'm smothering you,' Aunt Katherine says.

I nod. 'A little.'

A lot, but I don't want to hurt her feelings more than I have. Her overbearing qualities are from a good place, but there's a reason my cousins moved far away. They love their mum, but Katherine's love is of the intense variety.

She sighs. 'Christine warned me about doing this,' she admits.

'She did?' I ask, wondering when Mum had chance to speak with Katherine alone. I've been pretty much glued to Mum's side for the past nine months.

'Yeah,' Katherine sighs. 'She ordered me not to smother you after she was gone.' She shrugs and looks at me with watery eyes. 'I suppose I've failed already with that then. I just wanted to make sure you were okay.'

I grab a box of tissues from the kitchen table and offer it to her. She takes one and dabs her eyes.

'I'm doing okay,' I assure her.

She cups my face and studies my expression. 'You look so much like my sister,' she tells me. 'Sometimes just seeing your face makes my breath catch.'

'Except for my eyes, right?' I murmur.

Her gaze hardens for just a second, before she hides her hatred. I look so much like my mother we could've been mistaken for twins. My hair is the same shade of blonde and I have the same skin tone and features. Except for my eyes. Mum's eyes were the same blue as Aunt Katherine's. My onyx gaze is the only trait I inherited from my father, and I learned from an early age to never ask about him. Not that Mum or Katherine would ever tell me anything, but the sorrow in Mum's gaze was enough of a deterrent.

All I know is Dad left before I was born and broke my mother's heart. I have no doubt Mum loved me, but I saw the pain in her face when she looked at me sometimes. Aunt Katherine noticed too, and she developed a deep sense of bitterness for the man.

Me? I feel nothing for my father. He was gone before he knew Mum was pregnant. I can't blame him for abandoning me when he had no knowledge of my existence. I used to be angry that he broke my mum's heart, but over the years some of my anger transferred to Mum. How could she pine over someone like that? I've gleamed that she and my dad were only a thing for a few months in the spring I was conceived. Then he left without a word and it destroyed her. I don't understand how she could let it affect the rest of her life. It makes me angry when I think of the sad looks she gave me growing up. I made her sad, not because of anything I did, but because she let the memory of my father break her.

My mum was a fragile, delicate sort of person. She was easy to talk to and full of kindness. She was a bright star in the world, even days from dying. She loved me so much the darkness in me craved her presence. My darkness was drawn to the warmth of her love, wanted to bask in the sensation, and enjoyed nothing more than wrapping midnight tendrils around her.

I'm the polar opposite to Mum. There's nothing fragile or delicate about my manner or personality. I don't go out of my way to hurt people, but I'll only tolerate people for so long before my temper gets the better of me. People don't flock to be near me. I'm literally shadow compared to my mum's sunny persona. There's more than one reason why the eligible guys in the village don't ask me out. Forgetting that I spent the last nine months caring for Mum, I'm quiet, more than a little weird and I punched Kevin Spencer in the face when he grabbed my backside in the post office once. The cocky idiot whined like a little girl, blood dripping down the front of his shirt, as he stared at me in disbelief. Needless to say I ruined my chances of dating anyone that lives close by.

My mind drifts to the guy hiding in the hedgerow at the bottom of my garden. His voice had a way of curling around my insides and lodging an annoying nugget of sensation at my core. He's not here, but my awareness of the encounter hasn't faded.

'You're nothing like your father,' Katherine says, bringing my focus back to her.

'So you knew him?' I counter.

She purses her lips and releases my face, pulling me into a gentle hug. 'I'll back off,' she tells me, studiously ignoring my attempt to push for information.

'You're going to have to tell me about him one day,' I say when Katherine draws away.

'I promised Christine I wouldn't,' she admits.

I stare at my aunt in disbelief. 'What?'

'She was just trying to protect you,' Katherine answers. 'That man ruined my sister. You can't tell me you didn't notice.'

'I did,' I admit, feeling off kilter at how frank Katherine is being. It's the most open she's been with me concerning my father, and perhaps it has something to do with trying not to coddle me.

'I promised Christine I wouldn't talk about him, so don't ask,' she tells me. 'She doesn't want you to get your heart crushed in the same way hers was, and I happen to agree with her on that.'

'But-'

'Don't make me break a promise to my dead sister, Primrose,' Katherine cuts in.

I shut my mouth and concede. I've lived without knowing my father this long, what will it hurt to never know him? A small, desperate part of me despairs. I've just lost one parent and the hope of ever knowing the other is tied into a promise my aunt won't break. Anger at my mum's sneakiness burns through me. How dare she make this decision then leave? Dying wasn't her choice, but she has taken my choices from me. It's my future and I've got to navigate it without her now.

I walk Katherine to the front door. She kisses me on the cheek and I watch her walk away, until the road curves enough that she's out of view. I shut the door behind her and lock it with the key I confiscated from her bunch. I go back to the kitchen and make another coffee. I've slept about six hours in the last week and it's taking its toll. Makes me wonder if I hallucinated the amethyst light and the voice behind the hedgerow.

I grab milk from the fridge then have to squash the plastic carton back between the jars of homemade pickles. My fridge is full of food donated by people from the village. I understand the sentiment, knowing they're only trying to help. But the amount of stuff they've sent is ridiculous. There's enough to feed a family of four and I'm annoyed that most of it will go to waste.

I take my coffee back into the garden, going straight to where the light was in the hedgerow. There's no light or tingling sensation this time and I huff an annoyed breath. Hallucination or not, Aunt Katherine has impeccable timing. I sigh and take myself back up to the house, taking one last glance over my shoulder before going inside.

CHAPTER 3

I groan and turn my face into the sofa cushion. A crack between the living room curtains in letting sunlight hit me straight in the face, waking me from the first sleep I've had in forever. I reach over and grab my phone from the coffee table. The time flashes up on the screen and I sigh. The last thing I remember is watching crappy TV at three in the morning, while eating the family-size trifle Mrs Benton made me.

I push from the sofa and wipe sleep from my eyes. It's nearly nine, so I've slept almost six hours. I feel refreshed but need coffee and a hot shower to bring me around. I search the kitchen for my favourite mug then open the back door to take my drink outside. I pause before stepping outside, looking at the rose on my backdoor step. It's jewel-toned and a shade of purple I've never witnessed in a flower. I put my coffee down and retrieve the rose. It sparkles in the morning sunlight, the petals dusted with amethyst glitter.

I suck in a breath, thinking of the amethyst light in the hedgerow. Around midnight I convinced myself I'd hallucinated the whole encounter. But the flower in my hand is no ordinary flower. I turn it between my fingers

18

and realise there's a tag tied to the stem. One word marks the card in curling script.

Anya.

A shiver skitters up my spine and I scour the back garden with my gaze. The light was real, meaning a stranger was in my yard last night leaving flowers on my doorstep. It sounds sort of romantic, but I'm still fuming over his cavalier attitude. This guy, whoever he is, keeps doing stuff without my permission. If he wants to give me a flower then why not give it to me in person? He could just knock on the door and introduce himself, instead of hanging out in the bushes like a creeper.

I march over to the compost bin in the garden. It's a beautiful flower but I don't want it in my home, encouraging his behaviour. I lift the bin lid, ready to throw it inside, but don't get chance. The rose explodes into a cloud of purple dust and coats my skin. I cough and try to wipe the shimmering stuff off, but darkness rises from my flesh and sucks the dust inside. My knees go weak and I moan, gripping the edge of the bin in white knuckled desperation to stay upright. Energy pulses through me in blasts of intense…what? It feels too good, but it's so potent it splinters my body with pain.

I give in and drop to my knees, sucking in breaths of air in a battle to stay conscious. The pulses slow, ebbing, until I'm panting on my knees in the dirt. I catch my breath then stand up. I feel…wonderful. I flex my tingling fingers and take stock. The ache of fatigue is gone from my limbs, a pleasant tingling fizzing through me in its place. I'm confused and more than a little freaked out. What the hell was in that flower?

I slump into a chair at the kitchen table and take a second to absorb what just happened. Darkness is swirling around my insides and my skin tingles. My pyjamas are muddy at the knee and I've got dirt beneath my fingernails from clawing at the grass. I sigh and push to my feet. I can't seem to go a day without rolling in the mud.

I take a long shower and get dressed. The darkness has settled by the time I get downstairs, but the fatigue hasn't returned and I feel a little hyped. I use the extra energy to clean the cottage. I spend hours dusting and washing, ignoring one room, until there's nothing else to clean, except *that* room. My fingers curl around the door handle and I stare at the door. My heart is pounding as I depress the handle and push inside. Mum's scent hits me and my throat goes tight. I haven't been in here since she died, and I'm half expecting to see her smiling face.

But I won't. I'll never see her smile at me again.

I step into the room and take a pillow from the bed. I bury my nose in the fabric and breathe the scent of her. An ache yawns wide inside my chest and tears blur my vision. I can't bring myself to strip the sheets and wash her from the room. One day the scent will fade and I'll be forced to accept that she's gone, but until then what harm will it do to leave her stamp on this room? I put the pillow back and close the door softly on my way out. The darkness is unsettled again, reacting to my grief, like the day of the funeral. Onyx tendrils caress the door as I move away and my skin prickles.

There's a knock on the door as I make it downstairs. I turn left towards the front door, but the knocking sounds again from the direction of the kitchen. I hesitate for just a second, wondering if it's *him*. I shake my head and get it together. So what if it is the stranger from the hedgerow? So he's not normal. Neither am I.

I take a deep breath as I reach the back door. If I'm honest, I'm more excited than nervous. I've never met anyone with abilities outside of what's considered natural for a human. Then again, I'm the only one that can see my darkness, so maybe I've met loads of people with conditions like mine and just don't know it. I open the door, the breath of anticipation leaving me in a sigh when I see who is on the other side.

'Drew,' I mutter.

'A fine hello for your best friend,' he answers.

'You missed the funeral.'

'Because you text me about it at one this morning,' he counters.

The annoyance in his tone rubs me the wrong way. Well boo for him. I phoned him the day Mum died and he didn't pick up. That was over two weeks ago. He tried to phone me back the morning of the funeral, but I let it go to voicemail. I had enough to deal with trying to control my darkness. I didn't have the capacity to deal with Drew's grief as well.

'I phoned you the day she died,' I snap. 'Some best friend you are, Andrew Frost.'

Drew shuts his mouth, argument fading at my words. I'm right and he knows it. He's been away at university, living his life and I understand. I don't want to tie him down to the village and the small life I'm living. But you're supposed to be there for the people you love and he's failed epically in that department.

'You lost the title of Best Friend a while back,' I add just to hurt him.

It's a low blow but the bitterness I feel has risen to the surface. For a while Drew pressured me to be more than friends but I held off. I didn't want to ruin the best friendship I had. I've always been a bit weird, with the whole darkness thing, but Drew saw past that. I felt comfortable around him – safe. Then Mum got sick and he pulled away. When the chance came for him to go to university he bolted. He chose to escape and deep down I understand why. My mum was an important figure in his life and he was scared of seeing her waste away. But he left when I needed him most, and the hurt hasn't gone away.

Drew rakes long fingers through his blond hair, apologetic gaze meeting mine. It makes me angrier because I feel a stab of guilt for making him feel bad. Moisture gathers in his pale blue eyes and he looks away, scratching the back of his neck.

'I'm sorry, Prim,' he murmurs, voice thick with tears.

His gaze meets mine and I watch a tear roll down his cheek. I scowl at that tear because it's making me weak. I force myself not to pull him into a hug.

'You're still a giant wimp then?' I snap.

Drew's lips twitch into the semblance of a smile. 'Yeah,' he answers.

I sigh. 'You'd better come in,' I growl then turn back into the house, leaving him to close the door behind him.

I fill the kettle to make him a tea and me a coffee. Drew goes to the fridge and routes through the contents. I watch his eyes grow wide, before he pulls out a tray of caramel shortbread.

'Is this Mrs Chamberlain's caramel shortbread?' he whispers, tone reverent.

'Why do you think it's in the fridge?' I answer.

Mrs Chamberlain's caramel shortbread is famous in the village. She does something to the caramel that makes it gooey at room temperature, so you have to store it in the fridge or end up with a sticky mess. The shortbread is buttery and crumbly and the chocolate creamy. She must make at least ten trays a week at the request of people in the village. She gifted me this one at the wake.

Drew closes his eyes and sniffs the confection, humming in delight as he does.

'Stop sticking your nose in it,' I say thinking of all the germs he just exhaled over it.

He puts the tray on the counter and grins at me. It's a wicked flash of teeth that would have most girls fluttering their lashes. I roll my eyes and turn back to making our drinks. Drew will never be more than a friend. Not that I never considered more before he pushed for it. I did almost cave to his pressuring once, but he cemented himself in the Friend Zone when he baled on me.

I turn back to make the drinks and he comes to stand beside me, his arm brushing mine, and I feel his disappointment seep through my skin. I break the contact and purse my lips at the fact he still thinks he's got a chance with me. I've done nothing to encourage him. If anything, I've made it painfully clear where the boundaries of our relationship lie. Darkness pulses around me, dissipating the fog of Drew's emotion and allowing me to breathe.

'Thanks,' Drew says when I hand him a cup of tea.

I cut him a large slice of caramel shortbread and put it on a plate. He takes it from me and I smirk at his grateful expression. Drew follows me into the living room. Relief that I spent the day cleaning washes through me. I've cleared away the evidence of my sleeping on the sofa and the room gleams, like the rest of the house.

'Why are you here?' I ask once we're both seated.

'Because your mum died, Prim.'

'And?' I counter at his offended tone. 'You missed the funeral, Drew. There's nothing else to come back for.'

'There's you,' he argues.

'What about me?'

'Bloody hell, Primrose!' he barks. 'What do you think I mean? Are you okay? How are you coping? Is there anything I can do?'

Darkness flares around me in response to his anger. I stare at Drew, trying to temper the wild rage in my middle. It's harder to control since the day I killed the flowers in the meadow - stronger. Drew's worried about me and I'm trying my hardest to hold the bitter words inside. I remind myself it's not his fault. He didn't take Mum from me and I can't blame Drew for running away. Hell, I've wanted to run away everyday since Mum's terminal diagnosis. I just didn't have the option.

'I'm doing okay,' I answer, pushing the lie through numb lips.

23

'Is that why the cottage smells like disinfectant,' he asks, 'because you're okay?'

'Cleaning helps me process,' I answer, hating that he knows me so well. 'It's methodical and cathartic.' And helps me switch off from the depressing thoughts in my head.

'You need to speak to someone-'

'No,' I cut him off.

'Prim, you're grieving. It will help,' he argues.

'I'm not telling a complete stranger my personal issues,' I snap.

The idea of admitting anything to a professional scares the crap out of me. What if they analyse the dark thoughts in my head and realise I'm different to the average person. Hell no, not going to happen. I've watched too many movies where bad things happen to people deemed different.

'Then talk to Katherine,' he suggests. When I glare at him he adds, 'then talk to me.'

'No, Drew!' I push to my feet, look around then sit back down. I meet his worried gaze and get pissed off. 'Look, I know you're worried about me, which is why I haven't kicked you in the shin for suggesting this bull crappery,' I hiss. 'But understand this, Andrew Frost. My thoughts and feelings are private and will stay that way. If I need help then I'll ask for it. If you can't deal with that then get the hell out.'

Drew scowls at me then sighs and grabs his caramel shortbread from the coffee table. 'I can deal with it,' he mutters.

'Good,' I tell him, deflating a little. 'How long are you staying?'

He chuckles around a bite of dessert. 'Can't wait to get rid of me?'

'No,' I admit.

'Cheers,' he mutters. 'I go back in two days.'

'You stopping at your stepdad's?'

24

'Yeah,' he says, failing to hide the strain in his voice.

Drew and his stepfather have had a strained relationship since Drew's mother passed away when he was eleven. His stepdad has never been cruel or behaved in a negative way towards Drew. He even pays most of Drew's university tuition. But there's a rift between them that they've never been able to mend. Drew's mother was the bridge between them and she's gone. Her death was the reason Drew was close to my mum. He would come home with me most nights from school and have dinner with us. He enjoyed her attention and she enjoyed loving him like a son.

Another wave of guilt washes through me and I squeeze his hand. Darkness reaches from me to Drew, weaving over his hand then up his arm in intricate onyx swirls. I watch it for a moment then meet his gaze. His grief and confusion hit me, like a punch to the gut. I resist the need to pull my hand from his and sever the connection, not wanting to hurt his feelings. Instead, I let the darkness leach the negative emotions from him, until the pain clears from his gaze and claws at my insides.

'She loved you like a son,' I murmur.

'I know,' he breathes. 'Did she - was she hurt that I wasn't there?' he asks.

Mum never commented on Drew's absence, but I *felt* her upset. It's where my bitterness stems from. I needed him here for her, more than for me. Drew and I are the same age, but I feel so much older. He seems like a lost child in moments like this and I can't help but comfort him.

'She understood,' I say.

'I miss her,' he whispers.

I can't help feeling torn between smacking and hugging him. Part of me wonders why I'm the one comforting Drew, wondering how the hell he thinks I'm feeling right now. The other part pulls him into a hug and rubs his back, telling him it will be okay.

CHAPTER 4

Drew stays for a few hours, until I kick him out for eating half the food in my fridge. The idiot should be fat from his sweet tooth, but he's got that guy thing where he can eat what he wants and not gain weight. I slump onto the sofa and flick through the channels on the television. My mind won't focus enough to watch anything but the noise makes me feel less alone.

Knocking sounds from the back door and I stare in that direction. Drew is the only person who insists on going to the back door. I think it makes him feel like he's part of a secret club or something because he won't stop. I shove from the sofa and stalk through the house. I turn the key in the lock and yank the door open.

'Drew-'

I stop at the vacant space where I expected Drew to be. There's nobody here, but then I *feel* it. The hairs on my nape prickle and I know it's *him*. Excitement and fear duel for dominance in my middle. I want to know more about this stranger, but he's just plain creepy. Why won't he show himself to me? How the heck is he even keeping out of sight? If I'm honest, I'm a little desperate to find out more about him and it's overriding the fear. He's the only being I've met that seems stranger than me, and there's a magnetic draw to him I can't explain.

The feeling of being caressed mists over my skin. He's touching me again, only it's not a physical caress. He's touching my darkness and it's swirling around me in an excited cloud of midnight. I don't know if I'm more annoyed at him, or just my lack of control around him. I can admit I'm desperate to know more about him, but I don't want *him* to know that.

'Stop that,' I snap.

A deep chuckle sounds from the garden but there's no purple light this time to show where it's coming from. I feel like he's messing with me, and my hackles rise. I know it's stupid, but I step into the garden and scan the night. My temper is my downfall. Once the fuse is lit it's hard to rein it in.

'Where are you?' I growl.

Heat blankets my back, violet light bathing my skin from behind. My darkness weaves through the light, painting pretty patterns on my flesh. My heart races at the feeling of home, that deep voice sounding against my ear and sending a shiver down my spine.

'Anya,' he murmurs.

It feels like he's hugging me but we aren't touching. My darkness is fizzing at his nearness and I lock my knees to stay upright.

'My name isn't Anya,' I grit out.

Why the hell did I come outside? Stupid, stupid, stupid!

'I'll call you by your name, if you gift me the knowledge,' he answers.

Oh?

'Primrose,' I breathe.

'Primrose,' he purrs, turning my name into a caress.

'And you are?'

28

A rumble sounds behind me, like my need to know his name is pleasing. A pulse of pleasure ripples from him to me in confirmation, and my darkness drinks it in. Just being near him is intoxicating. He's making my mind lose focus and I don't like it.

'Zephyr,' he hums against the shell of my ear, accent thickening. I can't place it and it's driving me crazy. He's like mist; all around but I can't grab onto him.

'What are you doing in my garden, Zephyr?'

'You enjoyed my gift?' he asks, ignoring my question.

Gift? It takes my brain a second to understand.

'You mean the rose?'

'I can smell it on your skin,' he murmurs against my ear. 'It's taken the tiredness from your eyes and dusted you with my scent.'

Wait, what? I spin to face him but he isn't there. My gaze darts around the garden but Zephyr's gone. How is he doing that? I bolt back inside and lock the door behind me. Goose bumps prickle my skin and there's a soft sheen on it, like I've been sprayed with amethyst glitter. I scrub at both arms with hand soap at the kitchen sink, but the shimmer is still there when I rinse them under the tap. I lift the hem of my top, exposing my stomach, to find the skin shimmering too. It's only visible when the light hits it at certain angles, but it's definitely there.

I enjoy my scent on you.

I pause at the memory of his comment then sniff my hands. All I smell is hand soap, so I pull the neck of my shirt down and sniff my shoulder. An alluring fragrance teases my senses. It's faint, lying just beneath the scent of my body lotion, but it's there. It calls to something in my centre, like a memory I can't quite grasp.

Darkness vibrates inside me, like it's purring. It likes Zephyr but I don't know who Zephyr is. *I'm* harbouring some freaky secrets, but this guy? I can't move like he does. One minute he's there then the next he's gone, and I don't know what he looks like. My imagination is starting to get the better of me and it's not pretty. Zephyr's voice makes my insides do this weird wriggle, but for all I know he could look like a monster. I'd like to think I'm not shallow enough to discount someone for not being handsome, but I draw the line at fangs. Or gills - Or a third eye and scales.

I shake my head at the stupid direction of my thoughts. Zephyr is probably just screwing with me. I bet he's an average guy with a purple torch. I don't know how he moves so fast, but I've watched plenty of magic tricks on television. There could be a simple explanation for everything and my imagination is making things seem worse than they are. But then how does he *touch* me in the way he does? He makes my darkness pulse in anticipation and I lose rational thought. Zephyr's marked me in glitter and a fragrance that makes my toes curl. My brain wants to attribute everything to something simple, but it can't. I can't decide if I'm more fascinated or freaked out.

I think of his *touch* and fresh excitement rolls through me. What if Zephyr is like me? What if he has his own darkness but has learned to control it?

I microwave a piece of lasagne I saved from Drew's rampage of my fridge then eat it at the kitchen table. Every now and then the light catches the dust on my skin and I frown. I drum my fingers against the table and look at the back door. I'm agitated, wondering if Zephyr is out there, waiting until I go to bed so he can leave another rose on my doorstep. The smoke and mirrors act is tap dancing on my last nerve. I'm an angry person on a good day, and I'm not in an emotionally fit state to deal with all this tension right now.

I huff and push from the table, going back outside and march to the centre of the garden. It's quiet, no sign of Zephyr, but I get the feeling he's watching. I don't *feel* him, like before, but I *know* he's here, sneaking around, like the creep he's proving to be.

'I know you're here and I don't like it,' I announce to the seemingly empty garden. 'I don't like you sneaking around and I don't like the rose you left me, Zephyr. You need to leave.'

Violet light flashes around me and I shield my eyes from the glare. Hands grip my upper arms while I'm still blinking through bright spots in my vision. I'm pulled against a hard body then full lips meet mine. I gasp in shock and a tongue pushes into my mouth. With it comes the taste of the fragrance painting my skin, the scent left by Zephyr.

My brain catches up with what's happening and I start to struggle, despite my body urging me to surrender. Zephyr growls into my mouth, his grip on me tightening to the point of pain. I whimper and the pressure eases slightly but stays firm. I wriggle enough to wedge my hands between us. My fingers press into hard muscle then curl into fists when I fail to push him away. If I'm honest with myself I've wondered about his kiss, but not like this.

His lips heat against mine as light shines between us. It grows brighter and brighter, until I can't see anything except the amethyst shine. Zephyr bands his arm around me, weaving fingers through my hair to hold me in place. Heat fills my mouth and I gag when it pushes its way down my throat. I thrash against him, oxygen supply cut off. But I can't get free, and my darkness doesn't seem inclined to help me. Instead it's doing nothing, like it's rolled onto its back to show its belly.

Shadow creeps around the edge of my vision. I'm not afraid of dying, and I'm no stranger to the dark. But I'm angry at how weak I feel in this moment. I bite down in frustration and Zephyr snarls, ripping his mouth from mine. The light dies and the taste of his blood paints my tongue as I suck in a breath. I try to run but he pulls me close. I'm blind in the sudden darkness, Zephyr's heart drumming against the ear pressed to his chest.

'Mine,' he snarls.

31

I shut my eyes against another burst of purple light then fall to the grass, Zephyr's support disappearing. I pant against the ground, pressure wrapping around my chest. It feels like my lungs are filling with fluid, pain splintering through my ribcage in agonising shards. I crawl back to the house, making it to the kitchen before I can't breathe through the pain anymore. I pant into the floor, gaze locked on the open back door. A rectangle of night stares back, like a window to my future. I don't know what Zephyr did but I think I'm dying.

I curl into a ball when ice bleeds into my middle. It spreads to my extremities and I cry out. It hurts so much, a thousand agonies spiking over my skin. Something snaps in my centre and I scream, back arching. Pain steals my vision and lances through my skull. I try to suck in a breath but my lungs won't function. My palms slide over warm, wet linoleum and my mouth tastes like pennies. A scream crawls up my throat but I can't breathe to voice it. I scrunch my eyes shut and pray for an end.

The backs of my eyelids glow pink, like I've turned my face to the sun. There's light all around, but I can't open my eyes to see where it's coming from. Pain clenches my middle then slices through my centre. A sharp sensation rages from deep in my core and collides with my heart. The agony it causes flips me onto my back and I suck in a breath, voicing the scream lodged in my throat. My eyes snap open to blinding violet, which dims almost instantly under the shadow flooding my vision. I let the shadow take me, relief drenching my thoughts as consciousness fades.

CHAPTER 5

I think I'm in love,' Amy sighs drawing our attention.

She's gazing at a picture in her magazine with a dreamy look on her face, twirling a length of hair around her index finger.

'Is that Nile?' Charlotte asks.

'Who else?' Amy sighs.

'Lucas is better looking,' Charlotte says.

'No way,' Amy shouts and throws a pillow at Charlotte's head.

She squeals and throws it back. Amy ducks and it smacks into the wall behind her. I laugh, pressing against the opposite wall to stay out of range. Amy's bedroom door opens and her mum frowns into the room.

'Sorry, Mum,' Amy says before her mum has chance to speak.

'You girls should be asleep.'

'But, Mum-' Amy whines.

'I told Christine and Emily I'd have you in bed by ten and it's half past now,' her mum cuts in. 'Ten is more than reasonable for eleven-year-olds, so wash your faces, brush your teeth and into bed.'

Amy huffs but we all comply, going into the bathroom down the hall. I wash my face then brush my teeth, before going back to Amy's room and shuffling into my sleeping bag on her bedroom floor. Charlotte comes in a second later and slides into the sleeping bag beside me. We both look at the door when Amy squeals from the hallway. There's a loud thud followed by the sound of her brother laughing.

'Mum!' Amy shouts.

'Stop annoying your sister, Charlie,' her mum shouts back.

Amy storms into the room a second later and slams the door behind her. 'Stupid boy,' she huffs as she climbs into bed and yanks the covers up.

Charlotte grins at me and I grin back. Amy and her brother don't get on, and they go out of their way to prank each other.

'What did he do?' Charlotte asks.

'Sprayed me with a water pistol,' Amy grumbles, 'but I'll get him back.'

She reaches up and slaps the light switch, bathing the room in darkness. I hear her roll over in bed and I wriggle around until I'm comfortable enough to fall asleep.

Prickles skitter over my skin and I blink in the darkness. It takes a second to remember I'm not in my own bed at home. I'm at Amy's house for a sleepover, and that's Charlotte shifting on the floor beside me. I'm sleepy and warm, so why is my skin prickling? Something moves in the corner of the room and I stop breathing, straining my eyes in that direction. I can feel the heat of Charlotte beside me and Amy is snoring from her bed, so what else is in here?

A floorboard squeaks when the thing moves again, creeping closer to where Charlotte and I are lying. My heart picks up, thrumming against my ribcage so fast I think it might break a rib. My skin starts stinging, as the thing moves even closer, and something uncurls deep in my belly. The thing is so close I can hear it breathing. I want to curl into a ball on my side but I'm too afraid to move. A foot brushes my sleeping bag as the thing steps over me, until it's standing over Charlotte. I suck in a breath when something thick and oozing drips onto my cheek, my leg jerking out in surprise to kick Charlotte.

Charlotte sits bolt upright, smacking into the monster looming over her, and screams. I scream with her, clutching my

34

sleeping bag as the monster thumps to the floor. Amy's scream joins in and I'm blinded when the light blinks on. My vision adjusts to see Amy's brother Charlie squirming on the floor at Charlotte's feet. Darkness connects me to him, like a shadowy ribbon. It's circling his throat, choking him. His fear mixes with mine, making it difficult to tell what's mine, and what's his.

'Charlie!' Amy screams, scrambling from the bed.

She kneels beside him, tears streaking her face. The door crashes open and Amy's mum and dad rush into the room in their pyjamas. They drop beside Charlie too.

'He's having a seizure,' Amy's dad says trying to hold Charlie down.

The way Charlie's writhing on the floor makes it look like he's having a seizure, if you can't see the inky bands gripping his throat. He's in his pyjamas, a bottle of syrup oozing golden liquid onto the carpet. I touch my sticky face, where he must've dripped it on me on his way to Amy's bed, and it all makes sense. He was playing a prank on his sister.

'Please,' I whisper, glimpsing Charlie's blue lips.

My darkness is eliminating the threat to me. That's the biggest problem with the dark part of me. It doesn't understand that some threats aren't life threatening, and now Charlie might die because of it.

'He wasn't trying to hurt me,' I whisper and close my eyes, concentrating really hard on calming down.

If it thinks the threat is over it might let him go.

I take a deep breath and think of Mrs Spencer's ginger tomcat. His name is Montague and he's a peach Persian. He likes to roll on our garden in summer, leaving tufts of ginger fur on the grass. When it rains, the fur on his belly goes curly and he stretches out on his back while I brush it out. Mrs Spencer says he likes me so much he spends more time in my home than hers. She even gave me a box of the special food he eats for when he spends the night in our cottage instead of hers.

The sound of coughing draws my attention and I open my eyes to see Charlie half sitting up, my darkness no longer wrapped around his throat. His face is red instead of purple and his lips are

35

no longer blue. He's coughing like his throat hurts and tears paint his cheeks. Everyone is crying, including me, and a cloud of shadow halos my body.

'I want to go home,' Charlotte sobs.

Her caramel skin has turned almost as pale as mine. There's syrup in her hair and she's shaking. I want to hug her but I'm afraid because I don't know what my darkness will do. It feels prickly, and when it's like this it reminds me of a rattlesnake I saw on the television. The snake was shaking its tail, body coiled, ready to strike. My insides feel coiled tight, like that snake, the prickling sensation the rattle of its tail.

I hug my knees to my chest as tears drip from my chin. Amy's mum comes over to hug Charlotte and speak to her in calm tones. I don't hear what she's saying. I can't sleepover at Amy or Charlotte's houses anymore in case my darkness hurts someone else. It almost killed Charlie - I almost killed Charlie. I'm worse than a rattlesnake because nobody knows how dangerous I am.

Noise chips at my aching brain. I try to ignore it and return to peaceful dark, but the noise is persistent. I groan and roll away from it, but moving makes the noise grow louder. Bloody hell I feel worse than the time Drew and I stole the Russian vodka from his stepdad's liquor cabinet.

The thought of Drew makes the noise more distinctive, and it morphs into his voice. He sounds like he's shouting from the end of a long tunnel and it takes a while to distinguish what he's saying.

'Primrose.'

His voice gets louder then louder, like he's getting closer, and I realise he's shouting my name over and over again. It hurts my ears and I groan, trying to lift my hands to cover my ears. My left hand snags on something and I realise Drew's holding it. I take a deep breath and force my eyelids open. They stick a little, like they're glued together with sleep. I hiss against the daylight, head pounding, and snap them shut again.

'Don't close your eyes!' Drew shouts.

The raw panic in his tone has my eyelids slitting open. It takes a moment for his terrified face to come into focus, blue eyes filled with tears.

'Drew,' I croak, mouth dry. 'What's wrong?'

'Prim,' he sniffs. 'Don't close your eyes, okay? I'm going to phone an ambulance, just stay awake.'

Ambulance?

I grab his hand when he goes to stand. 'What are you talking about? Who needs an ambulance?'

He stares at me like I've lost my mind. 'Primrose-' his voice breaks and he stops to wipe his eyes with his sleeve.

I realise he means me, and start to panic. Memories from last night flash in painful snapshots through my brain, and I sit up. I groan, grabbing my temples when the room spins.

'Prim!' Drew barks, fussing around me but not actually doing anything. He gives in and pushes to his feet. 'I'm phoning for an ambulance.'

'No!' I shout and shove to my feet.

The room tilts and I stagger sideways, vision dimming. Drew swears and catches me before I fall into the kitchen table. I lean on him, while he pulls a chair out and sits me in it, crouching before me so he can look into my eyes. I bend forward and put my head between my knees, until the room stops tilting.

'Prim,' Drew whispers panic painting his tone. He's really no good in a crisis.

'No ambulance,' I whisper back meeting his gaze.

Whispering is good because it hurts my head less.

'But-'

'I can't go to the hospital. Not this soon after Mum.'

His mouth snaps shut, understanding dawning through his features. He wasn't here for the numerous trips to the hospital. He wasn't here for treatments or resulting days of sickness from the chemotherapy. He

37

didn't have to watch Mum waste away at the end. It took days to scrub the hospital stench from my skin, and I'll always associate the smell with those final hours of Mum's life. I can't go to that place right now. I can't.

'Okay,' he says then, 'can you tell me what happened?'

I blink at him, wondering how much I should say. I've never spoken to Drew about my darkness, and if I tell him I was attacked by a guy that pumped me full of purple light he'll change his mind about that ambulance.

I frown at him. 'How did you get in here?'

'The back door was wide open,' he answers.

I remember staring at the open doorway and nod. 'I didn't close it,' I murmur.

Drew rakes fingers through his blond hair. 'Did someone break in? Were you-' he closes his eyes and takes a deep breath, before meeting my gaze again. 'Did they…touch you?'

I choose my words carefully. I don't want to lie to him but there's no way I'm telling him about Zephyr.

'Nobody broke in, Drew.'

His relief floods the air around us, and it's difficult to keep the shock off my face. I can sense other people's emotions, but only if we're touching skin to skin. Drew and I aren't touching, yet I feel what he's feeling. His emotion mists the air and my darkness drinks it in. Intricate, midnight patterns swirl over my skin, different and I watch them fascinated. I can feel my darkness drawing Drew's essence to me, like it's breathing him deep.

'Then what the hell happened, Primrose?' Drew demands, his frustration cutting through the haze of shock. 'I came here at three, like we planned, to find you unconscious on the kitchen floor. And you're covered-' his voice wavers but he pulls it together. 'You're covered in blood and it's all over the floor, Prim. There's so much,' he says glancing behind him.

I follow his gaze to a large puddle of dried blood on the kitchen floor and what he's saying sinks in.

'What the hell?' I murmur.

Drew meets my gaze again. 'I didn't think a person could bleed that much and survive.'

'Me either,' I whisper.

You're covered in blood.

I look down to see my clothes stained the same red as the puddle on the kitchen floor. It registers that the blood came from me. I was bleeding last night; more than a person should and survive to tell the tale. I finger the rusty stain on my top, the material rigid.

'But I'm not injured,' I murmur, confused as to where it all came from.

'Your nose,' Drew whispers.

I meet his gaze again and touch my nose. I feel the blood crusted beneath it and push to my feet.

'Whoa,' Drew exclaims, grabbing me when I sway a little.

'I need to see,' I insist when he tries to push me back into the chair.

Drew studies my expression then sighs and helps me to the mirror in the hallway. I stare at my reflection. Blood paints my face in defined tracks, leading from my nose, eyes and ears. A knot of fear uncoils in my stomach then tries to crawl up my throat. I swallow hard, forcing it back down, when my pupils inch wider and black bleeds into the white of my eyes. I have to control it because I can't let Drew see.

'What are you doing?' Drew demands when I push past him.

'I need to shower.'

'You're too weak,' he argues.

Drew follows me as I force myself up the stairs. I think he's worried I'll fall back down and I'm sort of worried about that too. But I make it to the top and stumble into the bathroom. I turn in the doorway and press a hand to Drew's chest, stopping him from following me inside. I stare at my hand on his chest so I don't have to meet his gaze, unsure if my eyes have turned completely black.

'You're not coming in here while I shower, Drew.'

'Primrose-'

'There's no way in Hell you're standing in the bathroom while I'm naked in the shower, Andrew Frost,' I snap.

Drew tenses under my hand and his frustration taints the air. I don't care, he's not being in the same room as me when I'm naked.

'Fine,' he mutters and goes to sit on the top step of the stairs. 'But leave the door unlocked in case I need to get to you.'

I consider arguing but manage to rein it in, shutting the door on him instead. Sometimes I wonder if I'm short tempered because I can feel what others are feeling. Maybe if I felt worry from Drew instead of frustration I would've reacted differently. I turn on the shower and strip as the bathroom fills with steam. My body spasms with delight under the hot spray, and I brace both hands against the tile, letting water rain over me. Blood streaks my skin and I watch crimson circle the plughole.

I grab a towel from the rail and sit on the edge of the bath to dry. I don't feel as weak as I did downstairs, but my arms and legs are shaking. My skin is sensitive to touch, and I wince when I reach up to dry my shoulder. I crane my neck to see if it's bruised and onyx curls greet my gaze.

'What the hell?' I whisper.

I twist my arm forward to get a better view of my shoulder and see midnight swirls reaching down the back of my arm. I push to my feet and stumble to the mirror, turning so I can see the back of my arm and shoulder. My eyes go wide with shock. The swirls reach across my back and down the back of my other arm, like a giant tattoo covering my upper arms, back and shoulders. It's pretty, the black filigree seeming delicate against my pale skin. It curls down either side of my spine, in matching designs, ending just before the top of my backside. But the beauty is lost on me, because I sure as hell don't remember getting a tattoo. I rub at my shoulder, wondering if it's actually there, then hiss at how raw it feels.

'Son of a-'

'Prim?' Drew shouts through the door.

I grit my teeth until the stinging subsides then shout, 'I'm fine, Drew.'

The flesh on my shoulders feels raw, but I can't decide if the black filigree is real or if it's just my darkness acting strangely. I wrap myself in a fresh towel and check my eyes in the mirror. When I see they're normal again, I open the door and Drew's eyes go wide. He moves aside to let me pass then follows me into the bedroom. The weight of his stare heats my back but I can't tell if he staring because I'm in a towel or because of the tattoo.

I turn to meet his bewildered gaze. He licks his bottom lip, like he does when he's nervous, and scratches the back of his reddening neck. His eyes rake me from head to toe then meet my gaze.

'You got a tattoo.'

I take a deep breath to settle the panic clawing my insides. Nobody's been able to see my darkness before. I've lived my life hoping it's just a figment of my imagination – That my ability to sense the emotion of others isn't actually ability but borderline craziness. But if Drew's seeing this then I'm not crazy.

It means it's real.

'Yeah,' I murmur.

Drew's gaze goes to my shoulders then upper arms, where the edge of the black swirls curl into view. 'It's nice.'

'Thanks,' I say watching his gaze drop lower. His eyes go intense, like he's trying to see through my towel.

'Um, Drew?'

'Yeah?' he murmurs, still staring at my body.

'You can get out now.'

His gaze snaps to mine. 'Huh?'

'I want to get dressed.'

Mutiny flashes in his eyes but quickly fades, and his shoulders sag. I honestly don't know why he harbours any hope of anything more between us. That ship sailed a long time ago.

'I'll be right outside the door,' he answers.

I sigh at the forlorn look he gives over his shoulder on the way out. It grates at me, guilt ascending even though I know Drew's the one that should feel guilty for throwing that look my way. If he thinks I'll change my mind about him by making me feel crappy then he'll have a rude awakening.

I pull on clean pyjamas then brush my hair. I feel better, my body weak but no longer shaking. My stomach rumbles as I meet Drew outside my bedroom doorway. He offers a gentle smile then tucks a length of hair behind my ear and pulls me into a hug. I think of pushing him away then sink into his embrace. His emotions are all about comforting me and I can handle this from him. There's no suffocating wave of worry, like when Katherine hugs me. It's just warm and soothing, and I've missed Drew's brand of comfort.

'Come on, Prim,' he murmurs into my hair. 'Let's go downstairs and eat some of the goodies in your fridge.'

'You've eaten most of the goodies in my fridge,' I complain.

'I left you cottage pie and caramel shortbread,' he defends.

I chuckle against his shoulder then let him help me downstairs. I feel strong enough to manage the steps alone, but I feel Drew's need to help me, and I give him what he wants. I preheat the oven then supervise while he puts the cottage pie in to warm through. He places the tray of caramel shortbread on the counter to thaw and gives it a longing look.

'It's not the same unless the caramel is gooey,' I warn.

He smirks at my ability to read him like a book. 'I know, but waiting is a form of torture.'

'Delayed gratification,' I answer.

His eyes flash with want and I look away. Maybe I should address the elephant in the room before it gets any bigger.

'What time do you leave tomorrow?' I ask instead.

'Four,' he answers.

Betrayal slashes through me. I don't know why his words hurt so much. He already left me once, and he told me he was going back the day he got here, but he found me unconscious on the floor less than an hour ago and he's still okay with leaving tomorrow. *Running.* He's not leaving me he's running from the possibility I might be sick, like with Mum. Drew claims to love me, but you don't abandon the ones you love. You stick by them. You hide your fear and your pain, so they don't know you're hurting, and you suck it up. You be what they need you to be, putting your own wants and needs aside, until the end.

I open my mouth but nothing comes out. The panic in his eyes tells me he knows exactly what I'm thinking but he doesn't get chance to defend himself. Knocking comes from the front door and I push to my feet. Drew leaps from his chair and tells me to sit. I do, not caring who is at the door. I'm just relieved the ugly tension has been severed by the interruption.

I hear Katherine before I see her. I frown at how well I can hear her all the way at the front of the cottage. It's not a huge property, but the walls are thick stone, so noise doesn't travel as much as modern properties. Her voice is still a little muffled, but I hear what's being said. I listen to Katherine and Drew having a whispered conversation on the way to the kitchen. Drew, the snitch, is telling her all the gory details about how he found me earlier. The urge to slap him grows at the panic drenching Katherine's tone. Drew is such a selfish prick. He doesn't have to tell her anything, but he wants someone to know about it when he abandons me tomorrow. He's upsetting my aunt so he can feel better when he's gone.

I push to my feet and check the cottage pie in the oven, letting them have their whispered words. Drew's started, so he might as well finish. I turn the pie then grab two plates from the cupboard and put them on the counter. I fish cutlery from the draw and place it on the table, as Katherine sweeps into the kitchen. She hurries over and wraps me in a hug. I scowl at Drew over her shoulder and mouth a swear word at him. His eyebrows meet his hairline, the shock on his face almost making up for how annoyed I am. My mum hated swearing, so I never do it aloud, and it's a good way of making Drew aware of how much he just screwed up. He can't know I could hear everything they were discussing, but it doesn't take a genius to figure out it isn't that long a walk from the front door to the kitchen.

'Primrose,' Aunt Katherine breathes and draws away to look at my face.

I meet her panicked gaze. 'I'm fine.'

My tone is placating, like I'm the adult and she the child. It's the same tone I used with Mum on her really bad days. It seemed to soothe Mum and it appears to work on Katherine. Some of the worry leaves her face, but not her eyes. Anger flashes hot through my middle and I look at Drew.

'Drew was just leaving,' I tell Katherine.

Katherine's confusion coats my skin, in that weird new way that I sense people's emotions. I ignore it and cut Drew off, when he opens his mouth to argue.

'Katherine and I have a lot to talk about- Family things,' I tell him.

Hurt drenches his features but I glare at him in response. I haven't got the capacity to feel guilty right now.

'Yeah,' he murmurs at my hard stare. 'I, um, have plans with my stepdad.'

Katherine looks between us but doesn't comment. Drew pulls on his shoes and gives me a sorrowful look, before he leaves via the back door. I go to the door and lock it behind him. He's not welcome tonight and maybe not even tomorrow. I love the idiot like a brother, but he's overstepped the line too many times in the last few days.

'That was pretty mean,' Katherine tells me when I go back into the kitchen.

'Oh, don't fall for his crap,' I mutter and stalk past her.

'Primrose!' she scolds.

'No,' I snap and spin to face her. 'I know he just worried you half to death because I had a nosebleed and fell asleep on the kitchen floor.'

She frowns. 'He said there was blood everywhere.'

I glance at the floor, realising for the first time the dried blood is gone. Drew must've cleaned it up while I showered and I'm grateful. If Katherine saw the amount of blood I lost then she wouldn't believe my lie. I hate lying to her, but I'm not telling her I almost bled out.

'He was exaggerating,' I answer. 'He saw blood and freaked out. You know what Drew's like with stuff like that.'

'And you fell asleep on the kitchen floor?' she counters, unconvinced.

'I haven't slept in weeks,' I argue. 'Is it so hard to believe exhaustion finally got the better of me?'

Her shoulders sag and the fight dies in her eyes. 'So, you're okay?'

'I told you, I'm fine,' I assure her.

45

She studies me for a second longer then says, 'What smells so good?'

'Cottage pie,' I smile. 'You're staying for dinner, right?'

She matches my smile and her relief perfumes the air between us. Feeling emotion in this way will take some getting used to, but I can't say it's unpleasant when the emotions are good.

We chat for a while, until the pie is warmed through. Katherine tells me how Uncle David wants to take her away for the weekend. I sense her hesitation over leaving me alone and strive to reassure her. David must see the same stress lines creasing Katherine's face that I do. I remind myself that she lost her sister, and Mum's death isn't just about my grief.

'You deserve a break,' I tell Katherine, as I spoon cottage pie onto two plates. I place them on the table and sit across from her, interrupting when I feel her about to argue. 'You need it,' I say then go for the jugular. 'Uncle David needs it.'

Katherine hesitates. 'You think so?'

I nod, knowing I've got her. She won't take a break for herself but she'll do anything for those she loves.

'He's looking tired. Let him take you away and ease some of the worry I see when he looks at you.'

Katherine sighs and looks away, before meeting my gaze again. 'If you're sure you'll be okay?'

'I've got a whole village of nosey neighbours looking after me, I'll be fine.'

'You could always come with us,' she suggests.

I snort. 'And be the third wheel in your dirty getaway?'

'Primrose!' she scolds then laughs, her cheeks turning an interesting shade of red.

'I'm not five anymore, Katherine. Part of me wanting my key back was so I could have sex all over the cottage without the fear of being interrupted.'

Katherine's mouth drops open then she throws the dishtowel at me. 'Primrose Finley, I've never heard such filth!' she chastises but can't keep the laughter from her voice.

CHAPTER 6

I open a bottle of wine after dinner and Katherine joins me for a glass. We sit in the lounge and reminisce over memories of Mum before she got sick. There are so many good memories it's late by the time Katherine leaves. I lock the door and take the wine glasses into the kitchen. I'm a little tipsy, so I leave them by the sink to wash in the morning.

I lean on the bathroom sink while I'm brushing my teeth. The weakness from earlier is gone and the wine has left me warm on the inside. I wash my face then go to bed, lying on my back in the dark staring at the ceiling. The anger I felt for Drew is gone, diluted by the wine, until it dissipated to nothing. I don't feel guilty over the way I reacted about him upsetting my aunt, but I do miss him. I miss his easy smiles and how close we used to be.

I curl up on my side and think about David taking Katherine away the day after tomorrow. It's exactly what they both need, and maybe I need it too. Mum dying changed the landscape of my universe, but the stuff that happened since scares me. I've never experienced pain like last night. I thought I was dying, and now I have black swirls marking my skin. I think my hearing is better and I can sense emotion without touching people. I think of Zephyr lurking somewhere nearby and go rigid with fear. I don't know what he did, but maybe he was trying to kill me. Maybe he'll come back to finish the job. But how the hell did he almost kill me without my darkness taking him out? My need to get to know him has dropped to zero. He's not like me, he's something dangerous, and I don't think I'll survive another encounter with him.

I curl into a tighter ball and close my eyes. Sleep seems impossible but then I yawn so wide my jaw cracks. I'm so tired and the wine in my system is helping me relax. I take a deep breath and blow out the tension. Zephyr hasn't been back since last night. Even when he wasn't copping a feel in that creepy way of his, I still *felt* when he was close by, and haven't felt him since waking on the kitchen floor. I calm and the last of the tension leaves me. Another yawn stretches my jaw and I close my eyes to sleep.

I stare at the back door, hand wrapped around the handle. I can't *feel* Zephyr, but I don't trust it. My racing heart skips a beat when the knocking sounds again. My tongue feels thick in my mouth and I'm sweating. The fear I feel is unlike any I've experienced before. All I can think about is the agony from two nights ago, and I'm terrified Zephyr's returned to dish out more.

The knocking stops and a familiar voice curses from the other side. Relief blasts through me and I rip the door open, stopping Drew's retreat. His blue eyes meet mine, unsure but all I feel is relief that he's here. When Katherine gets back from her holiday with David I might take her up on her offer to stay with them. The fear of Zephyr returning is eating at me and I can't take being alone in the cottage.

'I didn't think you'd answer,' Drew says.

'You owe me an apology.'

'I just-'

'You scared Katherine half to death, Drew,' I cut in. 'She just lost her sister and you had her thinking she'd lost her niece.' I sigh and rub my temples. 'I know I scared you yesterday, but please don't do that to Katherine, okay? She's struggling to cope as it is.'

I see my words sink in before Drew nods. 'I'm sorry, Primrose.'

'Apology accepted,' I say then grab his arm and pull him inside. 'Now, get in here and help me pack.'

'What do you mean pack?' he asks.

'Katherine's gone away for a few days with David, so I thought I'd do the same.'

Drew stares at me. 'You're leaving the village?'

'Don't be an idiot, Drew,' I say and pull my overnight case from the cupboard under the stairs.

He stares at the case then meets my gaze. 'Come back to Liverpool with me.'

'What? No. You've got classes and live with three other guys. I don't even want to think about the state of your student digs.'

'It's Thursday,' he answers. 'I don't have any classes until Monday, and one of the guys I live with is a neat freak. The house is sterile, Primrose, I swear.' He blocks my path when I move to take the case upstairs. 'Come on,' Drew pleads. 'I'll put clean sheets on my bed for you and sleep on the floor. I'll take you out for drinks and we'll go dancing.'

I chew my bottom lip. 'Fine.'

Drew takes the case from my hand and sprints with it upstairs. 'Let's get you packed! Our train leaves at four,' he shouts over his shoulder making me laugh.

I follow him upstairs in time to stop him from opening my underwear drawer. I slap his hand away and order him onto the seat in the corner of the room. He shoots me a cheeky smile and I throw a pillow at his head.

'Perv,' I mutter.

'It's not like I haven't seen your knickers before, Prim,' he snickers.

'We were six,' I argue, stuffing underwear into the case before he can get a good look. 'And, I seem to remember stripping down because you covered me in slime.'

'Pond scum,' he corrects. 'We were looking for tadpoles and you fell in.'

'You pushed me,' I argue.

'It was slippery,' he counters.

I throw another pillow at his head and he laughs, making me smirk. We continue to argue the whole time I'm packing and it's nice to have my best friend back. Drew orders my train tickets using the app on his phone then helps me secure the cottage. I text aunt Katherine to let her know I'm going away with Drew, just in case she returns early and finds me gone. She texts back as our taxi pulls up to the station, ordering me to have a good time.

Drew gets our bags from the driver and carries them to the platform. He won't let me carry my own case, even though it has an extendable handle and wheels. I think he's worried if I do anything exerting I'll bleed again and our trip will be cancelled. How the hell he expects me to go dancing without exerting myself baffles me, but that's Drew's brand of logic.

'I can't believe it,' Drew says as the train groans into motion. The station disappears from view, the scenery beyond the glass blurring as the train gains speed.

'Believe what?' I ask.

'You're actually on the train.'

'I've been on a train before,' I drawl.

'But this time you're actually leaving the village for more than a day,' he argues.

I refrain from stating that the train station is located in the nearest town from the village, and we technically left it over an hour ago. Why he's getting so excited now is confusing. I've left the village for more than a day before. I've actually been on holiday, just not since Mum got sick. The only times I left for more than a day then was to sleep by her bedside in the hospital. I don't tell him that either.

'I've been on holiday before,' I say.

'But never as an adult,' he counters and a wicked grin stretches his lips. 'You're the legal drinking age now, Prim.'

I smirk. 'Just because I haven't been away in a while doesn't mean I don't drink,' I tell him.

'Oh yeah?' he smirks back.

'Yeah,' I say.

'What's your poison?'

'I enjoy a glass of wine, but gin doesn't give me a hangover,' I answer.

'I know a great gin bar we can go to in Liverpool.'

'I've never been to a gin bar,' I admit.

'Gin Bar Virgin,' he announces to the carriage.

'Drew!' I hiss, face warming with embarrassment.

He chuckles. 'I've missed that shade of pink.'

I smack his arm and a burst of his emotion hits me on contact. It's been difficult to read him since we got on the train. The carriage is filled with the combined emotion of everyone around us, diluting Drew's. But when I touch him, onyx tendrils reach out to caress his skin. His contentment washes through me and I resist the urge to give him a hug, to savour the emotion. It's been so long since I felt it.

'I've missed you, too,' I say.

His smile softens and he takes my hand. Drew's contentment floods my insides and I smile at him. We both go quiet, happy to just be together in this moment. I turn to watch the world pass outside the window, knowing this moment is fleeting. I can feel the fragile walls of its cocoon, like fine porcelain around me, and I draw as much of it in as possible. My fear from this morning seems a million miles away, and for the first time in a long time I'm happy.

Drew's emotion flexes then lightens. It's the strangest sensation and I pull my gaze from the window to look at him. I roll my eyes when I see he's asleep. The boy can sleep anywhere. My gaze drops to our interlaced hands. Darkness covers them, in a pretty lace pattern, taking lazy pulls of his contentment. I look back to his face and study his features. His strong jaw is dusted in three-day stubble, full lips parted in sleep. Thick lashes crest his cheekbones, blade-straight nose centralising his features. He's so handsome, and in moments like this I'm reminded of how easy it would be to be his.

Until life gets hard and he runs again.

I sigh and turn back to the window. If Drew were less of an emotional coward he'd be perfect. Not that I need someone emotionally stable in every way, just someone who's not afraid to deal with the dark parts of life. I'm part darkness, after all.

I step from the taxi and stare at the house Drew shares with three other guys. It has a green front door with a window at the top. Flowers decorate the circular piece of glass, and I can't imagine four males living beyond that door.

'This way,' Drew says, snagging my hand as he passes me. He has his bag slung over one shoulder, while he carries my case in his other hand.

'I can carry my own bag,' I say for the millionth time.

'I know,' he answers still not handing it over.

Drew drops my hand long enough to unlock the door then pulls me inside. He heads straight for the narrow staircase, pulling me up behind him then in through the third doorway along the landing. I don't get to see much of the house, but it smells clean.

He drops our bags onto a bed in the corner of the room and turns to face me. 'This is my room,' he declares.

I turn a slow circle to study his space. There's a small desk in the corner, a single bed and a slim wardrobe. The walls are painted light brown and the bedcovers match. I peer out the window to see a small but neat garden. I grin as I turn back, catching Drew in the act of kicking a pile of dirty laundry under the bed.

'You're still a pig then,' I say.

He offers a sheepish smile. 'I would've cleaned if I knew you were coming here.'

'We've known each other since we were five,' I counter. 'I kind of expected a lot worse.'

He opens his mouth then shuts it and shrugs. 'I can't argue with that.'

We leave our bags on the bed while Drew shows me the rest of the house. He points out the doors leading to three other bedrooms and the bathroom, on the way downstairs. He shows me the lounge and laundry room then takes me to the kitchen.

'Everything's so tidy,' I murmur.

'That would be my doing,' a deep voice with a Scottish brogue comments.

I spin to a guy sitting at the table in the kitchen. He has brown hair and hazel eyes, framed by thick-rimmed glasses. His face is lean, with prominent cheekbones and his smile is kind. He pushes to his feet and offers his hand.

'Primrose, this is Warren,' Drew introduces. 'Warren; Primrose.'

'Ah, the legendary Primrose,' Warren grins. 'It's a pleasure to finally meet you. I was starting to think Drew made you up.'

I slide Drew a curious glance to see him scowling at Warren. Drew's been talking about me with his house mates and I can feel he's worried Warren's going to drop him in it. I bite back the desire to ask Warren what he means but decide to save Drew instead.

'So, you're the reason it's so tidy in here?'

'Unlike my housemates, I can't live in a pigsty,' Warren answers.

'Don't you have some studying to do?' Drew grumbles.

'Don't you?' Warren counters but takes the hint. 'It was nice to meet you, Primrose,' he says, collects his coffee mug from the table and leaves.

'You didn't have to chase him off,' I say.

'Yes I did,' Drew answers.

I ignore his tone and go to peer out the window. 'Your garden is a suntrap.'

It's been days since I've been out to the meadow at home, mainly thanks to Zephyr, and I ache to be outside. I miss the wildflowers and untamed grasses of the meadow. They were my escape when Mum was sick, and the only thing able to calm the wild entity in my middle.

Drew unlocks a door at the end of the kitchen. 'You always did prefer it outside,' he smiles.

I return his smile as I sidle past him. I step onto the grass and lift my face to the sun, breathing a cleansing breath, and savouring the spring air.

'It's perfect out here.'

'Figures you'd like the garden more than the house,' Drew says. 'You always did like being surrounded by things that grow.'

He's right. Nature calms me, filling me with a sense of peace. It allowed me to breathe when life tried to suffocate me during Mum's illness. Lying amid the grass and flowers in the meadow is my escape. It's where I go when I need to be free.

'Do you want to eat out here or in the house?' Drew asks.

I move to the pond and peer at my reflection in the surface, before settling on the grass beside it. 'Eating out here is good with me,' I answer then look at Drew. 'What are we having?'

'My culinary prowess extends to cheese toasties, packet noodles or beans on toast,' he says.

'You've become such a talented chef,' I tease. 'I'll take option number one.'

He grins. 'You want crisps with that?'

'Salt and vinegar flavour?'

'Is there any other flavour worth having?' he smirks.

'Still not for you it seems.'

Drew laughs his way back inside to make our food. I grin at his retreating form then kick off my shoes and stretch out on my back beside the pond. The sun blinds me, so I close my eyes and inhale the earthy fragrance of the garden. I relax for the first time since leaving with Drew. Nothing strange has happened and my fear of Zephyr seems a million miles away.

The backs of my eyelids darken, the warmth of the sun fading from my skin. It must've dipped below the horizon and I shiver, sitting up to rub my eyes. Maybe I'll eat inside after all. I blink in my darkened surroundings then scramble to my feet, gaze darting around the unfamiliar space. I'm not in the garden anymore, but I'm also not anywhere I recognise.

The room is decorated in dark tones, with strange furniture and a spicy fragrance accenting the air. The floor feels like compacted earth beneath my bare feet, and the walls appear made from something similar to tree bark. An enormous bed lines one wall, vines curling around the posts at its corners. I stare at it, before my gaze finds a pair of ornate doors opposite.

'What are you doing in here?'

I whirl around to face a wall of muscle. It takes three steps back before I meet the man's midnight gaze, and I gasp when I do. Those eyes greet me every time I look in a mirror, except I'm not looking at my reflection. The man stares back at me looking as shocked as I feel.

'Christine?' he whispers.

If possible my eyes inch wider and I shake my head. 'Christine was my mother.'

'*Was?*'

'Mum passed away a few weeks ago,' I whisper. 'Cancer,' I add because it's usually the next question people ask.

Sorrow fills his handsome face and thickens the air around us. My heart starts pounding and the hairs on the back of my neck stand up. I can sense power in him and the immensity of it scares me, but more than that I recognise the pain in his gaze. It has been my companion for months and stops me from backing up another step.

I study his dark features, ebony eyes and midnight hair. He has powerful, angular features and muscle all over. He's naked from the waist up, hair hanging in dark waves over his shoulders. I see another set of doors behind him, explaining how he snuck up on me.

'You look just like your mother,' he murmurs, interrupting my perusal.

I meet his gaze. 'I know.'

He studies me as I've been studying him. 'Except you don't have her summer-sky eyes,' he says. 'Yours are more like-' he stops speaking, eyes growing wide, and stares at me. His gaze turns inward for a second then focuses back on me. 'I never knew,' he breathes. 'I didn't think it possible.'

The man steps forward and I back away from the immense energy pouring from him. Darkness rises inside me but it's acting like it did with Zephyr, like it wants to get closer. Fear clogs my throat and for a second I can't speak.

I push words through my dry lips when he takes another step in my direction. 'Stay back.'

He stops advancing. 'I won't harm you.'

His words do nothing to stifle the fear in my chest. It's a strange emotion that I'm struggling to process. The darkness in me has always had my back, so I've never really been afraid of anything. But it welcomed Zephyr and he hurt me, and I don't trust its judgement anymore.

'I don't know who you are, or this place,' I argue. 'The last thing I remember is dosing on my friend's garden then waking up here.'

'You're in my home,' he explains, tone soothing, like he's scared I'll bolt. If I knew how to get the hell out of here I would. 'I don't know why you chose to visit, but I'm glad you did.'

'*Chose?*' I scoff. 'I didn't *choose* to come here.' I glance around the unusual room. 'I want to go home now.'

'No!' he barks and I flinch, backing up another step. He raises his palms in surrender. 'Please,' he says tone placating. 'I'll show you how to leave, but only if you promise to stay for a short time.'

I glance around feeling trapped. I can't leave unless he shows me how to, so he's got me in a catch twenty-two situation. His expression is kind and a little wary, and I still don't trust him, but I need to cooperate or I'm stuck here.

'How long is a *short time?*' I ask.

'Just a few minutes,' he answers. 'I just want to speak with you, nothing more.'

I eye him warily. 'Who are you?'

His lips curve into a triumphant smile. 'My name is Aric, but you may call me Father.'

The blood drains from my face. 'What?'

'I'm your sire,' he grins, dark eyes twinkling. 'And you are named?'

Anger burns through the fear in my chest. This prick is claiming to be my long lost father? Does he think I'm stupid?

'What part of you is stupid enough to expect me to believe you could be my dad?' I snap. 'You don't look a day over twenty-five.'

'We age differently to humans,' he answers seeming confused by my outburst, before comprehension dawns through his features. 'But you know this?' he asks.

His words sear through my brain and my vision darkens around the edges. I realise I've stopped breathing and inhale a deep breath. If he thinks I'm his daughter then he's suggesting I'm not human. I feel my pulse beating wildly in my temples and a headache sparks to life behind my eyes.

'If not human then what are you?' I ask ignoring his question about what I know.

'You're yet to tell me your name,' he reminds me ignoring my question in return.

I chew on my lip debating whether to answer him then huff a frustrated breath. 'My name's Primrose.'

Aric smiles wide then closes the distance between us. I back up until I'm plastered against the nearest wall, but he ignores my behaviour and cups my face in his hands. His thumbs brush over my cheekbones, a blast of his delight pulsing through me on contact.

'My Primrose,' he breathes.

I frown, not liking the fact he called me his. He's missed the first twenty-two years of my life and I'm not *his* anything. Donating genetic material doesn't make someone a parent. My darkness doesn't seem to share my opinion, rising up to curl onyx tendrils over his hands and around his wrists, as if holding him to me. Aric's gaze dips to his hands and his delight flares brighter. My mouth drops open. Aric sees it – he sees my darkness and is beyond pleased by it.

'What are you?' I whisper.

'What are *we*,' he corrects.

'I'm human.'

I know I can't claim that anymore, judging by what's happening to me, but at least half of me *is* human, like Mum. As for the other half? I've always known I'm different, and Aric's the only one to ever see that part of me, which lends truth to his claims. But to find out I'm not human? It's difficult to admit that I'm different, so to believe I'm not even the species I think I am is proving impossible. I snort inwardly. Being here, in this moment, should be impossible, yet here I am.

'Can humans do that?' Aric asks and releases my face, dropping his gaze.

I reluctantly look down, to the trail of wildflowers blooming from the weird flooring. They're like a rainbow in the dark room, a mixture of exotic blooms in varying colours. They lead from where I found myself when I opened my eyes, seeming to accumulate around my feet.

'Are you suggesting I planted those flowers?' I hiss. 'Because you've been standing here the whole time and-'

He presses a finger to my lips. 'Walk to the mirror, Primrose.'

I shake his finger from my mouth and glare at him. 'Why?'

He smirks at my temper and I resist the urge to smack it from his face. Aric points to the adjacent wall and I gape when the organic material shivers then becomes reflective.

'How did you-'

Aric gives me a gentle push towards the mirror. 'Watch the flowers bloom in your wake,' he orders.

His bossiness rubs me the wrong way, but I take a few steps and look behind me, to the ground where I've walked. Green shoots sprout from the floor then bloom into exotic flowers in the places I've stepped. I turn, eyes wide, and watch the ground as I take a few backward steps. Flowers grow and bloom in my wake, just like Aric said they would.

'Holy crap,' I mutter.

Aric laughs, drawing my gaze back to his. He looks a mixture of smugness and pride, until my eyes brim with tears. He disappears in a cloud of black mist then reappears before me. I squeak at his reappearance and stumble back from his intrusion on my personal space.

'Did…Did you just teleport?' I rasp.

He counters my steps and rests his hands on my shoulders. 'Don't weep, my Primrose,' he croons. 'You have nothing to fear.'

My gaze slides to where my darkness is coiling around his hands on my shoulders. 'What the hell am I?'

'We're fae,' he answers.

'I, I don't know what that is,' I say meeting his gaze.

'Your mother called our kind faeries,' he tells me.

I feel my brow crinkle at his explanation, struggling to understand. Aren't faeries cute, little flying creatures that live in the woods? My thoughts turn to Zephyr and the purple glow in the hedgerow. Events from the last few days start clicking into place and making sense. Zephyr can appear from thin air, like Aric, and I *feel* him in the same way I *feel* Aric.

'Is Zephyr fae, too?'

Aric's brow crinkles. 'Zephyr?'

'I've always been different,' I admit gesturing to the flowers on the floor. 'But nothing like *that* happened until Zephyr kissed me. My darkness is different and he left tattoos on my skin.' I take a deep breath through the anger boiling up from my insides with each realisation. 'Zephyr did something that changed me. It hurt like hell and I almost died.'

Danger flashes through Aric's features. My skin prickles at the acute rage suddenly filling the space between us, as his hands flex on my shoulders.

'He marked you?' Aric asks in a deceptively soft voice.

Holy crap, and I thought Zephyr was scary?

'I don't know. I don't know what that entails.'

Aric's eyes bleed to black, shadow misting into the whites, until they're pure onyx, like mine on the day of

Mum's funeral. There's so much rage pouring from him it's difficult to breathe. It's raw and feral, and speaks to the wild entity in my middle.

'It means he tried to claim you,' Aric explains seeming unable to keep the snarl from his tone. 'But you can't do it to Halflings. Their bodies are too fragile in human form and they mostly don't survive the change into fae.'

'He did snarl *mine* at me, before he left me to bleed out on the kitchen floor,' I admit.

Aric's hands flex against my shoulders again. He closes his eyes and takes a few deep breaths, his power swelling around us. A series of fine, black lines web out from his eyes, like cracks in an oil painting. They're like fissures opening in his skin, allowing dark matter beneath to leak out. He has darkness inside him, just like me, only his *feels* so much more than mine.

Aric releases my shoulders then turns and stalks to the doorway across the room. 'Stay here,' he orders.

The doors blast open just before he reaches them and I panic.

'Where are you going?'

He glances at me over his shoulder, midnight gaze spearing mine. 'To arrange for Zephyr's mark to be removed,' he answers.

The doors slam shut, leaving me trapped inside his room. I stare at the doorway able to breathe now the oppressive weight of Aric's rage is gone. I take a cleansing breath and assess what just happened. A faerie? Laughter bubbles in my throat then turns to acid in my mouth. The need to be sick overwhelms me but I swallow it back down. I don't know whether to laugh or cry at the ridiculousness of it.

I sigh and lean against the mirrored wall behind me. There's no way I'm sitting on Aric's bed and there's nowhere else to sit in here, except the floor and it looks like compressed dirt. I grow annoyed that he just left me in here to stew over everything he's told me. He said he'd show me the way home if I stayed and talked for a few minutes, and he renegaded on his promise. I can't deal with this right now. I just want to go back to Drew's garden and go out dancing. I want to pretend I'm normal and none of this stuff is happening.

I squeal when the mirror disappears behind me, and blink to find myself sprawled on Drew's garden. I stare at the darkening sky wondering what the hell just happened.

'Do you want sauce with your toasty?' Drew shouts and I sit up to see him hanging out of the doorway to his student digs. 'I like mine smothered in brown sauce, but I know you're classier than me.'

'No sauce,' I murmur, trying to slow my racing heart.

He frowns. 'Are you okay? You've gone really pale.'

I force a smile. 'Just disorientated, you woke me up.'

Drew snorts. 'You can't sleep on a train but outside on the grass isn't a problem?'

I shrug and Drew goes back inside. I stare after him for a moment then look down at the grass to see flowers blooming around my bare feet. I reach over and snatch my shoes up, pulling them on before Drew comes out and sees it happening. It hits me that I'm not human and I choke back fresh fear. I don't know what to do. I don't know the first thing about fae, or why Zephyr is trying to claim me.

I think of Aric and my fear is momentarily eclipsed by the revelation that I just met my father. The abandoned little girl inside delights in the fact he seemed pleased with how I turned out. And he should, seeing as I'm not entirely human yet made it to adulthood without being certified crazy. That thought renews my confidence and I calm the hell down. All the changes I've gone

63

through don't mean I've changed as a person. I've navigated my way through some weird stuff growing up, but I've done it with no help from anybody, and I can bloody well do it again.

I shuffle away from the edge of the pond, now edged with pretty blooms. The flowers really are beautiful, and growing them isn't exactly a super power. Nor are the markings now covering my shoulders and back. It's not like I can suddenly shoot lasers from my eyes or throw cars around. So I can sense the emotions of others in a new way. I've always been able to do that to some extent. And my hearing is better, but that's nothing really. Nothing has changed to a degree I can't handle. I start to feel a little bit silly for freaking out.

'One cheese and tomato toasty,' Drew announces as he steps from the house. He plonks down on the grass beside me and offers me a plate.

'Looks delicious,' I tease.

'It's going to be the best toasty you'll ever eat,' he says as he smothers sauce over his own toasty.

'Do you want any toasty with that sauce?' I ask.

'Don't knock it until you've tried it,' he answers then takes a giant bite.

'Pig,' I scold him then hold my hand out for the bottle of sauce. 'Challenge accepted, hand it over.'

Drew grins and passes me the bottle. He watches me squirt a blob on a small corner of toasty then take a bite. I wrinkle my nose despite the fact I think it tastes good.

'Well?'

'It's not unpleasant,' I admit.

'It's awesome and you know it,' he scoffs.

Drew takes another huge bite, smearing sauce all over his face.

'You know you're disgusting, right?'

'I'm a guy,' he argues around a mouthful of food. 'I'm supposed to be disgusting. It's the law.' He swallows then says, 'You wouldn't want me any other way.'

I touch his hand with mine. 'You're right,' I tell him. 'You're perfect just the way you are.'

Emotion flashes through his sapphire gaze in the same moment his desire spikes through me. I pull my hand back but Drew snags it and holds it firmly in his. He leans in close and panic flares in my stomach. If Drew kisses me it will ruin everything.

'Drew, I-

He cuts me off by mashing his lips against mine. I start to freak out but he pulls away and grins at me like a loon.

'You've got a little sauce around your mouth,' he laughs.

I stare at the sauce on his face, which he just smeared all over mine.

'You dick,' I say but relief blasts through me.

Drew shovels more food into his mouth. I take another bite of mine and look away. I'm not in love with Drew, but I do love him. I look back at him and ache to tell him the stuff that's happening. But Drew has a safe, normal life and I don't understand what being fae means. I think of the agony Zephyr caused when he tried to claim me. I can't risk Drew over my need to confide in someone.

CHAPTER 7

Base vibrates the air and shakes the floor, in a way I've never felt. It's not that I've never been clubbing, just that it feels different this time. Drew pushes through the crowd, pulling me along in his wake. His hand around mine anchors me against the many emotions misting the air. My darkness is in a state of ecstasy, soaking in the collective emotion of those we pass. The sensation is warm and tingly, like I've had too much wine, yet I don't think it's got anything to do with how much I've been drinking.

Drew turns to me as we make it to the bar. His blond hair and blue eyes look so pale in the flashing lights of the club, like they're made of ice. There's a glittery hue to his irises that I find transfixing.

'What's your poison?' he shouts over the music, even though I can hear him fine. It's strange how I can hear so much better, yet the loud music doesn't hurt my ears. I don't understand it, but I'm grateful.

I blink to focus on what Drew's saying. 'You promised me gin,' I shout back.

He leans in close, so he can hear what I'm saying. He smells fresh, like ice and cold things. I'm confused by how much I like it. Drew gives me a puzzled look as he pulls away and orders our drinks. I can feel his confusion, matching my own, and give myself a shake. What the hell am I doing? Why am I so drawn to him all of a sudden? The need I feel to be close to him feels instinctual, and I have to force myself to ignore it. I'm acting weird enough for Drew to notice and I need to stop.

I take a sip of raspberry gin and look out into the club, curling the fingers of my free hand through the spirals I've put in my hair. The vibration of the music mixed with the emotional cloud inside the club is hypnotic. It's calling to the wildness in my middle and I can't ignore it. Drew gives me a quizzical look when I hand him my drink. The pretty brunette flirting with him glances between us, like she's worried we're a couple.

I lean in so she can hear me but Drew can't. 'He's my brother.'

She glances between us when I pull away and studies my blonde hair then Drew's and seems pleased. I decide Drew can thank me later, and push into the crowd. I hear him call after me but don't turn back. I make my way to the dance floor and squeeze between people to the centre. Emotion shoots through me in sharp blasts when I brush against those around me, and my darkness drinks it in. My arms are covered by the long-sleeve dress I'm wearing, but I can feel dark swirls curling over my skin. My eyes tingle and I feel the peculiar sensation of them bleeding to black. Part of me knows I should be worried that someone will see, but I can't ignore the consuming need to move in time with the music. My body sways with the sultry beat, the sound becoming a physical presence, guiding me into each move, until I feel it wrap around me in a heated caress.

'Anya,' a deep, accented voice purrs in my ear.

I realise I've shut my eyes, when they snap open at the sound of Zephyr's voice. What I thought was music wrapping around me is actually Zephyr. I'm plastered to the hard planes of his front, his hands spanning my lower back to keep me against him. He's the one moving us to the beat, our bodies flowing together as one.

My scalp prickles as I tilt my head back to look at his face. I suck in a breath when I meet his amethyst gaze. His eyes are stunning, dark pupils ringed with a jewelled corona. Black lashes frame each eye, making the purple irises extra surreal. I drag my gaze from his, taking in the rest of his features. Ebony hair frames an achingly beautiful face. It's almost too perfect to look at, and for a moment I just stare. His carved, kissable lips pull into a grin, displaying a set of white teeth. I see a flash of fang and sanity returns.

Fangs?

Zephyr has fangs!

I start to struggle, my flight instinct kicking in. Part of me can't believe that my imagination was right about his teeth. Okay, so his fangs aren't vampire sharp, but all the dangerous animals have teeth like that. Zephyr can easily take a chunk out of me. Maybe that's his plan.

He chuckles at my futile attempt to escape. 'Did you think to escape me, my Rose?' he purrs. 'Did you think I wouldn't find you?'

'Let me go!'

He strokes a spiral of hair from my face and leans closer, until his lips are by my ear. 'Never.'

I start struggling again and he chuckles against my ear. The sound and his scent do crazy things to my insides, but I shut the sensation down before it can take root. His lazy amusement at my fear terrifies me.

'Prim?' Drew says from behind me and I stop struggling, the fear for myself forgotten.

I look over my shoulder and meet Drew's furious gaze. He looks from me to Zephyr then back to me. The pretty brunette has followed him onto the dance floor and looks on with wide eyes.

'Get your hands off her,' Drew snarls at Zephyr.

I turn back to Zephyr when a strange vibration starts up between us. My eyes grow wide when I realise he's growling, but the other's can't hear it over the music. Static fills the air and my gaze drops to growing heat beside my left thigh. Zephyr's right hand is clawed, a ball of crackling, purple light forming between his fingers and palm. Power radiates from his hand, as the ball grows brighter. Realisation dawns on me and I stare up at his face in horror.

'No,' I whisper.

Fierce, amethyst eyes turn from Drew to me. 'Mine,' Zephyr snarls.

'Don't hurt him,' I plead.

Zephyr opens his mouth as if to answer, but a girl grabs his right wrist and hisses something at him in a language I don't understand. I glance between them, noting their similar features. She has Zephyr's golden skin tone, and her hair hangs in ebony waves down to her waist. She's as beautiful as he is, the lines of her body ultra feminine to the masculine lines of his. She glances my way and I glimpse purple irises. Zephyr glares at her then down at his hand. I follow his gaze in time to watch the amethyst light fade into his palm, the girl's body blocking the sight from those around us. She snarls something else at Zephyr and his grip on me tightens. He growls words at her in the same strange language she spoke to him, but she answers whatever he said with growled words of her own. Zephyr looks at me then glances around him. People are looking at us, and it's as if he only just realises.

He meets my gaze and his irises flash bright purple. Then he lets go and I stumble backward, until I feel Drew's reassuring presence behind me. Drew wraps a protective arm around my shoulder and pulls me into his side. Zephyr growls again, but Drew doesn't seems to hear it. My dark-haired rescuer uses her hold on Zephyr's wrist to keep him at bay. I don't know how she's handling the immense energy I feel pouring from him, but she seems to manage him with ease.

'I want to go,' I tell Drew.

Drew doesn't argue, his survival instinct apparently intact, as he turns me away and pushes me through the crowd gathered around us. The weight of Zephyr's stare sears the length of my spine. That non-physical part of him brushes against my skin. The darkness inside me rises to meet it then surprises me when it goes on the defensive, my skin going prickly as the wild thing coils to strike in my middle. My darkness didn't help me the last time I saw Zephyr, but maybe his attacking me made it realise he's a risk. If I die then so does my darkness.

The brunette realises Drew's a lost cause and disappears before we make it outside. Drew's too busy texting to notice, but doesn't take his arm from around my shoulder. His anger pulses through me at the skin-on-skin contact, but it gives me the strength to keep moving. He puts his phone in his pocket, and I realise who he was texting when another of his housemates appears from around the corner.

'Everything okay?' Max asks looking us over.

Max is tall with mocha skin and gorgeous, brown eyes. I'd kill for eyelashes like his. His hair it jet black, and has a wave to it, which he styles with gel and looks amazing. He plays rugby and is built all over, which is why I think Drew asked him to meet us. Max's nose is crooked from being broken more than once, but I don't think it would deter a majority of women.

'I'm taking Primrose home,' Drew answers. 'Are you staying out, or do you want to share our taxi?'

'I'm ready to head back,' Max says then winks at me.

Drew's anger fades in the taxi on the way home but I can't relax. I'm too busy wondering how Zephyr found me, miles from home, in the middle of Liverpool.

Drew's a little too drunk to realise how quiet I've gone. He's sharing a pizza with Max, and they both think the danger has passed.

Drew goes into the bathroom to brush his teeth when we get back to his house. I tug off my dress and stuff it into my bag. Onyx swirls curve over my body, in a restless pattern. The sight relaxes me because it's what my darkness does when it's on the defensive. And at least I know it's on my side again where Zephyr is concerned.

I spin to face the door when someone sucks in a breath behind me. Drew stands in the doorway with his mouth hanging open.

'My face is up here,' I snap when his gaze remains fixed below my neckline.

His eyes snap up to meet mine, and he offers a guilty smile. 'I was just checking your ink out.'

'The ink is on my back,' I drawl then pull my pyjamas on.

'Won't you let me take a look?' he asks.

'I'm tired,' I complain. 'Besides, standing around in my bra and pants, while you gawk at my back, isn't how I envisioned the night ending.'

'You could always take them off,' he suggests with a cheeky smile.

I throw a pillow at him. 'Behave.'

'A gorgeous girl is sleeping in my room tonight,' he answers. 'Can't blame me for trying.'

'You're a drunken idiot,' I answer and climb into his bed.

Drew turns out the light then dives across the room and lands on the airbed on the floor. I burrow under the covers and curl into a ball, rolling my eyes when Drew starts to lightly snore. The boy can fall asleep faster than I can blink. The sound is weirdly reassuring, though and I find my eyelids drooping. I shut them for just a moment.

Muffled tapping pulls me from the hazy world of sleep. I crack an eye open to see it's still dark then frown

71

into the room. I sit up at the outline of a person in the mirrored door of Drew's wardrobe. A scream builds in my throat, until I recognise the amused gaze staring back at me, and huff in relief. I push from the bed and tread carefully over Drew's sleeping form. He's facedown on the airbed snoring so loud I wonder how I heard Aric's tapping over it. Aric's grin flashes white in the mirror as I step up to it.

'How?'

Aric puts a finger to his lips, signalling for me to be quiet, and peers over my shoulder at Drew. I watch as my father presses a palm to his side of the mirror then meets my gaze with an expectant look. I don't know what he expects me to do, but he nods when I lift my hand in response. He nods again when I move it towards him, aligning my hand with his. The warmth of his palm meets mine, his fingers gripping my hand, before pulling me towards him. I stumble forward, into my father's waiting arms. He steadies me, while I look over my shoulder and gape through the glass into Drew's bedroom.

'Holy crap,' I whisper.

Aric chuckles. 'Your reaction to the mirror gateway surprises me,' he says.

I turn to meet his gaze. 'Why?'

'Because you used it to travel to me before, then again to leave during your last visit,' he answers.

I did?

'I didn't find or leave you on purpose the first time we met. Besides, there isn't a mirror in Drew's garden to do what we just did, so how would I know to use one?'

Aric nods in understanding. 'I wondered why I couldn't track your exit,' he murmurs, as if a mystery has been solved. 'You must've opened a gateway using a natural reflection. No wonder it took so long to find you.'

'You do know I have no idea what you're talking about?' I tell him.

He gives an indulgent smile. 'I have so much to teach you, my Primrose.'

I'm not sure I like the sound of that, but I nod. 'Okay.'

'Glass mirrors are traceable because they are constant,' he tells me. 'But any reflective surface can be used to open a portal, such as rivers, puddles-'

'Ponds?' I cut in thinking of the one in Drew's garden.

'Yes,' Aric says. 'Portals created from organic sources are harder to trace,' he explains. 'They fluctuate, flexing with the changing environment around them, and are easily lost.

'And you were looking for me? Even though you thought I'd left on purpose.'

'Of course,' he answers, like it's a stupid question. 'I wish to know you.'

My eyes sting with the threat of tears. I'm an emotional wreck right now, and I've craved those words from him for a very long time. I've hated my father for years, for leaving Mum and breaking her heart. But there were times I dreamed of meeting him. I imagined what he'd look like, wondering if we shared any features other than our eyes.

'You didn't know I existed?' I ask, needing to be sure.

'If I'd known Christine carried my heir, things could've been different,' he answers. 'But I left for her protection.'

Okay, this is new.

'You mean you didn't want to leave Mum?'

'I've lived a long time, Primrose,' he murmurs. 'Leaving your mother remains the hardest thing I've ever had to do. And knowing she no longer lives-' He closes his eyes and breathes deep, before fixing his raw gaze on me. 'Part of me has died with her, and when my light fades I pray she'll be waiting.'

'Mum loved you so much she found it difficult to look at me, because my eyes reminded her of you,' I admit.

He nods. 'Your eyes are how I first recognised you as my offspring.'

'You broke her heart, though' I add struggling to ignore years of resentment. 'And I hated you for it.'

Pain creases his features and pollutes the air around us. But he needs to know what it's taking for me to be here. Aric might have meant well when he left, but he broke my mum when he did. I don't doubt that she loved me, but part of her died when Aric left her, and she was a shade of the person she once was – a person I never got to know.

Aric takes my hand in his. 'I know I've failed as a father, but I promise to make it up to you, Primrose.'

He takes me deeper into the room I woke in the last time I visited. I look behind me to see the doorway gone from the mirror and my wary expression staring back. Flowers bloom from the floor in my wake. I've discovered it only happens when I walk barefoot on organic surfaces, which is good news for my carpets at home I suppose.

'Why do I leave a trail of flowers when I walk barefoot?' I ask. 'I've walked barefoot outside for years without this happening.'

'Something woke your dormant fae genes,' Aric answers.

'But how do you know that? You weren't there before it started happening, so it's not like you can contrast and compare.'

'You're not the first Halfling, Primrose,' he says.

I meet his gaze and purse my lips. I don't like where this conversation is leading.

'So there are others?' When he doesn't answer right away I ask, 'Were any of them yours?'

Aric's eyes widen and he shakes his head. 'You're my only heir.'

'That you know of,' I argue. 'After all, you didn't know about me until I showed up here.'

'Your mother was the only human female I took to my bed,' he answers.

Something inside settles, but I need more answers. 'Don't you mean, *someone* activated my fae genes?' I say returning to our previous topic.

Aric's anger prickles my skin, meaning I hit the nail on the head. Most of the weirdness in my life stemmed from Zephyr kissing me, triggering whatever had me bleeding out on the kitchen floor.

'When Zephyr marked you, his light triggered the dormant light in you, activating your fae genetics,' Aric explains.

'Marked me?'

'He put his mark on you,' Aric clarifies. 'It's one of the ways fae claim something as theirs, so other fae will know not to try.'

'Let's get one thing straight,' I grit out. 'I do *not* belong to Zephyr! I don't even know the guy, so he can shove whatever claim he tried to put on me where the sun doesn't shine.'

'Of course you don't,' Aric agrees, smirking at my tirade.

'Explain the light you keep talking about,' I say moving on now I have Aric's agreement.

'Our kind are beings of light, Primrose. It's a part of us, and we a part of it.'

'I hate to burst your bubble, but there's definitely no light inside me,' I tell him.

'What do you think is making the flowers grow in your wake?' he counters.

I glance at the flowers on the ground behind me, but can't fathom his words. I'm a creature of darkness and always have been. I've seen my darkness since Zephyr changed me. I feel it even now, deep at my centre. I'm yet to witness any sort of light.

'Your feet are bare,' I argue. 'There aren't any flowers sprouting wherever you step.'

'Flowers aren't part of my gifts,' he smirks.

'I'm glad you find my confusion amusing,' I mutter then glance around. 'Where are you taking me?'

Aric's smirk vanishes. 'To remove Zephyr's mark from you.'

Memories of the agony I suffered after Zephyr's kiss surface and I swallow hard, hating that I'm showing my fear. 'Will it hurt?'

Aric stops before a set of ornately carved doors and looks down at me. 'None will inflict pain upon you, Primrose,' he vows, a vicious edge to his tone.

He raises a hand to the doors and they swing open. Aric grins at my surprised expression and uses a finger to push my mouth shut.

'Sorry,' I mutter.

'The simplest things surprise you,' he smiles. 'And I find myself eager to witness everything you've yet to discover.'

He sounds so excited that the sarcastic retort dies on my tongue. Instead, I offer him a smile and let him pull me through the doorway. My smile fades when I realise there are fae waiting for us. I inch closer to Aric as we move through the room, the hairs on my neck rising at the many stares I'm receiving. I'm acutely aware that I'm in my pyjamas, and everyone here looks dressed for an upmarket party. The room Aric's pulling me through is huge. Trees line the walls, like pillars, branches reaching high into the vaulted ceiling. Everything appears made from intricately carved wood, and the floor is the same organic substance in Aric's room. I cringe, thinking of the flowers no doubt blooming in a trail behind me. I daren't look back to check, but I see others staring at the ground behind my feet.

Everyone we pass is beautiful in a way that's difficult to comprehend. There's a sparkly quality to their skin, like they're woven from a billion particles of light that shimmer when they move. I think of the purple dust Zephyr left on my skin. I haven't been able to get it off, and for some stupid reason it makes me feel a little better. I'm sparkly like everyone here, which is one less difference between us. But we *are* different, in more ways than I can count. I start with the fact that everyone is taller than me. At five feet, five inches, I've never really been classed as short, but I get the feeling I will be here.

'Who are all these people?' I whisper to Aric as we reach the opposite end of the hall.

I frown at the way he doesn't move around people. Maybe it's because he's pulling me along and they're scared I'll soil their pretty clothes, but everyone just moves out of his way.

'They're here to see the king,' Aric answers.

'What? I'm not exactly dressed to meet their king,' I squeak.

Aric chuckles. 'He doesn't care what you're wearing, Primrose,' he says, as he guides me up a set of steps, leading to where a large throne sits.

'Wait,' I say, pulling against his hold on my hand but he doesn't let go, and keeps dragging me towards the throne. 'You can't know what the king will do when he sees me,' I argue.

'Yes I can,' he answers and pulls me up the last few steps.

'Majesty,' a male fae greets Aric as we reach the throne, then bows at the waist.

Oh crap.

I stare at the man then look at Aric, who has an indulgent smile on his face. 'Malak,' he greets the male. 'I'd like you to meet my daughter, Primrose.'

'It's an honour, Princess,' Malak says and sweeps into another bow.

Holy crap.

'I, um-' I look to Aric for help and he grins back at me. '*You're* the king?'

Aric nods and a sinking sensation drops through my stomach. Laughter bubbles up my throat and I have to swallow it down. I'm guessing it will be of the hysterical variety, and I feel awkward enough in this moment. But seriously: a fairy princess? It's like all my childhood fantasies are manifesting. I glance around the room. It's less pink than my five-year-old self imagined, but still sparkly. All I need is for a unicorn to trot by and the fantasy is complete.

'Where's Darrak?' Aric asks, drawing my focus.

'Lord Darrak awaits you in the mediation chamber,' Malak answers.

'Very good,' Aric murmurs and pulls me past Malak to a set of doors directly behind the throne.

The doors lead into a room with a large, wooden table in the centre. One wall is just a long mirror, reflecting my wary expression. Flowers are already blooming from the organic floor around my feet, making me wish I'd worn socks to bed. A male stands from a seat around the table. He's blond and handsome, and it reminds me again that I'm wearing my pyjamas. Amber eyes rake over me as he strides in our direction. Other than Zephyr, he's the hottest male I've ever seen.

'Majesty,' he greets Aric with a bow then looks at me. 'And Lady-'

'Princess,' Aric corrects.

The hot guy glances between us. 'My apologies, Princess.'

'Primrose,' I murmur. 'Just call me Primrose.'

The title thing seems ridiculous. It doesn't even seem real. I'm not princess material, so hearing people call me it is starting to freak me out.

'I'd never deign-' Hot Guy begins but Aric cuts him off.

'It's fine in a private situation such as this, Darrak. Primrose is the reason I requested your presence.'

Darrak looks me over. 'How may I serve?'

'Primrose has been marked without my permission,' Aric answers. 'I want it removed.'

Darrak's gaze turns back to me, sweeping once more over my frame. 'I will be honoured to remove the marking from you, Primrose.'

My face heats under the gleam in his gaze. The look he's giving me suggests he'll enjoy whatever it takes to remove Zephyr's claim, and I don't get it. Darrak's like an Adonis, and I'm just me. Now I've seen Zephyr, I don't understand his interest in me either. I'm not tall and statuesque, like most of the female fae I've seen. And I keep it modest in the clothes department, compared to the skimpy garments I've seen some of them wearing. Why would either male be interested in me when they can have a female fae? It makes me feel like I'm missing something and I don't like it.

'Do you consent for Darrak to remove Zephyr's claim on you?' Aric asks.

I nod my head. Insanely hot or not, I want Zephyr's claim removed. Maybe then he'll leave me alone and I can go back to grieving Mum.

Aric gives me a gentle push in Darrak's direction. 'You may proceed.'

Darrak takes my hand and leads me to the table. I suck in a breath, when he grabs my waist and lifts me to sit on the edge of the polished surface. He parts my knees before I know what's happening and situates himself between them. Panic grips me at the compromising position. Darrak cups my face in both hands and brings his face close to mine.

'I can smell his mark on you,' he murmurs. 'But I can fix that.'

'What-'

He cuts my words off by pressing his lips to mine. My body goes painfully tight with shock. The last time I got kissed by a male this gorgeous, I almost died. But Darrak's kiss isn't forceful. His lips are a soft press against mine, and his hands on my face are gentle. He runs the tip of his tongue along the seam of my lips and my stomach flip-flops with desire. His tongue teases my mouth open then dips inside. He tastes like peaches and cream, and I moan in response.

Darrak slides a hand down the length of my spine then pulls me closer. Our bodies are so close I can feel the flex of muscle on his chest. A growl vibrates from inside him and he deepens the kiss. Something shifts in the centre of my chest and I flinch. I try to pull away, but Darrak holds me in place, his other hand weaving through my hair to stop my retreat. The thing in my chest heats up and uncoils. It snakes from my chest, until I gag when it lodges in my throat.

I rip my mouth from Darrak's but he doesn't let go. He uses his grip on my hair to pull down, forcing my face up, as a ball of violet light explodes from my throat. The light hovers above us for a moment, before shooting back towards me.

Aric appears at my side and snatches the ball of light from the air. He grips it in his palm and glares at it. His eyes grow wide and he looks at me, like he knows something. Then he snarls and throws the light at the mirrored wall. It passes through, sending ripples across the surface, as it disappears.

Darrak and Aric share a look, and I know something just happened that I don't understand – Something they weren't expecting. I open my mouth to voice my question but scream instead. Searing pain burns through my left wrist, and I stare down in horror, as a symbol appears in violet light on my skin. It circles my wrist, weaving around it, like a glimmering, amethyst bracelet.

Aric pushes Darrak aside and clasps my left hand to study the marking. My father's eyes bleed to black and his rage boils through the air. My darkness bubbles up in response, fizzing just beneath my skin. It's on the defensive again, waiting to see if it needs to attack. A growl vibrates the space around Aric and he leans forward to blow gently on my wrist. The burning eases, until there's just a dull throbbing. My darkness settles a little but doesn't relax.

'I'm going to kill him,' Aric murmurs.

'You said removing Zephyr's mark wouldn't hurt,' I pant, my heart still racing. I point to the shimmering mark around my wrist. 'And what the hell is this? You didn't tell me I'd get this as a result.'

How the hell am I supposed to hide a shining, purple mark on my wrist back home? I finger the design, feeling that it's raised against my flesh, and my eyes widen. It's a brand. Zephyr branded me.

'I didn't realise the Zephyr that marked you, is the heir to the Light Realm,' Aric growls.

I meet his furious gaze. 'What? What the hell does that mean?'

'This,' he snarls gesturing to my branded wrist, 'is a Mate Marking.'

Mate Marking? It doesn't take a genius to figure out what that means.

'No,' I hiss and shake my wrist at Aric. 'Take it off. Please, I don't want it.'

Aric shakes his head. 'It cannot be removed, Primrose. You and Zephyr are connected-'

'No!' I shout and push from the table. 'He can't do this to me. He never asked!' I claw at the marking, wincing at the raw flesh. 'There has to be a way to get it off.'

Aric catches hold of my right hand when my left wrist starts to bleed against my clawing. He pulls me against him, holding me close when I try to push away. I fight him until I don't have the strength anymore then curl into his embrace. A sob escapes and I can't help the angry tears that follow.

'Leave,' Aric murmurs.

I open my eyes to see Darrak turn back as he reaches the exit. 'I offer you my protection, Princess,' he vows before leaving.

'It appears you've captured another heart,' Aric says. 'Yet another of your gifts.'

I look up at his face. 'Why did Zephyr do this?'

'The spring equinox approaches and Oric's light is fading,' Aric answers. 'Zephyr needs to mate before he takes the throne from his father, and it appears he's chosen you.'

'I don't want to be mated to him,' I argue. 'Don't I get a say?'

Aric tucks a length of hair behind my ear. 'You won't be uniting with Zephyr.'

'But you just said-'

Aric puts a finger over my lips. 'Fae can only unite during the solstice or equinox, and Oric cannot hold on much longer. Zephyr needs to mate during this equinox because Oric will fade soon after. If Zephyr can't get to you then he can't mate you. He'll be forced to pick another and you will be free.'

Hope blasts through my anger, but it's twinned with an emotion that confuses me. Jealousy sinks deep claws through my gut at the thought of Zephyr choosing another.

'I thought you said we're connected,' I find myself saying.

'The Mate Mark means you and Zephyr are mates, not mated,' Aric answers.

'Well, that's not confusing in the slightest,' I growl, beyond enraged by the whole thing.

My temper is getting difficult to control, made worse by the strange emotions I'm experiencing where

Zephyr is concerned. Why in the name of fae everywhere would I feel jealous about another female claiming him? I don't even want him!

'The Mate Mark signifies that Zephyr claimed you as his and the request was accepted by you,' Aric say.

'I never-'

'It's a biological reaction, Primrose. Your mind might not want him, but you're biologically suited.' Aric snorts an irritated sound. 'Zephyr probably sensed the match and sought you out.'

'What do you mean?'

'Zephyr is of royal descent. He's a powerful fae, with a pure bloodline. It means there aren't many females that are biologically compatible as a possible mate for him.'

I pinch the bridge of my nose against the migraine forming behind my eyes. 'And I am?'

Aric nods. 'Mated pairs are linked by their light. Compatible pairs will sense each other and be drawn together. Zephyr will have sensed you, but your reaction to him will have been dimmed by the fact you were still human.'

'Until he changed me.'

Aric's expression is grim. 'Your light must've called to him enough for him to know you were a possible match, and his claim activated your fae genes.'

'So, he didn't actually know I was a match when he claimed me?' I scoff.

'If he didn't think it likely, he wouldn't have attempted it,' Aric answers.

'Why not?'

'Because most Halflings don't survive the transition into fae,' he reminds me. 'Fae light is too much for a frail human body to contain, and mostly it kills the human before their body has chance to become fae.' Aric sighs. 'It's why I left your mother.'

'Wait, Mum was a Halfling?'

He shakes his head. 'No, and I wouldn't have risked changing her if she was. As a human, my light would've slowly killed her.'

His words raise the tiny hairs on my neck. 'What?'

Aric lifts his arm, and my eyes widen when midnight tendrils snake over his forearm down to his hand. They reach out from his fingertips and cup my face. My darkness responds, reaching out to explore Aric's dark energy in return.

'You have darkness inside you, too?' I whisper.

'This isn't darkness, Primrose,' he says. 'It's my light.'

'But it's black,' I argue.

He nods. 'Only Royal Dark Fae carry it.'

'Dark Fae?'

'I rule the Dark Fae,' he answers. 'Oric rules the Light Fae.'

'So, I'm Dark Fae and the darkness inside me is actually a form of light?'

'It is,' Aric answers, sounding proud.

'But, my darkness — I mean, my light, didn't manifest when Zephyr claimed me. Sure, it's acting weird since he kissed me, but I've had my light for as long as I can remember.'

'Impossible,' Aric argues. 'You would've been too frail to contain it in your human form.'

I was too frail to control it.

I shrug. 'I'm only telling you what I know.'

My stomach churns and I swallow a lump in my throat. Aric's revelation about his light killing Mum has a knot forming in my stomach. My skin prickles and dread floods my insides.

'What did you mean about your light slowly killing Mum?' I ask.

Aric sighs. 'I adored Christine, but so did my light.' His brow wrinkles. 'My light couldn't get enough of her, and I had to rein it in around her, lest it damaged her fragile form. If I lost my focus for even a moment it would latch onto her, drawing her essence.'

Oh god. My heart is pounding by the time he stops talking, thinking of how much his explanation runs parallel to what I've experienced with my own light. I think of what it means and crushing weight presses down on my chest. Hot grief wells up inside, clogging my throat.

'I can't control my light,' I rasp.

'A human wouldn't have the mental ability to control fae light,' Aric agrees. 'If what you say is true-'

'It's true,' I snap, lashing out with the weight of my realisation.

Oh god, what have I done?

His gaze softens. 'Then I'm in awe you're alive,' he says. 'And I thank the Goddess for it.'

'But you know what it means, right?' I argue. 'I killed Mum.' Tears blur my vision at voicing the truth. 'My light craved Mum the way you said yours did. Whenever I was near her, it would leech her emotion.'

'Primrose-'

'She used to get headaches,' I say ignoring his placating tone. 'They got so bad sometimes she couldn't get out of bed. The doctors didn't know what was wrong with her for a long time. Then one day she got really sick, and they diagnosed her with a rare form of cancer.'

I take a shuddering breath as tears spill down my face. It feels like there's a vice around my insides, slowly choking me.

'There were drugs and chemotherapy,' I whisper, 'but nothing worked. I watched her die and it was slow.' I push from Aric's arms and back away at the memory. 'Maybe I didn't cause the cancer, but I made her sick and too weak to fight it.'

Aric rests a comforting hand on my shoulder but I shrug him off. 'I'm fae,' he reminds me. 'You can't hurt me that way, Primrose.'

His words are meant to console, but memories surface of my darkness leeching emotion from someone I love. I think of how tired Katherine's been, and the headaches she complains of. I'd thought they were because of Mum's passing. But Katherine worries about me and has spent so much more time around me than usual.

I feel eleven years old again, sitting on the floor of Amy's bedroom watching Charlotte cry. I feel like the snake I likened myself to back then. I've been coiled around my friends and family for years, my darkness slowly consuming them.

Monster.

I swallow back bile. 'How do I control it? How can I stop my light from hurting the people I love?'

'I'll teach you,' Aric assures me. I flinch when he takes my hand but he holds firm. 'It isn't your fault, Primrose. If anyone is to blame for Christine's death it's me. I should've been strong enough to visit and make sure she was well. But Christine was my weakness and I failed you both. I won't fail you again.'

I don't know what to say in response. The same numbness from the day of Mum's funeral creeps over me and I let it come. My light wraps me up in a cocoon, offering its brand of comfort, and I block out enough feeling to focus.

'How will you prevent Zephyr from mating me?' I ask, voice flat.

If Aric notices the change in me he doesn't comment. 'By keeping you in the Dark Realm,' he answers. 'To complete the bond, you and he will have to join intimately during the equinox. Without a physical joining your lights will not bind and Zephyr will be forced to choose another or miss his opportunity.'

'You said matches for Zephyr are rare?' I murmur.

'They are.'

'Then won't I be stuck here until he finds another match?'

Aric squeezes my hand. 'This is where you belong, Primrose.'

Aric speaks with such confidence, like I'll agree to give up my life and stay in the Dark Realm with him. I think of how Katherine and David will react when I don't come home. Then I think of Drew freaking out when he wakes up in the morning and finds me gone. All of my things are still in his room and he'll know something happened to me. He'll try to find me, and when he doesn't, he'll contact Katherine. I can't do that to her. I can't let her go through losing Mum then me.

'I need to go back and tell Drew I'm leaving,' I say.

'The male sleeping on the floor?'

I nod. 'He's my best friend. I can't just disappear on him. He'll worry.'

'It's too dangerous,' Aric answers. 'You carry Zephyr's Mate Mark, meaning he's able to locate you in whatever realm you're in. But he won't enter the Dark Realm without my permission.'

I see the resolve in his eyes and know I'm stuck until Aric lets me go. Panic tries to infiltrate the numbness but my light won't let it. I'm going through the motions, feeling detached from the situation. Discovering Zephyr can locate me anywhere should have me freaking out, but I'm taking it in my stride. And I can see Aric's logic. Perhaps staying in the Dark Realm is best, at least until he teaches me how to control my darkness.

'You said you'd teach me how to control my light.'

'And I will, but first I'm going to teach you a simple defensive move,' he answers.

I raise an eyebrow. 'You think I'll need it here?'

'I don't like how defenceless you are,' he counters. 'And learning this will teach you the fundamentals of how to focus the energy inside you.'

Oh. 'Okay then.'

Aric takes my right hand and turns it palm up. 'I'm going to teach you how to create an essence orb.' He lifts his own hand and a sphere of crackling, black light forms above his palm. 'Like this one.'

'Bloody hell,' I whisper.

It's a midnight version of the ball Zephyr made in the club. Heat radiates from it in the same way, and my skin prickles with awareness. Static fills the air, my skin humming with energy.

'It's called an essence orb because it's drawn from your essence,' Aric explains. 'The colour of a fae's light denotes their lineage, which is why I recognised which Zephyr marked you. Only royal Light Fae carry the amethyst light. Just as royal Dark Fae carry the black.' Aric closes his hand around the orb, extinguishing it. 'Now you try.'

I stare at my right palm but nothing happens. 'I don't think my light works the same way,' I mutter.

'Nonsense,' Aric answers and cups under my hand with his. 'Light fills you to the brim, Primrose. I *feel* it. Your palm is one place it can exit. You must draw it forth from here,' he explains pressing his other hand to my stomach. 'Focus your thoughts there, find where the light pools, and order it to your right palm.'

My focus turns inward, to the wild entity in my middle. The more I concentrate, the stronger the beast grows. It bubbles then flows up through my body. My arm tingles growing warm, as the sensation trickles down to my hand. A small, black spark crackles in my right palm.

'That's it,' Aric coaches. 'Now feed the spark. Let light pool in your palm, until it forms an orb.'

I imagine siphoning more of the fizzing sensation to my palm. I grin when the spark grows into a ball of crackling, black fire.

'I'm doing it,' I breathe.

Aric drops his hand from the back of mine and moves a few metres away. I glance between him and the black sphere in my hand, wondering what he's doing.

'Grip the orb and throw it to me,' he orders. 'You won't hurt me, Primrose,' he says when I hesitate. 'I'll catch it.'

I curl my fingers around the sphere and grip it tight. It's hot and alive in my hand, sizzling with power. It pulses, snapping with energy, as I pull my arm back and throw it at Aric. He snatches it from the air then plays with it, throwing it up and down in one hand, as if to test the weight.

'It's your turn to catch,' he says.

I nod and hold my hands out ready. Aric launches the orb at me faster than I expect and I flinch, ready for the impact. But my right hand darts out and snatches it from the air before it hits me. I blink at the ball in my hand, shocked I moved so fast.

'It belongs to you,' Aric chuckles. 'The light is part of you so you felt it and reacted before your mind fully registered it was there. Your light knows what to do to protect you, Primrose. You must trust it.'

'I *do* trust it – most of the time,' I answer then, 'I thought you said this was a defensive move, but you caught the orb and played with it. Won't everyone just do the same?'

'I can catch it because the light within you is also in me,' he says. 'You will always be a part of me, Primrose; my only offspring.'

His words make me feel warm, like I've achieved something just by being born. But it's a feeling I used to get with Mum; one I thought I'd never feel again. It infuses the numbness my darkness is creating, and I feel cherished.

'What will it do to Zephyr?' I say rolling the orb between my hands, feeling the energy crackle between my palms. 'Will it hurt him? Will it kill him?'

The idea of killing Zephyr turns my stomach. I don't care how scared he makes me I'm not a killer. I think of Mum and cringe, a wave of grief searing through the numbness to coat my skin. I already *am* a killer. I shake my head, trying to shake off the curved claws of loss in my middle. There's a difference between choosing to kill and doing it by accident.

Aric shakes his head. 'Your orbs won't kill Zephyr because he's a royal, but they'll hurt. Non-royal fae are a different story,' he warns. 'The light they carry isn't as powerful, so they're more likely to die. And humans would definitely perish.'

My gaze snaps to his. 'Die?'

'Your light is very powerful, Primrose,' Aric answers. 'It will never harm you, but you must learn to control it for the sake of others. Until then, I think it best you not create orbs around humans or common fae.'

'I won't,' I assure him. 'But what if Zephyr finds me? Can't he just use a mirror to get here, like I did?'

'Zephyr wouldn't dare enter the Dark Realm,' Aric says. 'He's never been here, so opening a mirror portal will be impossible anyway.'

'Let's just pretend I grew up knowing nothing about fae, and need you to explain that,' I say, frustrated Aric keeps eluding to stuff like I should know it.

'Dissolve your orb,' he orders. When I give him a pointed look he says, 'Hold it tight and return it to the well in your centre.'

I wrap my fingers around the orb and think of it returning to my core. It shrinks, sinking into my palm, until my hand is a clenched fist with nothing inside it. Aric takes my hand and leads me to the mirrored wall. He presses my palm to the surface and steps back.

'Think of a destination you'd like to go to,' he says. 'It has to be somewhere you've been to, or can picture perfectly enough to manifest a doorway there. And there has to be a reflective surface at that destination for a portal to open in.'

The image of my bedroom at home fills my mind, and I gasp when the same image fills the mirror. I'm staring at my bed from a sideways angle, and it takes a few seconds to realise I'm looking out from the mirrored door on my wardrobe.

'Is this real?' I ask.

'Push forward,' Aric answers.

I do, and my hand slips through the surface of the mirror. It feels like a thin membrane, solid to touch, but elastic in texture. It's viscous when I push through, like I'm passing through jelly, but isn't wet. I pull my arm back, losing contact with the mirror. The image on the other side wavers then dissipates, until I'm staring at my reflection.

'Zephyr won't be able to create a portal to the Dark Realm because he's never been here,' Aric clarifies. 'He has no memory or image to call upon to manifest a doorway. The only way of him getting here is by invitation or tracing another's doorway.'

'Tracing?' I ask, turning to face him. 'What's that?'

'This,' he answers and presses his palm to the mirror. The image of my room reappears and he looks at me. 'I've reopened the doorway last created between this mirror and the one in that room. I don't need an image of it, I just used my light to trace the last doorway opened.'

'Like pressing redial on a phone,' I say.

'Phone?'

'You don't know what a-' I shake my head. 'It doesn't matter. Is there a way to stop someone from tracing the doorways I've opened?'

Aric punches the wall, making me squeal in surprise and jump back. Cracks web out from the impact and parts of the mirror shatter, raining shards of glass onto the floor.

'Break the exit mirror,' Aric answers, like he didn't just make that clear enough. 'If either mirror is broken, the doorway loses its integrity.'

A dozen fae teleport into the room before I can say anything. They surround Aric in an arrow formation then aim a collection of weapons at me. A hand grips my throat from behind, pulling me backwards. My back meets a hard body and fear spikes through the numb layer my darkness provides. Energy crackles from the hand, stinging my throat.

'Stand down!' Aric roars.

The weapons are withdrawn as he pushes through the fae around him. The hand releases my throat and I stumble when the hard body disappears from behind me. Aric presses probing fingers to my throat. His eyes are full black and menace charges the air between us. My throat feels bruised, which surprises me because the hand on my throat was restraining, not crushing.

'You dare attack her?' Aric snarls.

'We heard the wall smash,' a male argues from behind me. 'We thought you under attack.'

'You have marked her,' Aric growls. 'Marked my heir.'

There's a collective gasp then a muscular fae moves around me, and drops to one knee at my feet. He presses a fist to the ground, head bowed when he addresses me.

'I accept the penalty, Princess,' he says.

'What's he talking about?' I croak.

'He injured you,' Aric answers. 'Such an act is punishable by death.'

I look from the kneeling fae to Aric, not quite believing what I'm hearing. 'What the hell are you talking about?'

'His life is yours to take, Primrose.'

'I'm not taking his life,' I hiss unable to mask the incredulous edge to my voice. 'He thought he was

92

protecting you,' I point out solidifying my point. 'Why would I want to kill him for that?'

'Your princess offers you mercy, General Denlyr,' Aric murmurs to the fae bent at my feet.

Denlyr lifts his face, vibrant orange gaze meeting mine. His skin is mocha, long, black hair tinged with orange highlights that match his eyes. When he smiles I see a flash of fangs. They remind me of Zephyr's, like the kind I've seen on wolves in nature programmes.

Feral.

The word whispers through my mind and I find it fitting. The Fae I've met have a regal elegance to them, but it's an illusion to hide the feral side they're masking. It fills the air around them, reminding me of the wild, green things I like to surround myself with – Like the untamed *creature* that lives in my middle.

'You honour me,' Denlyr says.

He's beautiful, like every other fae I've witnessed. But danger pours from him even as he smiles at me. His orange eyes glow like hot coals, unblinking, and I feel like I'm being threatened. Outwardly he's not doing anything, but there's an invisible presence, like when Zephyr touches me. Denlyr's using it to push a great weight into my chest, until it's difficult to breathe. My darkness rushes to the surface in response, and I feel my eyes bleed to black. My fingertips tingle and onyx swirls dance over my hands. Denlyr's eyes widen at the sight and he drops his gaze, the weight lifting from my chest.

'Forgive me,' he murmurs.

'Get out,' Aric snarls.

The fae blink away in flashes of brilliant light. Tension drains from my shoulders but the darkness remains on my skin, and my eyes stay black. Too many things have threatened me in too short a time, and my darkness is staying ready.

'What was that?' I demand.

'My sentinels,' Aric answers. 'They-'

'No,' I cut in. 'What did Denlyr just do to me?'

'He challenged you,' Aric says in a tone that's calm yet radiating menace.

'What the hell does that even mean? Stop speaking to me like I know anything about anything here!'

'I've never spoken of an heir because I didn't know I had one,' Aric explains not even blinking at my outburst. 'I think Denlyr thought you a fraud,' he muses. 'Especially because you showed him mercy.'

'So he was testing me to make sure I am who I say I am?' I scoff.

Aric shakes his head. 'He was proving you a fake, so he'd have the right to kill you.' Aric smirks. 'But your light stopped his challenge before it even began.'

Whoa, back up. Kill me?

The fading numbness in my body strains against the great well of emotion, threatening to take me over. Anger is already slipping out, but fear isn't far behind it. I've been in Aric's realm less than an hour and already somebody wants to kill me. I've had enough.

'Majesty,' Malak murmurs from the doorway leading back into the throne room. His gaze flicks to the broken mirror then back to his king. 'I have the reports you ordered.'

Aric turns his attention to Malak and my gaze slides to the broken mirror. Chunks are missing from the reflective surface, but parts of it remain. I inch backwards, until I'm level with a part that's big enough to view my reflection. I stare at myself in shock. My eyes are onyx pools against pale skin. Blonde hair is a nested frame around my face, looking like I've never used a brush. My pyjamas have long sleeves and legs, but the bare skin of my hands and feet are laced with black filigree, adding to the otherworldly effect of my image.

I glance at where Aric's moved to the doorway to speak with Malak in lowered tones. How long will it take before another fae tries to prove me a fake, so they can take my life? Dark Realm. Light Realm. Human Realm. They're all the same. I'm not safe anywhere, so I'll take this chance to say goodbye to the ones I love while I can.

I press my hand to the mirror and Drew's room appears. Drew's been the only real comfort in my life lately, and I can't let him wake up to discover me gone. I push through the mirror, into the dark space of Drew's bedroom. Light paints my back, and I turn to the image of Aric and Malak through the glass. Neither has noticed my absence, and I watch their fading figures replaced by my reflection.

I rummage around the small desk in Drew's bedroom until I find a pen. I turn his notepad to a clean page then write him a note, so he won't worry in the morning. Drew's still snoring on the air mattress as I pack my things. I kneel on the floor beside him and brush blond hair from his face, to press a kiss to his forehead.

'I love you,' I whisper and push to my feet.

I press my palm to Drew's mirror and think of home. My bedroom comes into view and I step through the glass. I look over my shoulder in time to see Drew's bedroom fade. I drop my case onto the bed and make it into the bathroom in time to throw up. The numbness continues to disintegrate, allowing the well of emotion to come crashing in. My body heaves, like it's trying to expel everything I can't handle. I'm not human. Heave. I'm Zephyr's chosen. Heave. I'm the daughter of the Dark Fae King, and there are fae who'll want me dead. Heave. Why else would Aric have a compliment of sentinels following him around? Heave.

I killed Mum.

I heave again, tears streaking my face. The emotion is suffocating, like a great wave crashing over my head, crushing me into the floor. And I'll do the same to every human I love, until I learn to control my light.

Light. My Darkness is a form of light, but it feels like a curse.

I wash my face and brush my teeth, before going back to the bedroom to pull on clean socks. Keeping my feet covered is a priority from now on, so I don't get caught out again. I dress in warm clothes, making sure to cover as much of my skin as possible. The less skin on skin contact I have with people, the less likely my light will leech from them. It's been syphoning emotion from the air around people since Zephyr changed me, but I don't think it hurts them unless I touch them. At least I'm hoping that's the case.

I pack a small bag then fish my boots from the wardrobe and pull them on. Sitting on the edge of the bed, I take a minute to text Katherine and tell her I'm going away for a few weeks. It's the middle of the night, so she won't get it until morning, giving me enough time to make it somewhere far from here before she phones. She'll either be happy I'm getting away or she'll freak out because I'm leaving the village.

I look up from my phone when something bangs downstairs. It sounds extra loud in the quiet of the night, and the hairs on my nape rise in response. I push from the bed and creep out onto the landing. I peer down the stairs but can't hear anything else. I move slowly, tiptoeing around the creaky steps on the staircase. I glance back when I'm nearly at the bottom, wondering if I should go back up and break the mirror in my bedroom as planned. Knowing that anyone with the ability to open a portal could trace my path makes me vulnerable.

Another noise sounds from the kitchen and my attention snaps back to the path before me. I take the final few steps and edge along the hallway. The kitchen is empty when I get there, standing in the doorway to scan the room. It occurs to me that I'm standing in the dark and can see, the space as visible as if it were the middle of the day. There's nobody here, not a dish out of place.

Movement catches my eye and I look straight into a pair of glowing, purple eyes through the kitchen window.

Zephyr smirks at me and I raise my middle finger at him. He quirks an eyebrow, like the gesture confuses him and I huff. The idiot doesn't even know I'm insulting him.

I turn and bolt for the stairs. Something crashes upstairs, making me pause. Quiet cursing reaches me in feminine tones, and I freeze on the bottom step. I race for the front door instead and run for Mr Windle's garden. He has a security light in his garden that lights the greenhouse up and turns it reflective at night. I can use it to open a doorway.

Violet light blinds me and I crash into a wall of muscle. The Light fades as Zephyr's arms band around my middle. I struggle against him but he's too strong.

'Let go!'

'Never,' he hisses.

I know I'm trapped and so does Zephyr, so I decide to play dumb. He can't know I've met my father, which means Zephyr probably still thinks I don't know what he is – or what I am. The less he thinks I know, the more chance I have of escaping. My fingers tingle with the urge to summon an essence orb, but Zephyr has me pinned, my arms trapped between us. Even if I summon an orb I won't be able to lift my arms to use it. And would it even be enough to stop him? Aric said my orbs would hurt Zephyr, but I need to disable him enough to get away. I need the element of surprise.

'Why are you doing this?' I demand.

'Because you're mine,' he snarls.

His eyes glow and I force mine wide, like the sight is new. I've grown good at lying over the years, and fear fuels my acting skills. He's so damn beautiful it stings my eyes looking at him. He's too perfect; with that wild edge all fae have. I don't trust it.

'What are you?' I whimper, giving myself a mental pat on the back at how convincing it sounds.

His eyes narrow into shining slits. 'Who removed my Mark from you?'

'Your what?' I squeak. 'Y-you mean the purple thing on my wrist? You put that there?'

Zephyr unwinds an arm from my waist and grabs my left arm. He lifts my wrist level with his face, and I watch in fascination as my sleeve pushes back from my hand. I don't have to fake the shock painting my face, at the feel of his psychic fingers sliding the fabric back. The glowing design banding my wrist is revealed and Zephyr makes a growling sound at the sight. Is he purring?

'Mine.'

His voice has turned animalistic, calling to the caged, wild entity in my middle. It claws my insides wanting out, and I swallow hard and regain my focus.

'What are you?' I whisper.

Zephyr's eyes narrow back on me. 'Tell me who removed my mark,' he demands.

I shake my head and push all the fear I'm feeling into my voice. 'I don't know what you're talking about.'

Amethyst eyes bore into me and I stare right back. Zephyr inhales a deep breath through his nose then snarls. He holds a splayed hand an inch above my chest, right over my racing heart. Heat washes over my skin, and I squirm, scared of what he's doing. I freeze when a faint, amber dust rises from my skin. It mists the air between us, until Zephyr does something that pulses energy through the air. The amber mist draws together, forming into a ball of amber light in the centre of Zephyr's waiting palm. His expression is feral as he grips the light then squeezes his fist tight around it. The amber orb crackles under the pressure and fizzles away.

'Mine,' Zephyr snarls into my face, baring his teeth.

I stare at his hand, unable to push the image of the amber orb from my brain. Dots are connecting and I don't like where they're leading me. When Darrack removed Zephyr's Mark, it manifested as an amethyst orb of light. What Zephyr just removed from my skin looked like Darrack's version of Zephyr's Mark. Did Darrack remove Zephyr's claim, to then put his own on me?

'What was that?' I ask, bewildered.

'It was another, trying to claim what is mine.'

Well crap.

I was hoping I was wrong, and Darrack hadn't tried to claim me. Anger flares bright in my middle at this latest revelation. If I ever see Darrack again his nose will have the indent of my knuckles across it.

'The man with the amber eyes did this to me?' I ask, blinking, like I'm only just figuring stuff out.

I'm angry, not stupid. If I want to escape Zephyr then I have an act to play. His frown deepens and his glare turns muted, confusion creasing his features.

'You know what you are?' he says.

'I'm a human being.'

Zephyr stares at me like I've grown a second head. 'But how can you not know?'

'Know what?' I huff. 'What are you talking about?'

He shakes his head. 'Your light was strong enough to draw me from my realm,' he murmurs confirming Aric's theory that Zephyr was drawn to me. 'What colour is it?'

I don't need to fake my confusion this time. 'What colour is what?'

'Your light,' he answers. 'It feels powerful and smells sweet, but I'm yet to witness the shade.'

So Zephyr doesn't know my light is black, meaning he didn't pick me because he recognised me as a royal fae. If I were planning on stopping with him then he'd get serious points for that. But he's still the creepy guy that showed up in my garden, messing with my head when I'm grieving my mother. Then he declared I was his and almost killed me with his Mating Mark. To top it off, he hasn't once asked my opinion in the matter. I think of what my father said, and wonder if I matter at all to Zephyr, or if I'm just a means to an end. He's found a compatible match and there's a time limit until he has to get mated.

'I don't know what you're talking about,' I tell Zephyr, looking him straight in the eyes.

He studies me, as if viewing something rare and unusual. 'Impossible,' he whispers.

'Please let me go,' I whisper back. 'I won't tell anyone about you.'

He shocks me when he releases me, but before I have chance to run he cups my face in his hands. 'I cannot.'

Amethyst light floods my vision and everything fades to black.

CHAPTER 8

I crack an eye open then hiss and roll my face into the bedcovers. How much did Drew let me drink last night? My brain is throbbing, and it takes a moment for it to catch up with the situation. I roll onto my back again and stare at the luminescent ceiling.

Luminescent.

Ceiling.

Crap.

I sit up and look around, the large room unlike anything I've seen. The walls are similar to the ceiling, like mother of pearl, highly polished with an ethereal gleam. The floor looks the same, though a shade darker. A large set of glass doors are opposite, light shining in through stained glass. I'm sitting in the middle of a huge bed, white-silk sheets tangled around my legs. My eyes widen and I rip the sheets away, breathing a sigh of relief when I find I'm still wearing the jeans and top I put on before Zephyr found me.

Zephyr.

I scramble from the bed, my boots silent against the shiny floor. I look like a silhouette against the bright space, a dark spot in the centre of all this light. It hits me that I'm in the Light Realm as I reach the ornate glass doors, searching for an escape. They open with a snick and I blink at the space beyond. It's a bathroom, though unlike any I've seen. I go to what I assume is the sink and hold my hand under a looping structure made from glass. Warm water gushes from the open end to wet my fingers and my lips tip into a smile. If I hadn't been abducted I'd think the glowing water kind of cool.

The smile falls from my lips and I turn back into the bedroom. Glowing water means I can't fill the bathtub and create a reflective surface to escape through. The only other doors are the glass doors opposite the bed. I go to them and push white voile aside. The double doors are beautiful, made from small pieces of glass, slotted together in an intricate pattern of coloured swirls. The light streaming through paints a rainbow on my skin, and I stare at it in wonder.

The doors make no sound when I push them open, stepping out onto a large balcony. There's no wall surrounding the balcony and I stare at the vista in disbelief. I thought the light shining in was daylight, but it looks close to dusk. Countless lights sparkle across the horizon, like fallen stars.

I force my gaze from the dazzling view to peer over the edge of the balcony. I've never been afraid of heights, but I'm so high up I can't see the ground. I drop to my knees and grip the edge of the balcony, leaning forward to get a better look. The tower I'm in gleams in the twilight, like the glow sticks you can buy at the funfair. Hundreds of crescents stick out from the main body of the tower below me; balconies, like the one I'm kneeling on.

'You're awake,' a female voice comments from beside me.

I squeal in surprise and shove back from the edge, spinning to face the fae behind me. She's beautiful, like all the fae I've seen. At first I think she's the female who stopped Zephyr from sending an essence orb Drew's way in the club. She has the same violet eyes, dark hair and willowy frame. But her eyes are sadder.

She studies me, as I study her, gaze sweeping my frame. Her expression is unreadable at the end of her perusal then she turns and walks into the bedroom. I stare at her bare back, gaze fixed on the intricate design on her skin. It looks like the design on my back, except hers is silver to my black. She pauses in the doorway when I don't follow and peers down at me.

'Come, Primrose,' she orders, tone soft but demanding. 'There's little time and much for you to learn, before you unite with my son.'

So this is Zephyr's Mum.

I push to my feet. 'I'm not marrying Zephyr.'

'Of course not,' she agrees confusing me. 'You and Zephyr will be mated on the equinox. Your lights will be united and bound until death.'

'I'm not *mating* your son,' I grit out.

She raises a perfect eyebrow. 'You have no choice, Primrose. Zephyr chose you for his mate and your lights are compatible. He'll accept no other.'

'But there *are* others,' I argue.

'They are weaker choices,' she states.

'But they want this,' I press, tone pleading. 'I don't.'

'Your wants are irrelevant,' she says and turns back to the bedroom.

Anger burns through me and my fingers tingle. I bite my tongue to curb the urge to blast an orb at the back of her head. Blood paints my tongue helping to cool my rage. The only way I can see out of this room is via the balcony, and I don't have a death wish. If I want to escape I need to play the game I started.

'I don't know what all this talk of light means,' I say as I stalk into the room behind Zephyr's mum. Like my dad, she doesn't look a day over twenty-five and it's just creepy. 'I already told Zephyr I don't have any light. He's got the wrong girl.'

'Zephyr told me you're ignorant of your true nature,' she answers and studies me once more. 'I feel your light from here, but then I knew you'd be strong. Most Halflings don't survive the transformation, and for your light to match Zephyr's spells your worth.'

'I don't understand anything you just said,' I lie.

'Zephyr has chosen you,' she answers. 'That's all you need understand.'

'I want to go home,' I whisper.

Emotion blinks through her gaze. 'Your home is with Zephyr now.'

I glance around the room, the air feeling thinner. Darkness licks at the underside of my skin, reacting to my growing panic. The surfaces in this room gleam but aren't reflective, so I can't use them to open a portal. I'm trapped and it's hard to breathe.

'When is the equinox?' I murmur.

'In two risings.'

My gaze snaps to hers in disbelief. 'Two days?'

'I'll give you a moment to digest everything,' she says then goes back to the balcony.

I follow her, stopping when the silver tattoo on her back, lights up. The glittery lines peel from her skin, stretching out behind her to form a pair of wings. The wings are transparent and veined with silver. They remind me of dragonfly wings but sparkly. The backless dress makes sense now, as I watch her step from the balcony. Her wings flutter then blur, as she floats out of view.

Holy.

Crap.

I back up from the doors then run to the bathroom. There's no lock on the door, but I rip off my top and try twisting enough to see the design on my back. It's futile without a mirror, and I huff in frustration. I unhook my bra and drop it by my top on the bathroom floor. I know from memory the markings on my skin are almost identical to Zephyr's mum's, and hers lifted from her skin to become wings.

The more I think of the way the lines on Zephyr's mum's skin just peeled from her back, the more my shoulders tingle. My skin starts to itch and awareness wriggles down my spine. Darkness pulses from deep in my middle then blankets my back. I feel it separate from my body and stretch out behind me.

I turn my head to glance at the unbelievable. I can see my wings are similar to Zephyr's mum's, except mine are veined with black instead of silver. The feel of them behind me ranks up there with one of the weirdest sensations I've ever experienced. They feel durable yet don't seem to weigh anything. I imagine fluttering them and squeak when my feet lift from the ground. Panic fills me and I tumble forward, face planting on the pearlescent floor.

I push to my knees thinking flying is way harder than Zephyr's mum made it appear. There was no grace in my landing, that's for sure. The fleeting hope of escaping via the balcony vanishes. Getting my wings to flutter took nothing more than a thought, but if I panic and fall from way up here I'm toast.

Voices sound from the bedroom and I stare at the bathroom doors. I'm naked from the waist up with a pair of wings out that will ruin any plan of playing dumb to knowing I'm fae. I close my eyes and pray it's easy to get rid of them. Energy prickles over my back and I glance over my shoulder to find my wings gone. Midnight filigree licks over the pale skin on my shoulder and I huff a relieved breath.

The doors swing open as I'm tugging my top into place, Zephyr's mum joining me inside the bathroom. An entourage of women follow her, lining up behind her when she stops before me. Though they're all beautiful, they seem different to Zephyr's mum, and they keep their gazes fixed on the floor. I scan their features, realizing a few of them look to be mid thirties. The reason hits me in the solar plexus and I feel sick. They're human, not fae.

'These females will be your maids in waiting,' Zephyr's mother states, bringing my attention back to her.

Her expression is unreadable, the flash of emotion I saw earlier replaced by indifference. I shutter my expression to match hers, not wanting her to see how intimidated she makes me feel. I don't know how she's doing it, but I can't *feel* any emotion from her. It's unsettling in a way I don't ever remember feeling.

'My what?' I ask.

'They will bathe and dress you ready for the Honour Banquet,' she murmurs.

'What's an Honour Banquet?'

'It's a celebration, to honour Zephyr's choice of mate,' she smiles, like the fact they're throwing a party to celebrate my abduction is going to endear me to her. Maybe she missed that the celebration is to honour Zephyr, not me.

'Right,' I drawl.

Her smile fades and the indifference returns. 'Tonight, Zephyr will present you to the court as his Chosen.'

'Just because he's forcing me to mate him, doesn't mean I'm going to slap on a smile and pretend I'm happy about it,' I warn.

Zephyr's mum steps closer eyes flashing bright violet. 'When Oric chose me for his mate, I knew I was fae and how to yield my light.' Her gaze rakes my frame, like I'm less that her. 'You don't stand a chance of denying Zephyr his every whim.' Fear blasts down my spine at her words. 'For your own sake, comply with Zephyr's wishes, for there is no other option.'

A human maid shifts behind Zephyr's mum, drawing my attention. She stares at the floor like she's willing it to swallow her, hands curled into fists. I wonder what the humans here have been forced to endure. At least I'm half fae and can create portals and essence orbs. I have a chance, whereas they have nothing. I shift my gaze back to Zephyr's mum and swallow my fear. Going to the banquet means I'll at least leave this room. Nobody knows I can open portals, and maybe I'll find a reflective surface beyond these rooms.

'I don't need anyone to bathe me and I can dress myself,' I say, aiming to maintain a sliver of freewill. 'And I'm not wearing anything too-' I study the opaque, backless dress Zephyr's mum is wearing and cringe, 'revealing.'

'You'll do well to rid yourself of modesty,' she advises. 'Fae are sexual creatures with strong appetites, and Zephyr is no exception.'

'Then he shouldn't have chosen me because I'm not interested in having sex with him.'

'I think it quaint you still believe you have a choice in the matter,' she murmurs.

Bile creeps up my throat. 'That's rape.'

'It doesn't have to be,' she counters, tone unnervingly calm, like we're discussing something mundane, like the weather.

'I'll never be willing,' I answer.

She purses her lips at my answer. 'The choice is yours.'

'So I actually *do* get a choice in something?' I snap.

'Choose your battles wisely, Primrose,' she murmurs, voice icy.

CHAPTER 9

Zephyr's smile fades as I'm escorted closer, gaze reading the distain in mine. Two enormous males bracket me, barely a breath between us, steely resolve painting the air around me. They've spoken to me once, when they collected me from my gilded cage. The maid fussing over my hair had backed away when they'd flashed into the room, terror glazing her eyes, like she expected them to take her instead of me. The males hadn't hurt me, though. They'd gripped my arms to teleport me from my room then promptly released me before escorting me into the banqueting hall.

Violet silk and lace hug my body, the same shade as Zephyr's eyes. It might be perceived that I chose the gown I'm wearing for that reason, but really it was the only option that wasn't backless. I need a dress that hides my wing markings, or this whole charade is over. The human maids seemed panicked when I'd refused nearly all the dresses offered, before an older woman dared ask why I didn't like the ones presented. They were afraid of me, and I'm ashamed at the fact I used it to my advantage. Their fear of me got me what I wanted, but the acrid taste of it still coats my tongue.

My gown is silk with lace overlay. It has a high collar, long sleeves and brushes the floor as I walk. There's a weird cut out in the front that shows what little cleavage I have, and the material hugs me like a second skin. I'm covered in all the places that count, but still feel naked. A band of silver filigree circles my head, sitting just above my eyebrows. My blonde hair has been braided into an intricate design around it, woven with violet ribbon.

The guards usher me into the seat beside Zephyr then melt into the crowd, giving the illusion of leaving. I resist the urge to snort. I can't see them but *know* they're there. My darkness is on the defensive, coiled tight and tasting the emotion in the air around us. It's wary of Zephyr, despite seeming excited to be near him. The weight of his gaze burns the left side of my body but I refuse to look his way, flinching when he takes my hand. Anger burns through me that he thinks he can touch me without permission.

'You're beautiful,' he murmurs.

The heat of his breath on my skin, mixed with the heady scent of his fragrance makes me shiver. I sense his pleasure at my response and rip my hand from his. I place it on my lap beneath the table and curl my finger into my palm.

'Don't touch me,' I say, keeping my outward appearance stoic. Who knows what punishment I'll receive for ruining the party?

'I don't like seeing you upset, my love,' he says.

'Perhaps you should take my right to be angry, too,' I suggest watching the other fae mingle. A lot of gazes turn my way and I don't like how they assess me. 'And I'm your prisoner, not your *love*.'

'You're not my prisoner,' he grits out.

I look at him. 'Then you'll let me go?'

'I can't.'

'What's your word for someone being held against their will then?' I ask not bothering to veil my sarcasm. 'Because I'm still happy to go with prisoner.'

'I need you,' he whispers.

'No you don't,' I whisper-hiss back. 'There are females who actually want to be your mate! You just don't want them.'

'They didn't call to me like you do,' he argues.

'You're talking like I understand any of this,' I snap.

'Your light called to me, Primrose,' he says. 'It drew me from my realm to yours, and you're just a Halfling. It's unheard of.'

'You've stolen my life; my choice,' I counter. 'You don't care about me. You care about getting what you want.'

Zephyr frowns. 'If I gave you a choice, would you choose me?'

My eyebrows creep to my hairline at the insecurity painting his tone. As angry as I am it's difficult not to be a little charmed by how unsure he seems of himself.

'I don't know you, Zephyr.'

'But if you did?' he counters.

I shock us both when my fingers curl around his on the table. His skin is hot against mine and I stare at our joined hands. What the hell is wrong with me? Why am I trying to console the guy who abducted me to be his wife? Perhaps a part of me wants it to be as simple as Zephyr letting me go, so we can get to know each other the right way.

'Maybe you should let me go and find out,' I suggest.

Zephyr stares at me with longing and a lump forms in my throat. His despair flows through our connected hands and I swallow hard against it. The moment opens, stretching out, and it feels like we're the only two in the busy hall. The fae around us fade and a

110

connection sparks in their wake. My hand on Zephyr's feels suddenly right and yearning stirs in my middle.

Zephyr sighs and looks away, breaking the connection. 'I can't,' he says. 'You'll leave and I'll spend millennia knowing you're out there.' He leans closer, breath brushing my lips. 'I'm aware it's selfishness, Primrose but you're young and I hope you'll learn to forgive me.'

I stare at him my thoughts stuck on the word millennia. He can't have said millennia. Nothing lives that long. Then I think of how he just denied my freedom, and instead of getting angry I just feel sad. The echo of his despair is bitter on my tongue, and I can't bring myself to feel anything but sorry for him. Zephyr is taking away my choices so he won't lose his own. I've felt that sense of powerlessness and empathise with his situation. The difference between us is I've never chosen to put my needs before someone else's before.

I slip my hand from his and return it to my lap. An empty plate is placed on the table before me and I stare at it so I won't have to look at Zephyr. I only lift my gaze when dishes of food start appearing in the centre of the table. I don't recognise anything in them, some of the food glowing with neon freckles. It reminds me I'm a long way from home and the need to hug my mum hits hard.

'Can I leave the party?' I ask. 'Your mum said it'll be a long day of preparing for the equinox tomorrow, and I'm tired.'

'You don't need my permission to leave the banquet,' Zephyr answers.

'Yes I do, Zephyr,' I whisper glaring his way. 'I've been locked in a room since I got here and was escorted to this party by two guards. If I try to leave they'll stop me.'

'The guards are for your protection,' he argues. 'Once we're mated you'll reside in my chambers, but until then I must keep you safe.'

Blood drains from my face so fast I feel dizzy. Not because of the possible danger Zephyr alludes to, but because his mum's words ring clear in my head. If Zephyr wants me he'll take me, willing or not.

'Primrose, are you unwell?'

Zephyr's light presses against mine, probing. It feels like another violation and I flinch, pushing into my chair to get away from him. I see Zephyr's parents turn in our direction, but Zephyr snatches hold of my hand and drags me from my chair. I stumble after him when he leads me from the hall, into an adjoining room. The doors slam shut behind us and he spins to face me, gripping my shoulders as he glares down at me.

'How many times must I tell you I won't harm you? Yet you flinch at my touch,' he growls.

Outrage blasts through me. 'Do you know I almost died that night?'

Surprise replaces the frustration on his face. 'What?'

I poke a finger in his chest. 'I'm talking about the night you kissed me in the garden,' I snarl. 'You did something that almost killed me then left. I was found the next morning in a pool of my own blood, so don't preach about never hurting me because you already have.'

'You were in pain?' he asks sounding genuinely confused.

'Agony,' I correct then shrug from his hold. 'Not that you care,' I add then chance a lie. 'Your mum told me you knew activating my dormant fae side would likely kill me, but I guess that didn't matter. As long as you get what you want.' I turn and walk to the doors leading back to the banquet. 'I'll find my guards and return to my cell.'

Zephyr doesn't stop me when I leave. Not that it matters, as my guards are waiting on the other side of the doors. I meet their stoic gazes and shrug, before letting them guide me away.

CHAPTER 10

I blink awake, not remembering where I am for one blissful moment. Light pours in through the glass doors, painting pretty patterns on the ethereal walls and I sigh.

'Finally,' someone exclaims.

I squeal and sit up, finding a gorgeous fae draped over the end of my bed. Recognition zips through me and I take a steadying breath. It's the girl from the club, the one that stopped Zephyr from toasting Drew.

'I've been waiting hours for you to wake,' she complains.

I study at her, looking like a supermodel stretched across the silk bedding. She shares Zephyr's olive skin tone and violet eyes, and has her head propped on one hand, regarding me with a catlike stare. Midnight hair curls in long ribbons around her shoulders and over her hip. It pools in a sensuous cloud around the elbow she has bent on the bed and I purse my lips. She looks like an advertisement for something sensual and she's not even trying.

'What the hell are you doing in here?' I demand.

'You've been sleeping for nearly eight hours,' she grumbles. 'And I've been waiting to speak with you.'

'Who the hell are you? Don't you know it's creepy to watch someone while they're sleeping?'

She sits up and grins. 'I'm Caligo, Zephyr's twin.'

Twin? 'And you're here because?'

'I need to speak with you before Zephyr gets here. And you can't tell him I visited.'

'I won't see Zephyr today. I'm being fitted for a mating gown and he's not invited.' I narrow my eyes. 'Besides, why would I do anything to help you? Unless you're here to help me leave?'

'I like you,' she answers surprising me. 'I know you don't want to be mated to my brother, but I hope we can be friends.'

'Is that what you came to tell me? That you want to be friends?'

Caligo shakes her head, sending a cloud of onyx hair around her shoulders. 'I came to ask you to give him a chance when he comes for you today. You're to spend this day getting to know each other.'

'It's a little late for that,' I scoff. 'I already know he's a selfish prick, what more is there to know?'

'It was never Zephyr's intent to hurt you,' she argues. 'Please, take this day to see beyond what you think you know and see what I see.' She sighs and looks away before meeting my gaze again. 'His decision isn't yet final. There's still the possibility he'll let you go.'

'Why are you telling me this?'

Caligo looks at the glass doors, like she hears something. 'I love my brother.' She meets my gaze. 'He has waited a long time to find you, longer than you can comprehend. You think he robbed you of your choices, but really you robbed him of his.' She reaches over and squeezes my hand. 'He deserves to be happy.'

I turn my face as Caligo disappears behind a wall of light. They should bloody well warn people before they teleport away. The light fades and she's gone, and I blink light spots from my vision. I'll never get used to everyone just popping in and out, like that.

I sigh and stare at the ruffled sheets. Caligo made Zephyr sound like a victim, skirting around the fact he *chose* to abduct me. Maybe he didn't intend to hurt me with his claim. He *did* look confused when I told him I nearly died.

I scramble from the bed and go outside, hoping the fresh air will help clear my mind. I sit with my legs dangling over the edge of the balcony, a sunrise unlike any I've seen lighting the horizon. The air is crisp and quiet and cleansing for my soul. It smells like nature and green things here, and I breathe it deep. This place is beautiful, and if I wasn't a prisoner I might actually admit that I like it here.

Thoughts of Zephyr permeate the calm settling around my mind. Last night he seemed desperate for me to like him, and it's more than confusing. The despair I felt from him was deep and hollow, and I struggle to comprehend how anyone can live that way. I finger the glowing mark circling my wrist, contemplating the mystery of Zephyr. I think of the sad look in his eyes at the banquet. For a moment we'd connected. It couldn't have been more than a few seconds but it felt so right. And I can't deny the desire I felt to comfort him. It's still there, buried beneath the resentment of his refusal to let me go.

I close my eyes and push all thoughts of Zephyr away. Sunlight glows through my eyelids and I pretend I'm sitting in the meadow behind my house at home.

'You're awake.'

My eyes snap open to find Zephyr's face about an inch from mine. I scream and slip from the edge of the balcony, gravity gripping hold of me. Zephyr snakes an arm around my waist before I fall and pulls me against him.

'Holy crap,' I whisper, heart racing.

I peer over Zephyr's bicep. We're hovering just in front of the balcony the ground so far down I can't see it.

'You shouldn't be sitting out here unattended,' Zephyr chastises. 'If I hadn't shown up you would've fallen to your death.'

'I wouldn't have fallen if you hadn't scared the crap out of me,' I argue meeting his gaze. 'What are you even doing here? Your mum said I'm getting fitted for my dress today and you're not allowed to attend.'

Zephyr sets us down on the balcony. I push from his arms and study his wings. They're bigger than his mother's, suiting his bigger frame, and veined with silver.

'You're spending the day with me,' Zephyr answers.

I eye him warily even though I know the reason. I don't know why I'm keeping Caligo's stupid secret. What will it matter if she came to see me?

'Why?' I ask.

'Because tomorrow we'll be bound for life,' he answers. 'I thought it'd be nice for us to know each other a little before that happens.'

'Are you asking or ordering?'

He considers my question. 'Asking.'

'Okay,' I say then turn to go get dressed. I stop in the doorway and look back over my shoulder. 'What about your mum?'

'She can wait,' he growls then sighs when I flinch. 'I've relented to all of her wishes, Primrose. The least she can do is give me this.'

'Right,' I murmur then leave him on the balcony.

Zephyr is sitting with his legs dangling over the edge of the balcony. He looks over his shoulder at me when I step outside, and his face lights with a smile. The effect it has on me is ridiculous. It's disarming, making a place in my centre grow warm. He pushes to his feet as I step closer.

'You look beautiful, Primrose.'

My face heats and I look down at the lemon dress I'm wearing. It has long sleeves, isn't backless and has a modest hemline.

'Thanks,' I murmur. 'It's all I could find.'

He's frowning when I meet his gaze again. 'Weren't you supplied with more garments to wear?'

I snort. 'I've seen porn stars wearing less revealing clothing than the ones provided for me.'

'What's a porn star?'

I shake my head refusing to go there. 'I'm just not comfortable showing as much flesh as the clothes provided for me reveal.'

Not all of the options are as hideous as I'm making out. There are some pretty dresses that I'd consider wearing, if they weren't backless. The lemon dress is the only one that doesn't showcase my wing markings.

'I'll take you to select dresses of your own choosing,' Zephyr tells me as he steps in close.

I shrug. 'Some jeans and t-shirts would be nice.'

He chuckles and takes my hand, before pulling me close. I suck in a breath when my front collides with his. Light blinds me and I shut my eyes, pressing my face into Zephyr's chest against the glare. Zephyr's body vibrates with laughter and I open my eyes to meet amused purple ones.

'It's easy to forget you're half human,' he admits. 'Though, I do enjoy your reactions.'

'Glad I'm keeping you entertained,' I mutter then push away, jaw going slack when I glance around us. 'Where are we?'

'The Jade Beaches, not far from the palace,' he answers, pointing to a tall, glittering structure in the distance.

I squint at the glittery tower, and what Zephyr is saying dawns on me. The palace he's referring to is where we were a few minutes ago, before he teleported us here.

'How did you get us from there to here?' I gasp.

He shrugs. 'Royal fae and a few other breeds can teleport within realms.'

'But not between realms?' I broach fishing for clarification.

Apparently only some fae traits realise in Halflings, like me. Full fae have fangs, like an animal. It gives them a vicious demeanour when they grin, adding to the feral aspect of their appearance. I don't have fangs or pointed ears. I'm guessing Zephyr and his family assume I don't have much going for me in the fae department. They don't know I have wings and I'm playing dumb over the whole light thing. I don't know if I can teleport because I've never tried, but it would be so helpful right now.

'We can't teleport through the barrier separating realms,' Zephyr says, drawing my focus.

'Then how do you get between them?'

'Mirrors make the best portals,' he answers tone wary, like he doesn't want to tell me anything about how to leave the Light Realm.

'That's the reason there isn't a mirror in my room?' I say, like I don't already know.

'Yes,' he admits.

'But I can't make doorways with mirrors,' I say, using the wrong words, so I sound like I don't know what I'm talking about.

'Because you're only half fae,' he answers. 'Different abilities manifest in Halflings after their light is activated. It seems many of them are lost to you,' he murmurs confirming my suspicion. 'We use our light to open doorways and you're not aware of your light.'

'It bothers you that I'm not fully fae,' I challenge. 'That I don't look exactly like you, and that I can't do the simplest fae thing.'

'No,' he denies then adds, 'We look the same.'

'Fae females are tall and willowy, where I'm short and curvy,' I argue. 'They have fangs and pointed ears, and

I don't. You all have wings and I'm stuck on the ground.' I shrug. 'I can keep going if you want?'

'You're beautiful,' he argues back. 'But it isn't your appearance that draws me to you.'

Well, it's not my stellar personality.

'My light,' I supply and he nods. 'Well, I find it difficult to exist without a reflective surface. How the hell am I suppose to see what clothes look like on me, or brush my teeth correctly?'

'You need only wait until tomorrow,' he answers.

'And why is that?'

'Because there's a mirror in my chambers for you to use,' he smiles.

Bile creeps up my throat at the mention of his chambers. I'll be moved there once we're fully mated, but by then it will be too late. If there's a mirror I'll use it to escape, before Zephyr has chance to force me. Failing that I can always maim him.

'So, the Jade Beaches,' I say looking at the sparkling jade sand. Lilac waves lap in lazy rolls against the shoreline, forming ripples in the sand. 'Everything is the wrong colour here,' I murmur.

Zephyr steps up beside me and we stare out at the ocean together. It isn't an uncomfortable silence and I feel myself relaxing. He takes my hand and leads me from the sea. I let him guide me to a blanket spread out on the green sand. There's a picnic arranged atop the blanket, dishes filled with food. I haven't eaten anything since before my abduction and I'm starving, but I don't recognise anything in the dishes.

'You didn't eat last night,' Zephyr says. 'So, I thought you'd be hungry.'

He pulls me down to sit on the blanket with him then releases my hand to fill a plate with food. I meet his gaze when he hands the full plate to me then fills one for himself. I study the food on my plate with suspicion. Things are weird colours and I don't know what to do with any of it? Do I need to peel any of it? Are there pips or stones in the things that resemble fruit? What if I'm allergic?

'You don't like the foods I've brought?' Zephyr asks, drawing my gaze back to him.

'I don't know,' I admit. 'I've never seen foods like this.'

Understanding dawns on his face. 'You should've told me you weren't familiar with the foods offered,' he answers.

I shouldn't have to tell him I don't recognise food from his realm. I've never been here and didn't come by choice. He knows I've lived my life as human, up until a few days ago. Why the heck would I recognise any of his stupid foods? I bite my tongue, remembering Caligo's request for me to give Zephyr a chance.

He reaches over and picks a neon berry from my plate. 'This is a Loka berry,' he tells me. 'It's sweet in flavour and can be crushed to make a refreshing drink.'

'Like a grape,' I say.

'I don't know what a grape is,' he answers.

I repress a sigh and pop the berry into my mouth. Sweet juice splashes over my tongue as I chew, reminding me of how strawberry mixed with melon might taste. Zephyr watches me, waiting for my reaction.

'It's delicious,' I admit.

His smile warms my insides. 'Loka berries are my favourite.'

Zephyr offers me another, this one from his plate. Instead of handing it to me though, he lifts the berry to my lips and waits for me to open. I fight the urge to tell him off for being presumptuous. It takes everything in me not to smack his hand away. Instead, I open my mouth and accept his offering. He pushes the berry between my lips, his index finger brushing my bottom lip as he pulls away. My stomach flip-flops and I bite back a moan. I try not to make it obvious when he looks at his plate and I shuffle away. He selects something and puts it in his mouth, and my eyes are magnetised to his mouth. He could be eating mud and it would look attractive. I shuffle a little further away and stuff another berry into my mouth. Warmth is pulsing through my belly and I don't like it. Why can't I feel this way about a nice, normal boy, instead of my kidnapper?

A breeze blows from the ocean ruffling my hair, and Zephyr's attention snaps my way. His nostrils flare and his irises blaze bright purple. His gaze grows intense as he breathes deep and he licks over his bottom lip.

'I scent your need,' he tells me.

My eyes go wide and my face blazes with heat. He can smell that? I breathe deep through my nose but all I smell is ocean, sand and the berries I've been eating. I guess I didn't get the fae-enhanced sense of smell then.

'I-'

'I know you feel the connection between us,' Zephyr says when I struggle for a response. 'But, I also know you're not ready to be intimate with me.'

'But your mum said after the equinox-' the words choke off in my throat and I can't bring myself to voice them. My mouth is dry and my palms are sweaty.

Zephyr makes an inhuman sound, reminding me of his feral side. It's easy to forget about when he lays on the charm. The lust is gone from his face, replaced by intense fury, and I have to force myself not to scramble away. Despite his anger, I sense he won't hurt me, but it's difficult to face such rage. His emotions call to me, clearer than any I've experienced, and my darkness vibrates at the taste of them.

'Alissa can only dictate so much of our mating,' Zephyr snarls.

'Alissa?'

He snorts a bitter laugh. 'I should've known she wouldn't introduce herself correctly, for all should know who she is without question. Alissa is my mother, Primrose and she has no right to tell you such things.'

Oh? 'Oh,' I murmur, voice trembling with relief.

'Let me make it clear,' he growls.

His anger strikes me as familiar, for it's so like my own. Compared to a human I'm an angry person, but not really when I'm compared to a fae.

'I'll never force you, Primrose. When we join, it will be of your own choosing.'

'Thank you,' I say and mean it.

He said *when* not *if*, but I don't bring him up on it.

I push from Zephyr's arms as the light fades, putting distance between us. It feels too right to be close to him, and I hate myself for it. A bead of sweat slicks the length of my spine with the effort it's taking to hold my darkness at bay. It wants nothing more than to curl around Zephyr and leech whatever magical mojo he has that's drawing it in.

'Where are we?' I mutter.

Trees surround us, so tall I can barely see the branches in the canopy. The trunks vary in shades of brown and cream, some so old and large it would take minutes to circle the base. Shimmering leaves litter the undergrowth, providing a sparkling blanket beneath my feet, and sunlight paints patterns through gaps in the canopy.

'We're in the Singing Woods,' Zephyr tells me.

I turn a full circle, soaking everything in. The air feels thicker, like an invisible presence is woven through the atmosphere. My darkness fizzes with awareness and the hairs on my arms stand up.

'The Singing Woods?' I ask, meeting Zephyr's purple gaze.

The forest answers before Zephyr can, warm breeze sweeping through the treetops and swaying the branches. My mouth drops open at the ethereal sound created by the movement and I smile.

'It's enchanting,' I whisper, afraid to break the spell.

'It is,' Zephyr whispers back.

When I look at him he's staring at me. Heat fills my face and he comes closer to pick something from my hair. He smiles and lets the silvery leaf fall from his fingers. It flutters to the floor, joining the others raining down around us from the swaying branches.

'Why do they make that noise?' I ask, heart racing at his nearness.

He's close enough to smell, and his scent is rich, adding to the woody aroma in the air. Zephyr smells like nature and I want to close the space between us and bury my face in his chest. I back up a step and turn away my reaction to him scaring me. I don't want to like him. I *can't* like him.

'Warm wind pushes down from the mountains to dance with the trees,' Zephyr explains. 'They call it the Dance of the Ancients. The wind is said to carry knowledge from those that have ascended, and if you listen in the quiet of the forest, the trees may share their secrets.'

His words make me think of Mum and grief wells inside me. I blink until the tears clear from my vision then look at him over my shoulder.

'Have you ever heard any of their secrets?' I smile.

'Once,' he answers, surprising me.

I turn to face him. 'Really?'

Zephyr nods. 'When I was a child, but that was a very long time ago.'

I frown. 'How old are you?'

'Not very old in fae terms,' he answers.

'What did they tell you?' I ask instead of calling him out on his vague answer.

I don't know why he's avoiding telling me his age but I don't like it. I like it even less when he frowns as if trying to remember.

'They spoke of me seeking darkness, but it made no sense,' Zephyr says. 'The trees speak in riddles and a language that's difficult to decipher.'

I think of my darkness and school my features to hide my shock. I thought Zephyr was joking, but they knew he'd come for me. He just doesn't understand because he doesn't know my light is black, and that I'm a Dark Fae.

'How do you even speak to a tree?' I murmur.

Zephyr chuckles, takes my hand and pulls me to the nearest tree. He presses my palm to the bark and holds my hand in place with his own. My darkness pulses at his nearness but I tamp it down and listen to what he's saying.

'If you were aware of your light, you'd use it to reach the energy inside the tree,' Zephyr explains. 'Your light would weave with the spirit of the tree and open a connection.'

He presses his other hand to the tree and his eyes glow amethyst. 'This tree is called Etnalla.' He frowns then looks at me. 'She wishes to speak with you.'

I glance at the tree then back to Zephyr. 'But, I can't use my light,' I argue. 'You keep saying it's there but I don't feel it,' I lie. 'And if I don't feel it, I can't use it to speak to a tree.'

Zephyr shrugs. 'Perhaps Etnalla wishes to sense you. She'll understand when you fail to make a connection.'

I turn back to the tree when Zephyr steps back and press both palms to the bark. I imagine my darkness reaching through the bark and feel an electric sensation latch on.

'Holy crap,' I whisper.

'*Welcome, Dark Fae,*' a feminine voice chimes through me, vibrating every cell of my body.

'*Um, hello?*' I think back and slide my gaze to Zephyr, to make sure he can't hear what's being said. He quirks a questioning eyebrow at me and I shrug, like I can't hear anything.

'*We celebrate your presence in the Light Realm,*' the tree says at the same time Zephyr tells me not to worry.

Zephyr talks some more, so I don't catch all of Etnalla's next words. She says something about Lumen and Unification, but I don't understand either of those words. Then Zephyr asks if I'm okay and I have to look at him. I tell Etnalla that I have to go, and thank her for talking to me. She sends a warm feeling through our connection and it makes me smile.

Zephyr sees my smile and steps close to pluck silvery leaves from the tangle of my hair. I drop my hands from the tree as the wind picks up, making the trees sing their ethereal song. More leaves rain down around us, fluttering to the forest floor. The air is thick with magic, as I stare up into Zephyr's mesmerising eyes.

'Primrose,' he murmurs, eyes glowing.

He cups my face and brushes his lips against mine. It's the softest caress and I step into him, resting my hands on his chest, feeling his racing heart beneath my palms. He whispers his lips over mine again and I whimper at the sensation. I don't want to like it, but it calls to that wild creature in my middle. My darkness undulates, soaking in Zephyr's nearness. He licks my bottom lip and my darkness grows electric. It feels like I'm lighting up from the inside, and I close my eyes when I feel them bleed to black.

I crush my lips to Zephyr's. He growls when I open for him, his flavour glorious on my tongue. He's sweet and decadent, and I've never tasted anything like it. I curl my fingers through his midnight hair and grip tight, desperate to hold onto this moment.

'Zephyr,' a familiar voice drawls, smashing through the magic we've woven.

I jerk from Zephyr and back away, until my back meets Etnalla's bark. Darkness scratches at the underside of my skin, pushing to be free and wrap inky ribbons around Zephyr. It wants him more than I think it's wanted anything. Everything has faded in his presence, like Zephyr is all my darkness sees. It's an eerie, sensory quiet I've never experience. I've never been around more than one being without knowing the emotions of everyone close by. Yet, Alissa's here, flanked by her entourage of women and all my darkness wants in Zephyr.

I shutter my expression when Alissa glides in our direction. She's dressed in another opaque gown, each movement graceful. Ebony hair hangs in waves to her hips, flowers woven into the midnight lengths. She looks like a forest nymph from a storybook and it reminds me where I am. Reality crashes in, chasing the pleasant tingles from my flesh.

'Mother,' Zephyr greets her.

'The time for preparing your Chosen grows short,' Alissa says.

'We're not finished,' he answers irritation lacing his tone.

'Primrose is to be fitted for her gown,' Alissa argues. 'You might insist on bonding with a Halfling, but she *will* look fae at the ceremony.'

Zephyr rolls his eyes, like his mother didn't just insult me. 'She's correct, Primrose,' he says and turns to me. 'There are traditions to maintain and rituals we must adhere to.' He lifts my wrist to his lips and kisses the glowing mark his claiming left on my skin.

'She'll be delivered to your chambers at moonrise,' Alissa says, like I'm a gift basket or something.

My gaze shoots to her. 'What?'

'Zephyr will lead his Chosen from his dwelling to the ceremonial alter,' Alissa answers. 'Your light will be bound with his at the height of the equinox, before you return to his chambers to consummate the mating by joining in flesh.'

Bile snakes up my throat when Zephyr doesn't correct her. He offers me a heated stare when I look at him and ice punches into my stomach. *Lies.* I fell for his lies. Alissa just said bonding needs consummating with sex and Zephyr didn't deny it. My heart beats so fast I feel like I might crack a rib. I don't know whether to be angry or scared. My darkness stops trying to reach for Zephyr and wraps me in a cocoon of numbness. It's then I realise my eyes aren't tingling the way they do when they've gone black. My darkness has blocked everything so I can think clearly.

'You have a mirror in your chambers, for me to see my dress before the ceremony,' I ask to make sure.

'Of course,' Zephyr answers then presses another kiss to my wrist. 'Until moonrise,' he murmurs and disappears in a flare of blinding amethyst.

'You're smart not to fight it,' Alissa says once he's gone.

Emotion flickers in her eyes and I recognise it because I've felt it before. Pain. It's gone before I can claim it's there and she holds her hand out for me to take.

'We both know I have no choice,' I answer and take her hand.

I look at our joined hands. I still can't feel her emotion, even when I'm touching her. It's like she feels nothing.

'No,' she agrees. 'But it pleases me how quickly you've adapted. When you are queen that skill will serve you well.' Alissa rakes me with an assessing gaze, like she's seeing me for the first time. 'My son has chosen well.'

Good grief, was that a compliment? If only she knew how much the hand she's holding would shake if not for my darkness. The fear is still there, buried deep beneath a thick layer of midnight. And queen? That word is poisonous to my brain. My grey matter throbs at the mere notion.

Purple light delivers us back to my glorified cell. I'm getting used to the teleporting thing and the burn it leaves on my retinas, but I stumble when Alissa releases me. The change in destination is disorientating, especially when I'm not in control of where I'm going. I glance at the many females in the room. I call them females because one has lilac skin and indigo hair. I study the beautiful creature and she smiles back.

'I've taken the discomfort of your body into consideration concerning the design of your mating gown,' Alissa say, pulling my attention from the lilac woman.

Alissa gestures to a silvery gown on the bed. It's floor-length and high-necked, with lace sleeves and jewelled detail. It's the loveliest item of clothing I've seen.

'It's beautiful,' I murmur, walking up to the bed.

I finger the fabric. It's silky and feels delicate, like I might break it if I grip too hard. I'm grateful beyond words that the gown isn't backless or opaque, as seems to be the fashion in fae realms. I don't want my private parts on show, and I still need to hide my wing markings.

'You approve?' Alissa asks.

I nod and meet her gaze. 'It's perfect.'

Alissa clicks her fingers and two of the women in the room hurry over to me. I recognise them as two of the humans from the day I got here, the ones Alissa assigned to wait on me.

'Wait!' I squeak when they start tugging at my clothing.

Alissa sighs. 'How are they to prepare you if you won't undress? You cannot bathe in those clothes, Primrose. Nor can you wear your mating gown over them. Desist with this nonsense.'

'I can bathe and dress myself,' I say and snatch the gown from the bed.

Alissa appears in front of me when I reach the doors that lead to the bathroom. 'You have no need for such modesty, child. Fae view our bodies as something to be worshipped, not hidden like a shameful secret.'

'I've noticed,' I answer then eye her opaque dress.

I knew the colour of the woman's nipples before I knew her name, and she thinks I don't understand fae views on nudity?

Alissa surprises me by laughing. Her face lights up with how amused she finds my comment, and I see how truly beautiful she is. It's the first time I've seen a real smile on her face, and it's more than unsettling.

'You may dress alone this last time,' she says, as her face grows serious. 'I doubt Zephyr will allow such freedoms after you're bonded.'

'What do you mean?'

Her mask is back in place when she answers, all emotion hidden beneath the regal façade I've come to associate with Zephyr's mother. She'd wipe the floor with anyone challenging her to a game of poker. Indifference paints her features and chills the air.

'I doubt Zephyr will allow you to wear clothing for at least the first decade of your bonding.'

Everything inside grows tight at her words, and I edge around her to get to the bathroom. Alissa turns, following my progress with a curious gaze, until I slam the door in her face. I clutch the pretty gown to my chest, as my heart hammers against my ribcage. Fear threatens to break through the layer of numbness but I force it down. I shake my head and pull myself together. Fear has no place in this moment. I've never taken crap from anyone in my life and I'm not going to start now. I need to put my game face on and get the hell out of the Light Realm.

CHAPTER 11

The same silent guards deliver me to Zephyr's home. When Alissa called it his chambers, I'd imagined a room like mine in the palace. Zephyr's domicile is separate from the palace though, on a vast estate of manicured gardens. His home is made of gleaming, white stone, standing stark against the vivid backdrop of exotic plant life in this realm. There are shades of red, blue and purple, punctuated with splashes of yellow and pink. Everything is so vibrant, and I don't think some of the shades even exist back home.

I feel the cold, stone path under the silk slippers on my feet, as the guards guide me to the entrance. Zephyr's home is a mansion, the stone carved into beautiful, intricate swirls around arching windows and doorways. The building has an ancient, elegant feel, without looking old or worn, and it's hard not to gape at my surroundings.

I stop to stare at a small tree in the garden. It's only a sapling, tiny with white blossoms on its branches. One breaks free and floats to land by my toes when I stop. I pick it up and smell the soft fragrance. I remember the sentient trees in the Singing Woods and feel like the flower is a gift. I tuck it into the woven strands of my hair and smile. One guard grunts and gestures for me to keep walking.

'You might want to be a little nicer,' I snap at him. 'This time tomorrow I'll be your queen, and don't think I won't remember the crappy way you've treated me.'

His eyes widen and I stalk down the path ahead of him. I don't think the guards will force me unless needed. They do a lot of gesturing and demanding, but they don't seem to like touching me. I get the feeling there's a rule about it. Nobody has outright said it, but the male fae I've been introduce to seem afraid to get close. And they give me a wide berth when passing like they're afraid I might brush against them.

Large, double doors open as we reach the entrance to Zephyr's mansion. He's there in the pristine foyer – shirtless. His dark hair looks damp, like he just stepped from the shower, and he's wearing black leggings that hug his muscular hips and legs, in the style favoured by male fae. I pull my gaze from his body to find his eyes raking my form. There's hunger in those purple depths and I repress my gag reflex at what it could mean if I don't escape.

'Primrose,' he breathes.

'Zephyr,' I answer, voice devoid of emotion.

His gaze snaps to mine then moves to the guards flanking me. 'Dismissed,' he growls.

The guards leave, closing the doors behind them, and a lump forms in my throat. I'm trapped with Zephyr in his home, with no mirror in sight. If I ask to see one will he grow suspicious? I need to play it cool, but the hungry look he's giving me has darkness prickling the underside of my skin. It writhes in a confusing mix of want and defiance. Its defences are up ready to protect us, yet it wants Zephyr with a need I can't voice.

'You look beautiful,' Zephyr says, moving closer.

I inch back and he stops advancing. 'I don't know why I have to wear my dress now, when the ceremony isn't until tomorrow,' I complain.

'It's tradition,' he answers. 'You'll wear it until I remove it after the ceremony.'

I stiffen at his words but don't correct him. Zephyr's frown deepens but he doesn't comment on my reaction. I'm not as good an actress as I'd hoped, and we've started a dance I can't back out of.

I give myself a mental shake and offer some truth. 'I'm nervous,' I whisper.

His features soften and he smiles. 'As is to be expected,' he answers. He holds his hand out to me. 'Come, let me show you our home.'

Our home.

I give him more truth to keep my emotions hidden, as I take his hand and let him lead me through the house. 'Your mum called this place your chambers, so I expected a room, like the one they put me in.' I look up at him. 'This place is so big but you knew we were here.'

He nods. 'Your light calls to me and I feel when you're near.'

'Oh,' I murmur and look away.

So he senses me the same way I sense him.

'But I *was* awaiting your arrival,' he admits.

I meet his gaze again and raise an eyebrow. 'You're half dressed.'

His smile turns shy. 'I was dressing for the ceremony when I felt you arrive. I didn't expect you so soon after moonrise.'

I look away again. 'Your mother insisted I came now.'

It takes a while for Zephyr to show me around his stupidly big house. There are more rooms than I can remember, and he lives here alone. Opulent is too feeble a word to describe his home. Yet, despite it's grandness, there's a homey feel to the place. It's full of warm colours and soft furnishings, making me feel welcome in each space. I can't hide my honest reaction, and Zephyr's pleasure at that is apparent. I feel myself relaxing and the tension leaves my shoulders, until he takes me upstairs.

I lose count of the bedrooms he shows me, each with an adjoining bathroom. It seems strange to have so many rooms and nobody to fill them. He pulls me into the last room and my back goes rigid. The biggest bedroom yet faces me, with a massive bed sitting in the centre. The room is decorated in deep purples and has a masculine edge the previous bedrooms lacked. And it smells like Zephyr, each breath I take filling me with his fragrance. Then I see it – a full-length mirror standing upright opposite the bed. My fingernails bite into my palms as I curl my hands into fists. If I run now he'll catch me. I still need the element of surprise.

Zephyr grips my arm and turns me to face him, breaking my train of thought. 'What's wrong?' he demands. 'Why ha-'

A bolt of purple light shoots from the mirror and hits Zephyr in the chest. He sucks in a breath and stares down at where the light hit him. I stumble back when he releases my arm and staggers towards the mirror. I watch him in morbid fascination, as he seems to fight every step he takes.

'What's happening?'

Zephyr meets my gaze but doesn't stop moving to the mirror. 'Caligo,' he growls.

'Your sister's doing this?'

He stares at me, even as his hand slaps against the glass and an unfamiliar room appears on the other side. I stare at the room, wondering if it's in my realm.

'This mirror only opens to the places I tell it,' Zephyr growls, drawing my gaze back to his.

A bead of sweat rolls down the side of his face, like it's taking everything he has not to step through the doorway he just opened.

'I can't open doorways, remember?' I hiss, using anger to disguise the lie. 'Where the hell are you going, anyway? Have you changed your mind about our bonding? If you have, I could really use a ride home.'

'Caligo is summoning me to the Realm of Man,' he snarls. 'I haven't changed my mind, but I must go to her.'

He growls, like he's in serious pain from denying her summons, but I'm stuck on where he said the doorway leads. The Realm of Man – home. I stare past him at the room through the mirror again.

'The Realm of Man?' I murmur.

Homesickness stabs through me. I'm so very close and yet so far.

'You're mine!' Zephyr snarls, tone so vicious it snaps my gaze back to him and jams my heart in my throat. 'You'll find it impossible to leave my dwelling, so don't try.'

My shock turns to rage and I glare at him. 'Goodbye, Zephyr,' I grit out.

He stares at me for a moment longer, like he's trying to decipher the meaning lacing my words. Then he cringes, like a wave of pain just hit him, and ducks through the doorway. He turns to stare back at me, our gazes connected until the doorway fades to my reflection.

I haven't seen my reflection in days, and what I see now is unfamiliar. I look elegant and polished. I was allowed to bathe and slip into the mating gown, but that's where the independence ended. My hair has been teased into an intricate braid, woven with silver ribbon and twined around a jewelled tiara that bands around my forehead. My hair is thicker and longer, the braid reaching past my hips in a golden rope. It's not an extension either. Alissa called one of her entourage forward and ordered the woman to 'fix' my hair. The woman simply combed her fingers through my tresses and they grew long and luscious in her hands. Then a fae female did something to my face that made it tingle. My skin looks flawless and my eyes, once framed with blonde lashes, are bordered with thick, dark eyelashes. I purse lips that are blush-pink, but I'm not wearing lipstick. The effect is natural and stunning, and freaking me out. No matter how gorgeous the effect, I get the feeling the changes are permanent. They've altered my appearance without my permission.

I press my hand to the glass, intending to open a doorway to my father but nothing happens. I remember Zephyr's words about this mirror only going where he tells it, which means it will only open to the place he went to last. If I open a doorway to the room I saw, the chances are Zephyr will be on the other side.

I drop my hand and back away. At least the doorway Zephyr went through leads to the Realm of Man. I might not know where the room is, but once I get there I can use the mirror on the other side to go home. I blow out a breath and look around the bedroom, shoulders sagging. It's been a long day and weariness is creeping in. I eye the enormous bed with distain. No way am I getting into that thing willingly.

I search through a few of the other bedrooms, settling on one with a view of a lake in the gardens. The moon is high, reflecting a near perfect disk on the surface of the water. I drag a plush chair over to the window and curl up in its softness. The scenery outside is stunning, but the trials of the day are weighing on my eyelids. I let them fall shut and submit to sleep.

CHAPTER 12

I yawn and stretch out. It takes less than a second to realise I'm in a bed instead of the chair I fell asleep in. It takes another second to register the fingers flexing on my hip. Zephyr sighs behind me and nuzzles the back of my neck. Desire pings through my insides, chased swiftly by a heavy dose of panic. I tamp both emotions down and carefully pry Zephyr's fingers from my hip. Halfway through rolling from his embrace, he clamps his hand back on my hip and drags me snug against him.

'Mine,' he mumbles against my neck.

'No,' I tell him and try to pull free.

But he won't let go. His grip tightens and his arousal presses against me. Fear wells in my middle and my darkness lashes out. Zephyr hisses, letting go, and I scramble away from him. He's lying on my dress and it tears at the shoulder when I try to tug it free. I fall from the bed in a heap and push to my feet, spinning to face him as he sits up. Zephyr blinks, a dazed expression on his face. He flexes his fingers, where my darkness attacked him.

'What happened?' he mumbles then looks at me.

I hold the torn part of my dress to maintain my modesty. 'You tried-' I swallow bile from my throat. 'You forced yourself on me.'

'I did not!' he denies.

'You were groping me,' I argue. 'You wouldn't let go when I said no, and you ripped my dress.'

He studies the torn fabric. 'I was sleeping. I didn't know what I was doing and I'd never-' he shakes his head and moves toward me.

I jump back, nearly falling over myself to get away. 'Stop!'

Zephyr's expression turns pained. 'I'm sorry.'

I know he wasn't conscious and, to be fair, if he felt half the lust I felt for him then I can't blame his subconscious for trying to relieve the ache. Heck, he's the hottest guy I've ever met and my girl bits melt just being around him. But I can't get my head around the fact he'd force me, nor can I trust him. One moment he's assuring me he'll never force me, the next he's agreeing with Alissa that there'll be sex after the ceremony.

'Just don't come near me,' I say and glance at my shoulder. 'I need to fix my dress.'

Zephyr nods, respecting my wishes for him to keep away. 'I can fix it,' he tells me. 'But I need to touch the fabric.'

I glance between him and my dress. 'I just need a minute alone.'

'I'd never force you, Primrose,' he whispers.

'But Alissa said-'

He snarls that vicious sound and I flinch away. 'So my mother is the cause for the change in you?'

'What chan-'

'We made progress in the woods this afternoon,' he cuts in. 'You smiled and it was real, not the false smiles you've been wearing since you arrived in my home.'

'What do you want from me, Zephyr? Your mum basically outlined how you'll rape me after the Bonding

137

Ceremony, and you didn't correct her. How the hell am I supposed to react to that?'

He shakes his head, violet eyes imploring. 'It's just a tradition to consummate the joining of light with the joining of flesh. I told you I'll never force you and you must trust that I won't.'

I repress a snort. Trust? The guy kidnapped me a few days ago and he expects me to trust him?

'And you must trust me to choose you,' I answer.

'Primrose-' he starts but I cut him off.

'You can't do it, can you?'

'I need you!'

'I'm a means to an end,' I snap. 'How romantic.'

'You're more than that,' he roars, the whites of his eyes bleeding to purple.

I stare at him and he stares back, before flashing away in a blaze of amethyst light.

I stare at the spot on the bed where he was sitting, knowing I probably have minutes before he comes back. I can't tell if my heart is aching for him or the future we'll never have. I wipe a tear from my face and go to the mirror, pressing my palm against the glass. A doorway opens to the room from earlier and I don't hesitate to push through.

I frown into what looks like a girl's bedroom. The scent of ocean hits me and I breathe deep, studying the pink décor. The colour makes my eyes ache, so I shut them to focus on my darkness. When I open my eyes an orb of black light forms in my palm. I wait for the doorway to fade then grip the essence orb and throw it at the mirror. It shatters on impact, destroying the exit mirror and stopping Zephyr from following me through.

Pain fills my chest at the shards of glass on the carpet. Tears blur my vision and I stifle a sob. The relief of being free is sharp but regret fills me. I scrub at my tears and turn away. I'm guessing Zephyr will sense I'm not near and come looking. It won't take a genius to figure out where I've gone and I need another mirror before he tracks me down. I reach the bedroom doorway, but a large male steps into my path, carrying a dark-haired girl. We all freeze and stare at each other. It's difficult to look away from the girl. Her skin glows with silvery light, calling to the creature in my middle.

'You're fae,' she murmurs, breaking the spell her light has cast over me.

I follow the direction of her gaze, to where the rip in my dress reveals part of my wing marking. I snatch the fabric up and press it over the design.

'Where am I?' I ask, eyeing what looks like a doorway to an en-suite bathroom.

'You're in the Realm of Man,' she answers.

She motions for the big male to put her down, and he does so with care. She frowns when he moves in front of her, almost blocking her from view. The girl sighs and pushes around him, ignoring his growl of annoyance.

'Are you well?' she asks, glancing at my torn dress.

'Just peachy,' I mutter.

'You're British,' the big male says.

My gaze jumps to his when I hear his accent. 'You're American! I'm in the States?'

And without my passport! Hysterical laughter bubbles up my throat but I swallow it down. My days just keep get weirder.

The male raises an eyebrow at me. 'You're in my home,' he drawls.

Whoops. 'Yes, sorry about that,' I say hoping he doesn't notice the broken mirror. 'It was the last place Zeph-' I clamp my mouth shut before I give myself away. Zephyr came here for a reason, so these people might know him. 'This is the only place the mirror would take me,' I explain.

'Do you need help?' the girl asks.

I slide her a sideways glance, trying not to look directly at her in case she hypnotises me with her silvery light again. It's obvious she isn't human. If you discount the light, this female sits right at the top of the beauty scale, which to me screams non-human. She has jet hair and navy eyes, offset by the gleam of her pearly skin.

'I don't recognise your accent,' I tell her.

'I'm from Lantis,' she answers.

I shake my head. 'Sorry, no idea where that is.'

She tilts her head, seeming surprised by my answer. 'I am mer,' she offers.

'You've lost me.'

'She's a mermaid,' the male sighs.

I feel my eyes go wide. 'Oh.'

My brain starts to ache, as it tries to reject this new turn in events. Mermaids are real? I eye the wardrobe, expecting a lion and witch to stroll out.

'How is it a fae knows not of my kind?' the girl asks.

I slide another glance at the other door. If it does lead to a bathroom there's a good chance of a mirror being in there. But I'm making assumptions. From this room alone I can tell this is a nice house. It might just be a walk-in wardrobe. I glance behind me at the broken mirror, a sense of urgency trickling down my spine.

'I have to go,' I murmur then look at the male. 'I'm sorry about your mirror. I'll send you money for the damage when I get back to-' I cut my sentence short, not wanting to reveal where I'm heading. 'Once I reach where I'm going.'

'You *do* need help,' the girl declares, concern staining her tone.

I open my mouth to deny it, but gasp when the mark on my wrist fizzes to life. What the hell? I pull my sleeve back to find the Mating Mark burning bright. It's always glowed against my skin, but now it's filling the room with amethyst light.

'Oh hell,' I breathe and yank the sleeve back into place. 'I've really got to go,' I say, darting another gaze around the room, as the feeling hits me.

Zephyr.

I *feel* his presence prickle over my skin. My heart starts racing and the air grows thick with his scent. I dart across the room and through the other door, slamming it behind me. Sliding the little lock into place doesn't make me feel better. Doors mean nothing to fae and I know I've got to get the hell out of dodge before Zephyr finds me.

I was right about this room being a bathroom, but the only mirror in here is the one over the sink. I eye the frame, wondering if I'll get my backside through it.

'Primrose!' Zephyr shouts from the bedroom. 'Where is she? Where's my mate?'

'Zephyr, what's going on?' the girl demands.

'I smell her in here and your mirror is broken,' Zephyr snarls. 'You can't hide her from me, Nima!'

'You mean the blonde with dark eyes and a ripped dress?' the male cuts in, tone accusing.

I stare at the door for one more second then haul myself onto the sink and press my palm to the mirror. Home is the first place I think of and my bedroom appears beyond the glass. I push through the doorway, panicking for just a second when my hips snag on the frame. I grip the edge of the mirror on my side for leverage and push. I fall onto my bedroom carpet with a thump then scramble over to my desk in the corner. I snatch the paperweight Drew brought me back from his trip to Great Yarmouth and throw it at the mirror. The glass explodes under the impact, raining glass over the carpet.

I look around, thinking of my next move. I can't stay here. Breaking the mirror will stop Zephyr from opening a doorway to it, but he knows where I live, and I get the feeling he doesn't need a mirror to get here.

I glance at my ruined dress and my brain fires into action. I pull the gown off and tug on some of my own clothes. Calm washes over me at the familiarity of wearing my own clothes, and being in my own home. I pull on my favourite boots then hurry downstairs. It takes a second to locate my mobile phone. I frown at the dead battery and reach for the landline, thanking God that I know Drew's number by heart. I look at the clock on the wall. It's the middle of the day and I hope he hasn't switched his phone off while he's in class.

'Primrose?' he answers after only one ring.

'Drew I-'

'Where the hell have you been?' he cuts in. 'I've been freaking out over you just disappearing and now you're ringing me from your house phone?'

I cringe at the worry in his voice but what the hell can I tell him? 'I'm sorry, but the last two days have been-'

'Two days?' he snaps. 'Prim, you've been AWOL for nearly a week! Where the hell have you been?'

'Wait, a week?'

'David and Katherine are going crazy,' he answers. 'They think you've taken a long walk off a short cliff because of your mum.'

I hear Drew talking but I'm stuck on the fact I've been gone for a week. I wondered after visiting Aric how the whole night had passed at home when I'd only spent an hour with my father. Time moves differently in this realm compared to the fae ones. I've spent two days in Faerie and nearly a week has passed in the Realm of Man.

'Primrose!' Drew's panicked tone pulls me from my musings. 'Are you still there?'

'A week,' I whisper.

'Thank God,' he declares. 'What the hell is going on, Prim?' he pants.

'Why do you sound breathless?'

'I came home when you went missing,' he says. 'I'm running through the village, on the way to you.'

'No!' I blurt, worried for Drew. 'Don't come here, I'll come to you.'

He's quiet for a moment, except for his laboured breathing. I hold my breath, praying he'll listen.

'I'm on the corner by the post box,' he answers.

'Give me five minutes,' I tell him.

'I'm giving you two,' he counters. 'Then I'm coming to get you.'

I jam the phone back into its cradle and scribble a note to Katherine. I tell her I've gone travelling for a few weeks and promise to text her, so she won't worry. I prop the note on the counter and run from the house, not bothering to lock the door. I took Katherine's key and need her to see the note.

I reach the end of the road then suck in a breath when I feel him.

Zephyr.

I up my pace, skidding around the corner onto the main road that dissects the village. The village square comes into view half a minute later and I see Drew's burly frame leaning against the post box. He straightens when he sees me, and steps off the kerb.

My steps falter when Zephyr shouts my name. I glance over my shoulder to see him sprinting after me. I realise there are too many witnesses for him to teleport to get to me, and I give him the one finger salute. He didn't know what it meant last time, but from the look on his face I think he gets it now.

The relief bleeds from Drew's face as I near him, his pace to meet me increasing. He must see the panic in my expression and doesn't resist when I snag his hand and keep on running.

He glances over his shoulder at Zephyr. 'Who the hell is that?'

I glance back. Zephyr is gaining on us because Drew is too slow. I'm faster since my fae side was woken, and Zephyr is even faster than me. My head start gave me an advantage, but I'm slowing my pace for Drew.

'We're royally screwed if he catches us,' I say.

'What is he, an Olympic medallist?' Drew pants. 'And when the hell did you get so fast?'

Drew looks tired already and I'm not even breathless. My heart is racing, but I feel like I can keep going for a while. But sweat coats Drew's face and he's panting hard.

'He's more than that,' I answer and tug Drew into a sharp left, into the churchyard.

'There's no way we'll outrun this guy, Prim,' Drew says and looks over his shoulder. 'I can probably take him if we-'

'No you can't,' I cut in, meeting his gaze.

He must see something in my glare because he asks, 'Then where the heck are we going?'

'Dragon Pond,' I answer, tugging him between the last few trees in the churchyard then under Saint Mary's Gate.

The large pond comes into view at the bottom of the hill and I pull Drew down it at a dead run. For a moment it feels like my legs are moving too fast for my body, and I worry we'll fall. But Drew squeezes my hand and steadies my gait, like he knows what I'm thinking. I suppose that's what happens when you know someone for as long as we've known each other. We used to run down this hill as children, to go play by the Dragon Pond. It gets its name for all the dragonflies that can be found here during the summer.

'Primrose!' Zephyr roars as we reach the bottom of the hill.

I refuse to look back, forcing Drew to run a little faster. Zephyr is so close it makes the hair prickle on the back of my neck.

'Prim,' Drew pants as we near the water.

His eyes grow wide when I don't slow our pace.

'We're jumping,' I tell him.

'What?'

'Don't stop!' I snap when he hesitates. His gaze meets mine. 'Just trust me.'

'Okay,' he pants.

I squeeze his hand in mine. 'And don't let go of my hand.'

Drew nods and ups his pace a little more to meet mine, even though I know it must hurt. We reach the edge of the pond and jump from the grassy edge. I grip his hand a little tighter and think of Aric's room in the Dark Realm. Zephyr shouts my name, and instead of sounding angry he sounds scared. But scared of what? Of me hurting myself? Of losing me? I remind myself I'm just a means to an end for him.

You're more than that.

More.

In a sick way Zephyr woke me from a cycle of grief. He pulled me from my funk and permeated my life with feelings I didn't know existed. There could've been so much more, but what is more without trust and respect?

Without love?

I don't want to be someone's solution to a problem. I want it all.

I land on my back in Aric's chamber then groan and push up to look at the mirrored wall. It shivers, the image of the sky above the pond disappearing until I'm staring at my dishevelled reflection. I lift my hand to create an essence orb and destroy the mirror, but the mirror shivers and turns into a wall before I get chance.

Okay then.

'That did just happen?' Drew coughs beside me.

'You'll have to be more specific,' I mutter, dissipating the orb.

'We just jumped into the Dragon Pond and ended up here, right?'

'Yep,' I answer, bracing myself for him to freak out.

'How?' he asks, the picture of calm.

'I opened a doorway,' I say, still waiting for him to freak.

'I figured that bit out by myself, Prim,' he drawls. 'I want to know *how*.'

'Well, I'm sort of, maybe, half fae.'

Drew quirks and eyebrow. 'What's a fae?'

I huff. 'A faery, Drew; I'm half faery.'

He stares at me. 'You're a little tall for a faery, aren't you?'

'Why aren't you freaking out?' I demand.

'Do you want me to freak out?'

'It's what a normal person would do.'

He shrugs. 'You're still you, aren't you? I've known you all my life, Prim. You could be half zebra and I'd still love you. Besides, this isn't the strangest thing that's ever happened to me.'

I stare at him in shock. 'What's happened to you that's stranger than this?'

He glances around the room. 'Can we talk about this later, after you've told me what the heck is happening? Why was that guy chasing you and where have you been?'

My eyes burn at the reminder of my predicament and I sniff back tears. Drew's expression softens and he holds his arms open. I crawl into his lap and cry against his shoulder. I've wanted to tell him everything for so long, but worried he'd hate me. I've carried the secret of my darkness for as long as I can remember, scared people would reject me. But here Drew is, accepting me as though it's nothing that I'm not human. It makes me wonder what secrets he has of his own.

'Easy,' he murmurs.

'I'm sorry. It's just been so hard to keep this from everyone,' I admit.

Drew kisses the top of my head. 'Anytime, Prim,' he says. 'So, are you going to tell me where we are?'

I look around, suddenly nervous about bringing Drew here. 'We're in my father's home.'

146

'You met your dad?'

I bite my lip. 'Yes. We're in the Dark Fae Realm, and he's sort of the king.'

Drew blinks at me then starts laughing. 'You know what that means, right?'

'Why the hell are you laughing?'

'You're a faery princess, Prim.' He laughs even harder. 'Princess Primrose!'

I shove away from him and push to my feet. 'Shut up, you giant moron,' I snap but it's a challenge to hide my grin.

Drew teased me endlessly whenever I did anything remotely 'girly' as a child. He's called me Princess Primrose to annoy me for years.

'Don't make me blast you,' I warn when he keeps laughing.

He sobers a little. 'Blast me?'

'Don't tempt me,' I mutter then change the subject. I don't want to talk about my ability to kill Drew. Instead, I prop my hands on my hips and stare at the wall where the mirror used to be. 'Look, it's not that I don't trust Aric-'

'Who's Aric?'

'My dad,' I answer and meet Drew's gaze. 'It's not that I don't trust him, but I don't think it's a good idea for him to find you here.'

'Why?'

'I don't know what the rules are,' I admit. 'I brought us here to escape Zephyr-'

'The guy chasing us?'

I nod. 'He kidnapped me and took me to the Light Realm. It's where I've been for the past week, except time is different there and it was only two days for me.'

'Prim-'

'Let me finish,' I cut in. 'There are humans there and they didn't look happy, Drew. I don't want Aric to find you here and decree that you can never leave. We need to get you out while we still can.'

I trust Aric as much as I can trust someone I just met. I once thought myself a good judge of character, but everything I've seen has me questioning what is real. Fae are masters of deception and I doubt my ability to see through their glamour. It's a risk for me to leave the Dark Realm before the equinox is over, but Drew is important.

Drew's face pales. 'No offense to your dad but I don't want to be stuck here, Prim.'

'Agreed,' I say and press my palm to the wall.

Drew stares at the wall when the mirror shimmers into place beneath my hands. 'Where are we going?' he murmurs.

'I can't take you back to the village while Zephyr's there,' I say.

'Take me to Liverpool then,' he answers.

I hold out my hand and Drew takes it, lacing our fingers together. He gapes when his student bedroom appears on the other side of the mirror.

'You'll never need your passport again,' he says mimicking my thought from earlier.

'I'd rather need a passport to travel than be forced to mate a fae with a god complex,' I mutter.

'What?' Drew asks.

'Nothing,' I say and pull him through the mirror.

The feeling hits me as soon as we step into Drew's bedroom. I swear a second before Zephyr pops into the room.

Drew curses behind me. 'He teleports?'

I meet his incredulous gaze. 'After everything you've seen, this surprises you?'

'You've got to admit, it's kind of – Watch out!' Drew yells and leaps in front of me.

Purple light smacks him in the shoulder, throwing him against me. His head connects with my jaw, as we crash to the carpet. I hiss in pain but ignore it and scramble to my knees. I push Drew onto his back as his body arches from the floor. I search his shoulder for injury but there's nothing there. Purple light crackles over his body and his jaw is clenched in pain, but he's not dead.

'What did you do?' I shout at Zephyr.

'It won't harm him,' Zephyr answers.

'How do you know?' I screech.

'Because it was meant for you!' he shouts back then his tones softens. 'I'd never hurt you.'

'Looks pretty painful to me,' I snarl.

'It would only have knocked you out,' he argues.

I get what he's saying. I'm fae, so whatever Zephyr threw would have rendered me unconscious. But Drew's human.

'Drew,' I murmur and shake him gently.

Zephyr snarls when my hands make contact with Drew's torso. My gaze snaps to Zephyr and his irises are glowing bright purple.

'What the hell is wrong with you?'

'You're touching another male,' he snarls. 'It's forbidden.'

I feel my eyes bleed to black as anger blasts through me. Zephyr's eyes widen in response but I don't care. I'm done hiding what I am from everyone. The fact I can open doorways using mirrors should've clued Zephyr into the fact I've been lying.

'If Drew dies I'll never forgive you.'

Zephyr's eyes narrow into slits. 'You love him,' he growls.

'Of course I love him!' I shout, curling my hands into fists against Drew's chest. 'You've taken everything from me: my humanity, my life and now my best friend. And you expect me to trust you? Lay down and mate you?'

'Prim,' Drew croaks, drawing my attention.

I gasp when I look down to find him staring up at me with glowing, blue eyes.

'What the hell,' I whisper.

'Help me up,' he whispers back.

I help him to stand then steady him when he staggers back and bumps into the mirror. He pinches the bridge of his nose then groans and grips his temples.

'It hurts,' he groans, as blood trickles from his nose.

'Oh God,' I breathe panic blooming.

'It's too late to reverse it,' Zephyr says.

Drew and I both look in Zephyr's direction. 'What's happening to him,' I demand.

'The same thing that happened to you, when I activated your dormant fae genes.'

My eyes snap to Drew. 'He's half fae?'

'Ironic, isn't it?' Zephyr says. 'Halflings are a rarity, yet I've activated two of you in less than a decade.'

Drew stares at me, a bead of blood forming in his tear duct. It rolls down his cheek, followed by another and another, until twin streams paint his face. I stare at him in horror, remembering Aric's words about most Halflings dying during the change into fae. My heart thumps a heavy beat and tears fill my vision. The relief that Zephyr's shot didn't kill Drew shrivels to nothing, and I choke back a sob.

'I'm dying,' Drew whispers.

'No you're not,' I answer.

'Probably,' Zephyr counters earning a scowl from me.

Drew leans heavily on the mirrored door of his wardrobe and closes his eyes. Sweat sheens his skin and he's panting hard. He opens his eyes and looks at me. There's so much sadness in his eyes I fail to hold back another sob.

'Sorry, Prim,' he whispers.

'For what?'

'I let you watch your mum die, I won't make you watch me,' he says then falls backward through the mirror.

150

I stare at the mirror in shock, Drew standing on the other side of the glass. He's in woodland that I don't recognise and could be anywhere. He opened a doorway. How the hell did he open a doorway? Forget the fact that he even knows how to do it, where the heck do you find a reflective surface in the middle of the woods? Drew drops to his knees and clutches his head, and I move for the mirror. It closes before I make it through, and I hit the glass so hard it shatters.

'No!' I scream and smack my palms against the wardrobe door, where the glass used to be.

Drew's gone, and I don't know his destination enough to open a portal to get to him. I think of the agony I went through during the change and cry harder. He's going to die alone and I won't be there to help him through it.

'Primrose,' Zephyr murmurs behind me.

He grips my shoulder in a gentle hold and turns me to face him. I stare up into sympathetic eyes and fall against him. He wraps his arms around me and just holds me while I cry. I cry for Drew, who's dying in a field alone somewhere. I cry for my mum and the grief still simmering beneath the surface. And I cry for the human life I had that was stolen.

By Zephyr.

My skin prickles against the force of my anger, an essence orb forming in the palm of my hand. I conceal the orb behind my back and push away from Zephyr, wiping the tears from my eyes with my free hand. I take a deep breath then throw the orb at Zephyr. It hits him in the chest and launches him across the room. He smacks into the opposite wall, creating a crack in the plaster, before hitting the floor.

Zephyr groans, face down on the carpet. I run from the room and across the hallway, into the shared bathroom and lock the door behind me. A tiny part of my brain is wondering why all this noise hasn't brought

Drew's housemates running, but then they're probably in classes right now. I press my hands to the mirror on the wall then scream when the bathroom door blasts open. Zephyr stands in the doorway, expression furious.

'You've been keeping secrets from me,' he snarls.

I throw another orb at him, aiming for his feet so he's forced to look down to dodge it. I take that moment to open a doorway I know he won't be able to follow me through. My hips snag on the frame of the exit mirror, but I push through with enough force that I don't get stuck this time. I hiss in pain when I crash to the floor, knocking items from the sink on my way down. I meet Zephyr's gaze through the mirror, as I push to my feet. He watches me from the other side and I see my name on his lips. I shake my head and back away, watching him until the doorway closes between us.

'Zephyr's worried about you.'

I gasp and spin to find the dark-haired girl from earlier, standing naked in the bathroom doorway. That mesmerising, pearlescent light shimmers over her skin, seemingly brighter in the diminishing daylight.

'He's here?' I ask, worried he figured out my destination already and arrived through a different mirror.

The girl shakes her head. 'He left to search for you? Why do you run from your mate?'

'You know you're naked?'

She nods. 'And you've disposed of your ripped dress. But you didn't answer my question.'

'I didn't choose him,' I tell her. 'And I won't be forced.'

The girl's eyes widen. 'Zephyr wouldn't-'

'He put his Mate Mark on me without my permission,' I cut in. 'Then he stole me from my home and imprisoned me in the Light Realm.'

'Because he loves you,' she says.

'What part of abducting me and holding me prisoner sounds like love to you?' I snap. 'He stole me because I'm compatible. Zephyr doesn't love me. He wants me for the light I carry and he'll take me whether I agree or not.'

'This doesn't sound like the Zephyr I know,' she murmurs.

'It's the Zephyr *I* know,' I counter. 'I've seen many emotions from him over the last few days, but not one of them was love. Being compatible doesn't mean he owns me.'

'No,' she says, surprising me with her agreement. 'It does not.'

'Then, you won't tell him I'm here?' I hedge.

She shakes her head. 'Zephyr is my friend but I won't aid him in acts of wrong doing.'

A tiny bit of tension leaks from my shoulders. 'I've, um, never met a mermaid before.'

'It's strange to meet a fae that doesn't know of my kind,' she tells me. 'And I've never met one with such dark wing markings.'

Tension creeps back into my shoulders. 'I get the trait from my father,' I mumble. 'Look, it was really nice meeting you, but I don't suppose you can direct me to another mirror? I really need to leave.'

'I will show you to a mirror but I have conditions.'

'What conditions?' I ask, wondering if I should just squeeze back through the bathroom mirror. I rub my sore hip at the thought.

'You won't tell Zephyr I assisted you in evading him,' she says.

'Done,' I agree.

'And you'll consider mating him,' she adds.

'Didn't you hear what I just told you?' I scoff.

'You must know how rare it is to find a female who has light compatible with Zephyr's,' she says.

'There are other, willing females,' I argue.

'Not compatible ones.'

'But Zephyr said-'

153

'His parent's are fading,' she cuts in. 'The time for him to mate grows short.'

'Fading?'

'Dying,' she clarifies.

I suck in a breath, heart squeezing in my chest. The grief at losing Mum grows unbearable at times, but Zephyr's about to lose both his parents?

'I didn't know.'

'You don't seem to know much about fae culture, for a fae,' she agrees.

'I wasn't raised with other fae,' I tell her. 'I know almost nothing about them.'

'Then I must tell you that finding a compatible mate is akin to Zephyr winning the lottery. Your kind live so long, Primrose,' she says, shocking me with the use of my name. Of course, Zephyr *was* shouting my name like a maniac the last time we were here.

'Wait,' I say hoping I'll finally get some answers. 'How long are we talking?'

'Fae are one of the longest lived of the Archaic Races,' she answers. 'Your kind can live millennia.'

Archaic Races?

'Are you serious?' I bark, making her flinch.

'This upsets you?' she asks, perplexed.

'Thousands of years; Zephyr is thousands of years old?' I scoff.

Does that mean I'll live thousands of years? I don't think I want to live that long. Hopefully the fact I'm half fae will mean I'll die sooner. No wonder Aric was so vague when I asked him his age. How does anyone even live so many years and not go mad with boredom? I shiver at the thought then think of Zephyr and try to imagine things from his perspective. The loneliness since Mum died is suffocating, and she's only been gone weeks. It almost chokes me to think of years without her, and Zephyr's gone millennia. He had his parents, but the relationship seems cold and indifferent. He doesn't appear to have the bond with his mother that I shared with mine. I've only seen his father once, from afar at the banquet, and he didn't even acknowledge his son. Mum and I were more like best friends than parent and child. I could tell her anything and know she'd support me. It makes me sad that Zephyr doesn't have that.

The girl nods. 'Did Zephyr not tell you of the time he's spent dreaming of finding a compatible match?'

'No,' I snap, angry as hell at him.

'That's how rare you are,' she tells me. 'Zephyr is over two millennia old and you're the first compatible mate he's found. Can you understand his rash decision to claim you now?'

It upsets me that I can. I want to hate Zephyr with every fibre of my soul for what he's done, but I can't. I can't even bring myself to imagine the years he's lived, let alone the loneliness of not having someone to share his deepest thoughts with.

'He should've told me,' I mutter, 'asked my permission.'

'A mistake on his part,' she agrees. 'But now he's chosen you there can be no other.'

'What do you mean?'

'Zephyr put his Mate Mark on you, Primrose. Only if you die can he claim another,' she answers.

'Then what happens if his parents fade and Zephyr has no mate?'

'Zephyr will ascend the throne unmated,' she says. 'His chance to mate lost.'

'But why?'

'It's fae law,' she answers.

'That's stupid law!'

I don't know what to think. I'm angry at Zephyr, but I empathise with his plight. What the hell am I supposed to do? Am I stupid to feel sorry for the guy, or am I just a nice person? It makes me angry that I want to help him.

I want to help him.

I shake my head, dislodging the thought. He kidnapped me and was about to force me into mating him. But if I don't mate him he'll be alone for the rest of his life, which sounds like a very long time.

'It's their way,' the girl says. 'There are reasons for fae laws, but I'm not privy to all of them.'

Something occurs to me. 'If putting his Mate Mark on me prevents him from taking another mate, what does that mean for me? Please tell me I can mate whoever I want?'

The girl bites her bottom lip and shakes her head. 'I'm sorry-'

'You've got to be kidding me!'

It's one thing to ruin his chances of mating anyone but me, but to steal the choice from me on top of everything else he's done? Darkness fills my vision and prickles over my skin. The girl gasps and I follow her gaze to the onyx pattern swirling over my hands. I'm wearing jeans and a long-sleeve top, so only my hands are visible, but I feel the darkness all over my body.

I glance over my shoulder to see my reflection in the mirror. My eyes are two pools of midnight and black filigree curls in complex patterns over my neck and face. I take a deep breath in and let it out slow through my nose, trying to calm the storm brewing in my centre. My darkness is raging and feels like it did the day of Mum's funeral. But I'm not frightened of it this time. Instead, I feel empowered. The only thing that scares me is if Zephyr were here, I'd use it on him.

I meet the girl's worried gaze. 'I'm not mad at you,' I tell her. 'I'm just struggling to understand how he can do this to me.'

'Please, consider my words and don't punish Zephyr too harshly,' she pleads. 'He has waited for you for such a long time, and I know he feels deeply for you, as I see you do for him.'

'I *do* feel deeply for him,' I agree. 'Deep-seated anger for what he's done.'

'It's more than that,' she argues.

I stare at her. 'Thank you for explaining all of this stuff to me,' I say. 'I'll consider your words.'

The girl sighs at my flat tone and leads me from the bathroom. She must realise there's nothing she can say that will endear me to Zephyr. I glance at the bed as we pass through the pink bedroom. The huge male is sleeping there and I look away fast when I realise he's as naked as the girl. I catch sight of the mirror I broke the last time I was here and see it's mended. A shiver zips down my spine at the sight and I hurry away from it. It's only a matter of time before Zephyr figures out where I am, and I expect him to step through it any second.

The girl leads me to another bedroom with a large mirror fastened to the wall. I breathe a sigh of relief at the sight and press my palms to the surface. A doorway opens to Aric's chamber and tears fill my eyes. I'm trading one prison for another.

The girl squeaks when I turn and pull her into a hug. 'Thank you for helping me.'

She wraps me in a comforting hug. 'You're welcome, Primrose.'

I chuckle. 'I'm hugging a naked stranger and don't even know your name.'

'Anima,' she laughs, offering a smile as I let her go.

'It's a pretty name,' I whisper.

I wipe my eyes and step through the mirror, waving at Anima once I'm through. She waves back, before the doorway closes between us, and the mirror turns back into a wall. I take a deep breath and try getting myself together.

'Primrose,' Aric says from behind me.

I turn to see him standing in his bedroom doorway and run into his arms. He catches me and gathers me close, his earthy scent an instant comfort.

'You're safe now,' he murmurs.

'They didn't hurt me,' I answer, feeling a strong need to defend Zephyr.

'There are only a few hours left until the equinox,' he says looking down at me. 'Once it has passed you'll be free.'

My lip wobbles as I try to smile. I should be happy that I managed to escape, but all I feel is empty. I've made my decision and we'll both suffer the consequences. Then there's Drew.

'Happy tears?' Aric asks, wiping a pearl of moisture from my cheek.

I shake my head. 'I found out Drew is a Halfling like me.'

'Your friend?'

'Yes.'

'That makes you sad?'

'Zephyr activated Drew's fae genes and now he's dying.' More tears spill from my eyes and bead my lashes. 'He went through a portal to a place I don't recognise and I broke the mirror before I could trace the doorway.' I wipe at my eyes to clear my vision. 'Is there a way I can find him?'

Aric nods. 'If he survives the transition and we know which fae line he heralds from.'

'But he probably won't make it, right?' I sniff. 'Most Halflings don't, and by then it will be too late. Drew's going to die out in the woods somewhere, and I won't be there to comfort him.'

'My Primrose,' Aric murmurs and uses his thumbs to wipe my tears. 'You have your mother's generous heart, and deserve a devoted mate.'

'Zephyr's Mating Mark has stolen my chances of mating anyone other than him. He'll be alone and so will I.'

Aric's eyes go completely black. 'There's still time for you, Primrose.'

'But they said-'

'You're a royal fae,' he cuts in. 'Like Zephyr, you have until you ascend the throne to find a mate.'

'I don't get it.'

'What you say is true for common fae, but I'm guessing the light fae that told you the laws didn't know you are my daughter,' Aric answers.

Oh hell, this is getting too complicated. I don't tell Aric it was a mermaid, not a fae who told me. I don't think my brain can handle the resulting questions.

'But Zephyr's put his Mate Mark on me, and you said there's no way of reversing that,' I say.

'No,' he agrees. 'You and Zephyr will be connected until the day he dies, but your royal status means there are other avenues open to you.'

A chill rakes my spine at the way Aric said, until the day Zephyr dies, like it's a given he will die before I do. The hairs on my nape stand up but I shake the feeling away.

'What other avenues,' I ask.

Aric smiles and tucks a length of hair behind my ear. 'We'll discuss this after you've rested,' he tells me.

'But-'

'I feel your exhaustion, Primrose.'

I sigh and sag against him, admitting I'm running on empty. 'Okay,' I murmur.

Aric takes my hand and leads me from the room. I glance back at the mirror disguised as a wall on my way out, wondering what this means for Zephyr. I worry I've sentenced us both to a life of loneliness.

CHAPTER 13

I sense the moment Zephyr enters the Dark Realm. I wonder at what point I grew so attuned to him. The first few times I met him he seemed to be able to control whether I felt his presence or not. Then he turned me fae, and the more time I spend around him the more I've been able to sense him. It used to be I could sense when he was near, but in such a short time it has grown to knowing when we're occupying the same realm.

Our connection is getting stronger and I don't know why. I'm too afraid to ask my father, for fear he'll ask how I know. If I tell him Zephyr is here, Aric will murder him for sure. I was certain Zephyr would never dare to follow me here, but it seems I was wrong.

I look up when Aric reaches over and takes my hand. It's then I realise the tall, elegant glass I was holding is in pieces on the floor, the contents a blue puddle at my feet. I must've dropped it when I felt Zephyr's presence curl around me in warm bands. I open my mouth to tell Aric as such then force an apology out instead.

'It's just a glass,' Aric smiles. 'Don't be so nervous, you have nothing to fear,' he tells me, thinking it's the reason I dropped my drink.

I force a smile, something akin to panic flooding my insides. My eyes scan the room, skipping over groups of entitled Dark Fae in search of Zephyr. I wonder why he'd risk coming here in the midst of so many powerful Dark Fae, here to meet me, the lost Dark Fae princess, who found her way home. But I know the answer already. Zephyr doesn't want to be alone and part of me can't blame him. I'm just surprised he thinks mating me is worth the risk of dying.

I cringe at the amount of Dark Fae here. They all assume I want to be their princess, including my father, when all I really want is to go home to my cottage. I want to curl up in my bed and pretend the last few weeks never happened. Instead, I find myself sitting in a throne beside Aric's, dressed in a backless amber gown to showcase my wing marking, a crown banding my forehead.

Elegant, Dark Fae circle the room before us, reminding me of sharks, each taking a turn to approach the throne for introductions. It's boring and sinister in the same instance. My eyes bled to black during the first introduction, when a Lord questioned my legitimacy, and have stayed black ever since. My darkness senses the challenge in the room and has remained visibly present in warning. The swirling cloud of onyx around me has stopped any further questions regarding my claim to the Dark Fae throne, while putting a smirk on Aric's face. He seems to be enjoying the stinging sensation my darkness is pulsing through the air around me, despite the grimace it causes any other fae that nears me.

Aric tilts his head toward me when I lean closer to him. 'I don't think I can do this,' I say.

'Do what?'

'I'm not princess material,' I whisper. 'I don't know the first thing about how to behave in a fae court.'

Aric gives me an indulgent smile and brushes his knuckles over my cheek. 'You're behaving perfectly,' he says. 'Your instincts are sharper than I'd hoped, reacting to every challenge issued without any effort on your part.'

'Challenges?'

Aric booms a laugh, making me jump. 'You didn't even realise they were challenging you?' he asks.

'No,' I mutter. 'Except for the first guy who asked if you were sure I'm your daughter.'

Aric laughs again, like my admission is the best thing he's heard in a long time. His laughter dies and his face grows serious.

'You're better at this than you think, Primrose. There are fae in this room powerful enough to rule, should my line die out.'

'They were hoping for it,' I say reading his meaning. 'Then I came along.'

'You needed to prove yourself able to withstand a challenge from them,' he says then smirks. 'I think you surpassed their expectations.'

'How do you know?' I murmur, staring out at the sharks before me.

'Because you surpassed mine.'

I meet his gaze, the panic I feel that Zephyr's in this realm notching higher. Aric hasn't said it, but everything he's told me hints at the fact he has plans for me. They involve me inheriting the throne from him. A throne I don't want. He refused to let me leave when I asked to go searching for Drew, claiming I have to wait for the equinox to pass. When I insisted on not giving up on Drew, he placated me by sending a team of Tracker fae to locate him instead. The most Aric let me contribute was to open a doorway for the Trackers, leading to Drew's student bedroom. I understand Aric's reasoning, but I get the impression he's not going to let me leave once the equinox is over. He looks at me like I'm precious, and I'm starting to feel as much a prisoner in the Dark Realm as I felt in the light.

I stifle a sigh. 'Can I return to my room yet?' I ask. 'I'm tired.'

'You don't need permission, Primrose,' he answers. 'You're Princess of the Dark Realm and are free to roam it.'

As long as I don't try to leave it, goes unsaid.

'Thank you,' I murmur and push to my feet.

'But remember the Welcome Ball later,' Aric reminds me. 'Many have travelled from distant realms to greet you.'

To challenge me.

'I remember,' I tell him, forcing a smile onto my lips as I leave the throne room.

I smirk as I traverse the hallways, sensing at least six guards behind me. I can't see them but *know* they're there. I'm the fae version of being grounded and I'd laugh if the thought didn't freak me out so much.

'You look beautiful in that gown,' a familiar voice whispers by my ear, making me scream.

Lord Darrack shimmers into view as if from thin air. He's laughing, a deep, rich sound and his eyes glow amber with mirth.

'Bloody hell,' I hiss at him. 'What the hell are you doing, sneaking up on me like that?'

My heart is racing from thinking he was Zephyr, until I registered the amber glow. I remember the amber dust Zephyr removed from my skin and anger flares hot inside me. My fingers curl into my palms and I resist the urge to punch Darrack in his smirking face. He tried to claim me while removing Zephyr's claim and thought I wouldn't know. But Zephyr knew his claim had been removed, so I'm assuming Darrack does too. Yet, he seems okay with it. My anger abates and I wonder if I was wrong about him trying to claim me. Punching him seems a little harsh when I'm not certain of his intent.

He tucks a length of his blond hair behind one pointy ear. 'I apologise for startling you, Princess,' he says looking anything but apologetic.

Darrack's looks are on a par with Zephyr's, which puts me on edge. He already has the advantage of me finding him attractive, and I trust my instincts even less because of it. He doesn't cause my stomach to flip-flop, like Zephyr though, so it's easier to keep my focus around him.

'Don't pretend you weren't out to scare the crap out of me,' I say, some of the venom leaking from my tone.

I suck in a breath when he takes my hand and presses a kiss to my palm. 'Forgive me,' he murmurs, gold eyes fixed on mine. They give him a leonine appearance from this angle. 'I simply wished to convey your beauty in the gown I selected for you.'

I look down at the amber silk hugging my frame. 'You picked this dress for me?'

'It was my honour,' he answers.

Something about his demeanour makes me uneasy, and I tug harder on my hand until he lets go. He's being familiar with me in a way no other has dared, and surely the guards shadowing me will report it back to my father.

'It's very pretty,' I offer, not knowing what else to say.

The dress is beautiful, backless but tasteful. My back might be bare, but it has a high neck and long sleeves. The amber silk drapes to the floor, in elegant folds that make me seem taller, which is a bonus when surrounded by tall fae. Black lace overlays the silk, giving it an opulent appearance.

'It's a combination of our combined lights,' he says.

I stare at the black and amber material and realise he's right. The amber is an exact match to the amber hue of his light.

'You were in my room?' I say thinking of how I found the dress laid out for me after I'd finished bathing.

'I had one of your attendants take it to your room,' he counters.

'You shouldn't have,' I grit out, meeting his gaze.

Hurt flashes through his features. 'You don't like it?'

I've offended him, and I wonder if I'm reading too much into the gesture. Maybe this is some weird fae custom, and I'm taking it too personally.

'I already said it was pretty. You just-' I stop and sigh. 'Thank you.'

'You honour me by wearing it, Princess.'

I refrain from telling him that I wore it because it was laid out on the bed for me, and I assumed I was supposed to.

'Please just call me Primrose,' I mutter.

The constant reminder of being a princess is freaking me out, adding to the long list of things that are doing that right now.

'Primrose,' he breathes, like I've gifted him the moon.

'And don't pop in on me like that again,' I order. 'I'm still getting used to the teleporting thing.'

'I didn't teleport,' he says.

'But, you appeared from nowhere,' I argue.

'I was using glamour to disguise my presence,' he says. 'It can be quite entertaining.'

'Entertainment for bored immortals,' I mutter.

Darrack laughs. 'I'm not immortal, Primrose.'

'Close enough, though.'

'Perhaps it seems that way to you,' he agrees. 'You'll learn that time is short, even to those of us who are considered long lived.'

'So that's what you were doing, using glamour to sneak around for your own entertainment?' I say.

His smile fades. 'Your father requested I watch over you.'

'Spy on me, you mean.'

'No-'

'So how do you explain the other five fae with you?' I cut in.

I hadn't known how they'd been shadowing me without being seen, but Darrack did me a favour by putting a name on it. Glamour was something I hadn't been aware of, until now. I just assumed when fae popped in and out of rooms they were teleporting. Saying that, Darrack appeared in the hallway in a shimmering cloud of light, rather than just popping in to existence in the usual flash teleporting creates, so I should've noticed the difference.

Darrack sighs and signals to the space behind him. Five fae shimmer into the hallway, filling me with a smugness that I guessed the correct amount based on the emotions I sense. *That* I can do, since I've been fine-tuning the skill for years.

'If Aric wants me to have a guard then he should ask me, not ask you to sneak around after me,' I snap.

'You don't want me as your guard?' Darrack asks, the hurt back in his tone. 'You don't like me,' he says flatly.

'What?'

How did the conversation turn from me being spied on to whether I like Darrack?

He grasps my hand again. 'You don't like spending time with me?'

'It's not that,' I argue. 'It's-'

'Will you come with me now?' he cuts in.

I glance over my shoulder in the direction of my room. 'I don't think-'

'I'll teach you how to glamour,' he says.

My gaze snaps back to his. 'Really?'

Darrack smiles. 'Of course.'

'Can you teach me how to teleport?'

He grins. 'I can teach you all you wish, my flower.'

'I'm not your flower,' I tell him. I glance again in the direction of my room then at the males standing behind Darrack in the hallway. 'I'll go with you, but they're not invited.'

Darrack glances at the other fae. 'Dismissed,' he tells them.

They bow to him then pop from the hallway, until I'm standing alone with Darrack. He turns to face me, and grins. Being alone with him makes me nervous. He's in my personal space more than is comfortable, almost like he has a right to be there, and it's triggering an internal alarm.

Darrack takes me to a beautiful room, filled with light. The walls look made from wicker, white branches woven into pretty patterns as they reach up to form high, arched ceilings. White fairy lights peek from tiny spaces within the weaving, creating a starry effect.

'It's beautiful in here,' I murmur, taking in the enormous space.

'Come, we'll practice up there,' he says, pointing to one of many woven platforms jutting out from the walls. They look like balconies but with no safety rail, like the one in my room in the Light Realm.

'How are we supposed to get up there?' I ask, not seeing any steps.

'We'll fly, of course,' he answers, like it's a silly question.

I suppose it *is* a stupid thing to ask a fae.

'I can't,' I murmur.

He stares down at me. 'Why not?'

'I can't, um-' I feel my face heat with embarrassment then huff and look away. 'I don't know how to fly.'

I gasp when Darrack wraps his arms around me and pulls me close. My gaze snaps back to his to find him smiling down at me.

'What are you doing?'

Energy ripples between us and a set of wings lift from Darrack's shoulders. They're similar in design to Zephyr's and my father's, the shape more angular than mine. It's a difference I've noticed between male and female fae. Darrack's are veined with amber and I stare at them in fascination.

'I'm going to teach you how to fly,' he announces, drawing my gaze back to his. 'Release your wings.'

I take a deep breath and do as he asks, feeling my wings peel away from my back. Energy trickles down my spine, like someone's pouring it between my shoulder blades, as my wings stretch out and flutter behind me. I glance over my shoulder at them, looking like black-veined glass behind me.

'Beautiful,' Darrack murmurs.

'What now?' I ask, feeling uncomfortable under his scrutiny.

It takes a second for him to stop staring at my wings. His eyes are burning with amber light, when he finally looks down at me again.

'Beat your wings,' he says.

'I almost broke my face the last time I tried this,' I warn him.

Darrack laughs. 'I'll catch you,' he promises. 'Trust me.'

Trust him? I don't think we're at a stage of trusting each other. I haven't met one fae I feel I can trust, and that includes my father. But I don't want to offend Darrack and lose this chance of learning to fly.

'Right,' I answer.

My wings open and close a few lazy beats, before picking up speed to flutter rapidly behind me. They get so fast that they blur and my feet lift from the ground.

'Don't look at them, look at me,' Darrack coaches.

I turn my face back to his, to find him grinning. I stare at the pointed tips of his canines, before my eyes shift to the dimples either side of his smiling mouth. This guy is going to make some lucky fae female very happy one day, but all I see when I look at him is Zephyr. I don't know why, but being with Darrack makes me miss Zephyr more.

I miss him. The realisation is jarring.

'You're doing it,' Darrack praises, interrupting my thoughts of Zephyr.

Darrack's wings blur and he joins me in the air, until we're hovering level with each other.

'This feels amazing,' I admit.

'Shall we go higher?'

I look down at the ground, currently about a metre below us. 'You'll catch me, right?'

'Of course,' he answers then pulls us higher.

We stop just short of the woven ceiling and I laugh at the lack of fear. All I feel is elation and the sensation of freedom.

'Such a lovely sound,' Darrack says.

'What?' I ask matching his grin with one of my own.

I squeal when he spins us, the sound turning into laughter as we complete the turn.

'I could listen to your laughter for the rest of my days,' he tells me.

His words are sobering and my laughter fades. He releases my hands to grip my waist and pulls me close. I realise I have no idea how to get down, without Darrack showing me how. I'm stuck up here with him.

'Darrack, I think-'

'All other females pale in your wake, Primrose,' he tells me. 'I've thought of no other since our kiss to remove Zephyr's Mate Mark.'

'What?'

'Aric's acceptance of my mating request pleases me greatly.'

His words feel like tight bands around my ribcage and it becomes difficult to breathe. My heart starts racing at what I think he's saying.

'What mating request?' I ask.

Darrack frowns. 'Didn't your father inform you of our plans?'

I stare at him, while trying to swallow the boulder lodged in my throat. Everything starts to slide into place and the alarm sounding in my head grows louder. Aric's reassurance that I had options other than mating Zephyr. Darrack's tolerated intrusions of my personal space. The gown he sent for me to wear. They're all making sense now. Aric's planning to mate me off to Darrack and didn't even tell me.

'Aric told me,' I lie, hoping to coax the truth from Darrack. 'But when you mentioned mating I panicked, thinking of Zephyr.'

Darrack's frown eases. 'Zephyr cannot reach you here,' he assures me. 'After the ceremony tonight, you won't ever have to fear him again.'

'Because we'll be mated,' I hedge.

Darrack smiles, eyes glowing bright with triumph. 'We'll be bound before the visiting dignitaries, and my Mating Mark will replace the uninvited one on your wrist.'

I look down at my wrist, where Zephyr's Mating Mark pulses beneath the sleeve of my gown. Darrack's speaking like his Mating Mark is wanted in place of Zephyr's, when all I can think of is getting the hell out of the Dark Realm. My darkness scratches at the underside of my skin but I force it back, not wanting Darrack to discover my intent.

'It's getting late,' I tell him. 'I should return to my room and prepare for later.'

Darrack cups my face. 'I'm a highborn fae from a good line, Primrose,' he says, like it should mean something to me. 'Our offspring will prosper with such a strong pairing.'

I feel nauseous at his speech. Not once has he asked my opinion in the matter, which puts me in the same situation as my time in the Light Realm. Why the hell does everyone want to mate me?

'How do you know my light is compatible with yours?' I say, latching onto the first reason I can think of not to mate Darrack.

'From the moment I removed Zephyr's claim,' he answers.

My brain starts to ache at everything I'm finding out. It is pretty obvious Aric has no intension of letting me go, even to the extent of making me Mrs Darrack. Anger burns through me that I didn't see this coming, and my eyes sting with tears. The little girl inside that rejoiced at finding her father curls into a ball and cries.

'Hush,' Darrack murmurs and wipes a tear from my face. 'Zephyr can't get to you here.'

I repress a snort, wondering how Darrack would react if I told him Zephyr was in fact in the Dark Realm. Even now I can feel his presence, and it offers its own brand of comfort.

'I'm just so relieved,' I lie. 'I won't have to worry about Zephyr anymore.'

Darrack presses a kiss to my lips and I force myself not to pull away. Are mating rituals in the Dark Realm the same as in the Light? Does Darrack think he'll be mating me in light first then in flesh later? I wonder if he'll force me, if I don't want to consummate the bonding. Zephyr was adamant he wouldn't ever force himself on me like that. Darrack has made no such promises.

'I want to get down,' I say.

'You don't want me to teach you glamour?'

I shake my head. 'I was on my way to prepare for tonight when you intercepted me in the hallway,' I tell him then construct a smile. 'You're an easy distraction,

Darrack. Besides, we'll have plenty of time for you to teach me how to be the perfect fae, later.'

The crease between his eyebrows disappears and he grins. 'You're right,' he says then coaches me on how to land.

He speaks of our future as he walks me to my room. I ignore him and think of escape to blunt my need to punch him in the face. The feminist part of me is reeling at the way I've been treated by the fae I've encountered. I've met so many powerful, female fae that I know they're not a gender bias race. It's my weakness they're exploiting. First Zephyr then Aric and Alissa, and now Darrack have commented on the great power inside me. I just don't know how to utilise it, and they're taking advantage before I have chance to learn how.

'I'll collect you as the moon reaches its zenith,' Darrack says when we reach my room.

'Can't wait,' I say plastering a smile onto my face.

I stand on my tiptoes to give him a peck on the cheek, but Darrack has other plans. He grips my waist and lifts me to his level, before planting his lips on mine. His peaches and cream flavour fills my mouth, when he pushes his tongue inside. He tastes great and isn't a bad kisser, but I don't want to become Mrs Darrack.

'Delicious,' Darrack whispers against my lips before putting me down.

I turn and stumble into my room, shutting the door behind me, and kick off my shoes. I lean against the wood and wipe my mouth with the sleeve of my dress, heart racing. Tears blur my vision and I take deep breaths. Darkness rolls around inside me, restless and impatient for something I can't grasp. I feel myself teetering on the edge of an abyss and don't know how to escape it.

'What do you want?' I ask and look up into a pair of amethyst eyes.

CHAPTER 14

Zephyr stares at me like he's seeing me for the first time. My wings are still out, fanned against the door. They do that when I lean my back on something, reacting reflexively, like any of my other limbs.

'You're Dark Fae,' he accuses.

'You're powers of observation are outstanding,' I answer. 'But let's not forget who did this to me. I wasn't anything fae until you came along, Zephyr.'

Something flickers in his gaze and I don't dare entertain the idea that it's remorse. 'I don't regret claiming you,' he states.

It scares me that I'm relieved by his comment, that it matters to me he might despise my being Dark Fae.

'No, I don't suppose you do, as long as you get what you want,' I tell him. 'You do know they'll kill you if they find you here?' I say. 'After all, Light Fae are forbidden to enter my father's realm.'

'I only wish to speak with you,' he answers. 'I need you to know-' Zephyr stops and his face goes pale. 'Your father's realm?'

I arch an eyebrow. 'You mean you've been here hours and haven't figured it out? Does the black veining on my wings not give it away?'

'You're Aric's daughter,' he murmurs.

'Someone give the male a prize,' I drawl and push away from the door, moving closer to him. 'How did you get here?'

'I followed you through the mirror in Caleb Harrison's bedroom,' he says.

'Caleb Harrison?'

'Anima's mate,' he clarifies, confirming my suspicions. 'She said she spoke to you.'

'She told you where I was,' I say feeling betrayed by the mermaid.

'No,' he answers. 'I followed the pull of your light, like when I found you in the Realm of Man. Anima reprimanded me to within an inch of my existence though, when she realised I can track you.'

So Anima didn't give me away, even though Zephyr is her friend. The mermaid has integrity.

'Why are you here?' I demand.

In this death trap, where there's not a cat in Hell's chance of abducting me.

He sighs a defeated sound. 'To ask you to choose me, Primrose.'

I stare into his purple eyes. 'Can you find your way out of the Dark Realm, without getting caught?'

Zephyr's expression turns crestfallen and he nods. 'I can locate a return portal,' he answers then walks around me to the door. 'I wish you a happy life, Primrose.'

'So you followed me into the realm of your enemy, to ask me to mate you, and aren't going to wait for my answer?' I snap.

Zephyr turns back so fast the movement is a blur. 'You agree to join with me this equinox?'

'You haven't exactly made the best impression,' I argue.

'I know.'

'But you're making up for it?'

Zephyr didn't have to come here and risk his life, which I'm hoping means we'll work through the billion issues we've got going between us. I don't picture a fairy tale relationship in our future, but Zephyr's offering an olive branch and I'm hoping it will be my ticket out of the Dark Realm. Not that I'm committing to bonding with him, but I am already connected to Zephyr. Mate Mark or not, I get the feeling the connection is irreversible.

Knocking prevents him from answering and we both look at the door. The knocking sounds again when I don't answer and I panic that they'll come in uninvited.

'Who is it?' I shout.

'It's Thalla and Wynn, Princess. We're sent by Lord Darrack to deliver a gown for the ball.'

'Lord Darrack?' Zephyr whispers.

'My latest bridegroom,' I whisper back.

'What?' he snarls.

'Oh, so mating me off to someone I barely know is shocking to you now?' I hiss. 'It's your fault, Zephyr. Aric thinks mating me off will save me from mating you.'

'And you agreed?' he hisses back.

'Hell no! I'm not supposed to know about it, but Darrack let it slip earlier and I let him think I knew.' I scrub at a traitorous tear that dares slide free at my father's scheming. *Stupid inner child!* 'Seems I can't trust anyone,' I mutter.

'Tell me how to make it better,' Zephyr whispers.

I meet his gaze at the sincere edge to his voice. 'Wait here,' I tell him, ignoring his protest and go to the door, whispering, 'Cloak yourself in glamour, idiot! I can still see you.'

Zephyr stares at me in shock then disappears in a mist of amethyst sparkles. I study the spot where he's standing, startled that he actually did something I asked then open the door. Two females enter when I gesture them inside, with a dress draped between them. I feel the colour drain from my face at the silver material and sense a spike of anger from Zephyr. Silver is the traditional colour fae females wear to be mated, which means I'm staring at a mating gown. The females lay the gown out on the bed then turn to face me.

'It pleases us to prepare you,' the dark-haired one says.

'I'm not ready for you,' I tell them.

'But, Princess,' the blonde female argues. 'Time grows short to ready you.'

I glare at her in response and she drops her gaze, which then fixes on the ground by my feet. I frown when the dark-haired female sucks in a breath and stares at the same patch of floor. I look down at the rainbow of flowers that have bloomed around my bare feet, remembering I'd kicked my shoes off when I got inside.

'Out,' I snap, causing their gazes back to mine.

'But, Princess-'

''I won't tolerate your staring,' I snarl, unleashing a little of my darkness for effect. Onyx light crackles over my skin and my eyes go black. 'Get out.'

The females pale and flee the room, closing the door behind them. Zephyr glitters back into sight and stares at me, mouth agape. I've never seen that look on his face and it scares me. He's lived such a long time and has such power. It must take a lot to shock him.

'What?' I ask, checking behind me. 'What is it?'

'You're a Lumen,' he answers.

'I'm sorry, what?'

He points to the flowers around my feet. 'You're a Lumen Fae.'

I glance at the flowers then back to his face. 'Zephyr, you need to be more specific,' I say. 'I was raised a human remember? I don't have a clue what you're talking about.'

'The flowers,' he tells me. 'They grow in your wake, when you step on organic ground?'

'Maybe,' I answer, not sure where this is going.

Aric didn't seem this shocked to see flowers growing from my footsteps. He just seemed pleased. Really pleased.

Zephyr shakes his head, awe filling his features. 'It's your light,' he says. 'It's so powerful that your form can't contain it and, as a result, connects to all living entities around it.'

I think of my darkness and how it connects with everyone around me. It's how I read the emotions of people near me. I know they're there because I can feel them. My light leeches emotion from them, sucking the essence from their beings and into me. I don't think it means to do it, but its power is so vast it acts like a magnet to organic energies around me. Except for when I'm with Zephyr, and it reaches only for him.

Zephyr.

'You,' I whisper having a light bulb moment.

'Me?'

Why didn't I see it before? I stare at him, mind churning through everything I know. I've had my darkness for as long as I can remember, meaning my fae light manifested way before I ever turned fae. It killed my mother by leeching the life from inside her. I think about each time I was around her, and how the darkness would seek her out, the same way it seeks out Zephyr. There was something about her it wanted; something it searched for deep in her centre. Aric had the same problem, but he knew what his light was and how to control it.

'Light,' I whisper, thinking of how my darkness reacts to the bright heat at Zephyr's core.

'You're speaking nonsense,' Zephyr growls.

'No,' I correct. 'It all makes sense.'

'What does?'

'I had my light before you turned me fae, Zephyr.'

177

He shakes his head. 'That's not-'

'Possible? Aric said the same thing, but it's the truth.'

'The human body is too frail,' Zephyr argues. 'Your light would've killed you.'

'I think it killed my mother instead,' I whisper.

'What are you saying?'

'As a human, I lacked the ability to control my light,' I explain. 'So it controlled me; did what it wanted unrestrained. My mum was the person closest to me, so she suffered the majority of the fallout.'

'You can't know this, Primrose,' he says.

'I call it my darkness,' I answer, needing him to know. 'I didn't know what it was before you turned me fae, Zephyr. It's been my saviour and my curse, for as long as I can remember.'

His eyes soften. 'Primrose-'

'I killed my mum, Zephyr. You need to know, in case you change your mind about me.'

The more I say it the realer it feels. There's no actual evidence that I killed her, but the pieces fit. It all makes sense and points to me being a murderer. Maybe Mum would've survived if I hadn't been there, sucking the life from her. My mind flickers to that day on the beach when I was six; a day I try not to think of. I was a murderer way before I took Mum's life.

Zephyr is in front of me before I can blink, holding me. I drop my head on his chest and let him comfort me, with no hope or agenda. His scent fills my insides with warmth, while his heart drums steadily in my ear.

'You can't blame yourself for something you've no control over,' he murmurs, his compassion suffusing the air around us.

'It wants you,' I whisper.

Zephyr pulls away enough to look down at me. 'Your light?'

I nod. 'It senses a brightness at your centre,' I answer, not really knowing how to describe it any other way than that. 'It's all my darkness wants when I'm near you.'

Zephyr grins. 'Thank the goddess, you feel it too!'

I frown. 'What are you talking about?'

He cups my face. 'Primrose, haven't you listened to anything I've said? I've told you over and over how your light calls to me. The pull of it's so strong it summoned me from my realm to yours.'

'Your light seeks mine?'

'Yes!' he answers, like he's been trying to tell me exactly that since we met. 'Do you think I would've claimed you for anything less?'

'There are others-'

'Goddess help me, there are no others!' he barks. 'I see no other beyond the call of your essence, Primrose. My light will accept none but yours.'

'Oh,' I murmur.

'Oh? That's your answer?'

'Well, you didn't tell me! Not properly,' I argue.

'I've been telling you since I found you,' he snaps.

'Growling 'You're mine' isn't as clear as what you just explained,' I snap back.

'You *are* mine,' he shouts his frustration stinging my skin. Zephyr calms a little and his expression softens. 'And equally I am yours.' He sighs. 'When I found you in the Realm of Man, I thought you knew all this.'

'I told you to leave me alone,' I argue.

'I tried,' he says, like he's admitting a dirty secret. 'I couldn't, and your rejection angered me.'

'Because you thought I knew about fae?'

Zephyr nods. 'I felt your light even before I claimed you. I could smell the human in you, but I'd never encountered a Halfling up close. I thought you smelt human because you'd been born one, not because you still *were* one.'

'Because I had my light.'

'Yes,' he answers. 'If you were human you wouldn't have had any light, so I thought you were fae. We were compatible but you rejected me.'

I snort. 'Because nobody has ever rejected you before?'

'Because I've waited millennia for my match, and when I find her she doesn't want me,' he huffs.

I see the hurt in his eyes and try to imagine it from Zephyr's perspective. It must have been a relief, finding a compatible mate before his parents fade. But I rejected him and his hopes were broken.

'I'm sorry, Zephyr.'

He drops his forehead to mine. 'My Rose,' he whispers.

I close my eyes and breathe deep. Mum used to call me Rose, and memories well up inside me.

'So, what now?' I murmur.

'We escape the Dark Realm,' he answers.

I open my eyes and step back. 'Okay, let's do this.'

I retrieve the mating gown from the bed.

'You're not wearing that,' Zephyr snarls.

'And what do you think will happen if we get caught running around the palace, and I'm not dressed for the celebration?'

'It's a mating gown, Primrose.'

'It's cute that you think I don't know that,' I tell him heading for the bathroom to change.

CHAPTER 15

Zephyr grabs me before I step around the next corner, pressing me against the wall. He puts a hand over my mouth and flattens his body against mine, caging me in. The air around us grows hazy, like looking through rising heat in the desert. He puts a finger to his lips, signalling for me to be quiet then drops his hand from my mouth, as three male fae round the corner.

Sentinels.

Denlyr isn't among them, but the ebony uniforms are duplicates of his. They all have black hair, but with different colours staining the tips. Unlike regular palace guards, these fae radiate danger in choking amounts. Darkness curls over my skin in response and Zephyr sucks in a breath. I look up into burning, amethyst eyes. He's staring at the midnight swirls on my skin, with a look that makes my stomach clench.

'Her chamber is empty,' the sentinel with bronze staining his hair says.

'Nor with Lord Darrack,' the ruby-haired one adds, frustration painting his tone.

'Aric ordered a lockdown of all portals until the ceremony is over,' the third sentinel intones. 'She cannot leave the Realm.'

'The moon is rising,' Ruby argues. 'Time runs short.'

'We'll find her,' Green answers.

The sentinels stare at each other, expressions intense, before disappearing behind glittering walls of glamour. I watch the space where they were standing, not knowing if they're still standing there. No need to guess who they were talking about. I've been gone from my room less than twenty minutes and already everyone's freaking out over not being able to find me.

'They're gone,' Zephyr murmurs.

I meet his gaze. 'How do you know?'

Using glamour creates a flare in a fae's aura,' he answers. 'You can see it if you're trained how.'

'They know I'm missing, Zephyr. They've closed the portals.'

'Not all of them.'

Zephyr steps back, allowing me to push away from the wall. He traces a finger over a dark swirl on my shoulder, eyes flaring bright. A shiver ripples through me at the barely-there touch. Darkness peels away from my skin and curls around his finger, and Zephyr's skin lights with purple fire. I bite back a groan, knees going weak.

'Your light is black,' he breathes.

'They were sentinels, Zephyr;' I answer, 'my father's personal guards. We need to go.'

Zephyr gently tugs his finger from the ebony curl then lifts his purple gaze to mine. 'They won't find us.'

He pulls me around the corner then through an arched doorway at the end of the hallway. We step into a room with vaulted ceilings. They make sense, since witnessing fae using their wings. The hallways are wide with high ceilings for the same reason. Fae can easily pass each other with their wings out and not worry about crashing into each other.

'What is this place?' I breathe, staring around the room with wide eyes.

The only light is coming from a circular pool in the centre of the flagstone floor. It's filled with liquid light, shining white in the dark.

'Every fae palace is built around a light pool,' he answers. 'They're a source of replenishment for our kind.'

'You mean healing?'

Zephyr nods. 'They feed the light inside us, creating the ability to mend.'

'So why are we here?'

'Light pools are a link between realms,' he explains. 'They're naturally occurring portals that can't be closed.'

'A doorway that can't be closed,' I murmur.

'Yes,' he answers, sounding pleased with my analogy. 'I knew if I were discovered in the Dark Realm I'd be killed, and that they'd seal the portals if they suspected my presence. So I sought this place on arrival.'

Clever.

'You came here, despite the strong possibility of dying?'

'What's a life without your other half?' he answers.

I stare at him, his words shaking me. 'Zephyr, I-'

'Come,' he cuts in, like he's afraid of what I'm about to say, 'we must leave before they remember this function of the light pool.'

I purse my lips and follow him to the edge of the pool. I look down into the luminous water, looking like a moon in the dark stone floor. It's the first room I've encountered in the Dark Realm that doesn't have the organic flooring, so I feel comfortable slipping off my shoes. I dip a toe into the liquid light, sending a rainbow ripple across the surface. It's warm around my toes and sends energy fizzing through me.

Wow.

I stare at the light in fascination, my darkness soaking it up. It's not enticed by this light in the way it seems to be by Zephyr's. There's something about his brand of energy it craves, and everything else pales in comparison.

Zephyr climbs into the water and turns to face me, light hugging his hips. He reaches up to help me down, the heat of his hands scorching through the fabric at my waist. Light hugs my skin as he lowers me into the pool. It's like slipping into a warm bath, without getting wet.

'How does it work?' I ask.

'Light intersects the realms of our universe,' Zephyr explains. 'We can use our fae light to open doorways to the light that links the realms. That's what happens when we use mirrors to open portals. We're tapping into the pathways between realms.'

'But this doorway is already open,' I say, understanding.

'Correct,' he answers. 'We don't have to open a doorway to access it. We simply have to think of a destination and it will open a portal in that place.'

'Where are we even going?' I ask. I'm not sure I'm ready to go back to the Light Realm, but I think of Darrack and how he's expecting to mate me. 'Actually, I don't care where we go, as long as it's away from here.'

'Close your eyes,' Zephyr orders.

'Why?'

'I'm going to temporarily link our lights, so we end up at the same destination,' he answers.

'How will you do that?'

He cups my face and brings our faces close. His mouth is a breath from mine; his exhales heating my inhales.

'When we're connected, feel what I do with my light,' he murmurs. 'It will help you navigate the Light Ways should you ever need to do it again.'

'But how-'

Zephyr presses his lips to mine, stopping my question with the softest of kisses. The second his lips meet mine his energy infuses me, weaving around my darkness in a complicated knot. The bottom of the pool shifts and we're surrounded by light. It feels like we're floating, before the light fades and gravity returns.

Zephyr's lips leave mine and I realise I'm gripping his hair. I let go and step back, putting space between us. I suck my bottom lip as I look around, tasting him. It's daytime wherever he's taken us, but it's not the Light Realm. I study the familiar lines of the room, wondering why I recognise it.

'You know, I didn't believe Nima when she said you'd found a match, Z.'

I turn in sync with Zephyr to a redheaded male smirking from the doorway.

'Navi,' Zephyr greets. 'How Anima puts up with you continues to remain a mystery to me.'

Zephyr's mention of Anima brings the room back into focus. I glance over my shoulder, to the exit mirror behind me. It's the mirror I went through to get to the Dark Realm after I escaped Zephyr – The one Anima escorted me to. We're in the mermaid's house.

Navi shrugs. 'She loves me.'

Zephyr's expression softens. 'I heard about her soul.'

'All thanks to Caleb Harrison,' Navi answers.

Zephyr frowns. 'How is that possible?'

'The Goddess,' Navi says keeping with the cryptic conversation.

'Do either of you want to explain any of this to me?' I ask.

The dark-haired male, who was with Anima the first time we met, pushes around Navi into the room. 'You should know Navi is annoying as hell,' he tells me. 'And he hates wearing clothes, so don't be surprised to find him naked and flashing his junk.'

'Humans have such warped ideas about nakedness,' Navi counters. '*Your* opinion is biased, Caleb Harrison.'

Ah, so this is Caleb Harrison.

'Your opinion has been noted,' Caleb drawls, like he's had this argument with Navi a million times before, then looks at me. 'You should also know Anima and Navi aren't human.'

'They're mermaids,' I answer.

He hesitates. 'Sort of.'

'Sort of?'

'It's complicated,' he tells me. 'The only thing you need to know is that we're not the bad guys.'

I blow out a breath. My gut instinct is to trust this guy, but my ability to judge people has been compromised. I don't trust my instincts enough to make a decision on anyone anymore, leaving me with one last option. I'll have to wing it.

'You're mated to Anima, right?'

'I am,' Caleb answers.

'But she loves Navi?' I ask, unsure what the dynamic is between them. Do mermaids mate more than one person?

'He's like her very annoying big brother,' Caleb answers.

I nod in understanding. 'And you love her?' I shake my head as soon as the words are out. 'Wait, that was rude.'

'No, it's okay,' Caleb says. 'Anima's my soul mate.'

'That's terribly romantic,' I say.

'I guess it is,' he answers. Caleb glances at Zephyr. 'I take it you're here because you want to be and not because he's forcing you?' he asks me.

I elbow Zephyr when he growls at Caleb. Navi snickers and I glare his way.

'I'm here because I want to be, Caleb.'

'Where's Anima?' Zephyr asks.

Caleb turns his attention to Zephyr, his frustration permeating the air. 'She's out swimming. Why are you here, Zephyr?'

'We require concealment until morning,' Zephyr answers, surprising me.

Caleb's frown deepens. 'Why here?'

'More than one fae has passed through here in a short amount of time,' Zephyr explains. 'Tracing our light will be difficult enough in this place for us to remain hidden until morning.'

Caleb sighs and turns back to the doorway, shoving Navi aside as he leaves the room. 'It's a good job Mom and Dad are still on vacation,' he calls over his shoulder on the way out.

'Your parents know about the mermaids?' I ask hurrying after him.

Caleb goes to the pink room I associate with Anima. 'Hell no,' he answers. 'My parents don't know anything about this stuff.'

'You mean the supernatural crap that happens to be real?' I grin. 'I half expect a werewolf to knock on your front door and ask to borrow a cup of kibble.'

'Don't even joke about it,' Caleb groans. 'I'm too afraid it will come true.'

'I'm unaware of any shifter territories in this area,' Zephyr muses. 'The nearest lupine community I can think of is two states over, but it's been a while since I frequented the Realm of man.'

I join Caleb to stare at Zephyr.

'Are you saying werewolves are real?' Caleb asks.

'Werewolves are fantasy based around a real species,' Zephyr answers.

'You called them shifters,' I murmur. 'Is that what they're called?'

'Don't answer that,' Caleb cuts in. 'I'm still wrapping my head around the fact mermaids and faeries exist. I don't want to deal with anything else unless, in fact, it turns up on my doorstep, which seems to be the trend at the moment.'

'We're called Fae,' Zephyr corrects.

'My species aren't called mermaids, either,' Navi stage whispers to me, while eyeing Caleb.

I can already see why Caleb finds him annoying. It seems Navi goes out of his way to do just that.

'Whatever,' Caleb huffs, 'it's the same thing.' He looks at Zephyr. 'You can stay until tomorrow. This room has fresh sheets and Anima can bunk with me.' He moves to the doorway, pushing Navi with him on his way out. 'Just shout if you need anything.'

The door clicks shut and I turn to find Zephyr watching me. Sunlight streams through the window behind him, silhouetting his frame.

'You have the strangest friends,' I mutter.

He grins. 'Wait until you meet-' His grin fades and the light dims in his eyes.

'The colour of this room,' I say, trying to fill the stretching silence between us.

'It's painful,' he agrees.

A few more seconds pass and the silence turns awkward.

I huff. 'Okay, what is it?'

'I don't-'

'Bull crap! You're acting weird.'

'You never answered my question,' he blurts.

Oh? *Oh.* I don't need to ask which question he's referring to. I scratch the back of my neck and pretend to study the eye-watering décor, while searching for the right things to say.

'Is that why you brought me here, instead of the Light Realm?' I say.

'You know what will happen if I take you home,' he answers.

'It's *your* home, not mine.'

'I want it to be *our* home,' he murmurs.

'And what if I want the Realm of Man to be home?' I argue.

'I can't rule a kingdom if I'm not residing in it, Primrose.'

He's right and I know it, I'm just talking us around in circles. He's giving me the choices I asked for, being reasonable for once, and I'm making it harder for the both of us. I take a deep breath and close my eyes, turning my thoughts inward.

'Primrose-'

'Give me a second,' I tell him.

I take a moment to think things through. My life has never been what a human would call normal. My darkness made sure of it. But what is normal? I don't know what being fae really means. What I've seen has been wild and brutal, mixed with graceful elegance. They're bi-polar beings and so am I. The few things I do know all point towards Zephyr being the answer. It's difficult to admit that the thing I've been running from this whole time could be the thing I need most. My darkness wants him with an intensity I can't describe. When Zephyr touches me, it calms that wild place in my centre and brings it to life. He's got the key to the cage it's been locked in, and I know without him it will never be free. I try to imagine living millennia feeling caged this way, and open my eyes to look at Zephyr. How has he done it?

'I agree,' I whisper.

'You agree?'

I take a deep breath then blow it out. 'To mate you,' I clarify. 'I agree to mate you, Zephyr.'

Zephyr closes his eyes. 'Thank you.'

'Tomorrow, you can take me back to the Light Realm,' I say.

'Tomorrow?'

I nod. 'I'm not ready to go tonight.'

Emotion flashes in his eyes and I wait for him to say something, but he doesn't. I close the distance between us, and push onto my tiptoes, pressing a kiss to his lips. He stares at me in surprise. I swipe my tongue across his bottom lip to steal a taste, and he opens for me. Relief pours through me and I press my palms to his chest, steadying myself as I deepen the kiss. I haven't felt in control for such a long time, and Zephyr is gifting me this moment. He yields to my advances, letting me make the choices and take the lead. He's getting what he wants but it's my decision to give it.

I curl my fingers into his hair, pulling his face down to mine. Zephyr comes willingly, following my lead when I guide him across the room to the bed. An ache yawns wide inside me, as darkness crawls in midnight swirls over my skin. Inky tendrils reach from my skin to wrap around Zephyr and pull him close. His olive skin lights with amethyst. Ribbons of sparkling purple weave with my light, lacing together in intricate swirls.

I turn us around and push Zephyr onto the bed. Our bodies break apart but our lights remain laced. We're not touching but remain connected, and there's rightness to it that I can't describe. Zephyr watches as I peel the dress from my body, letting it pool in a heap of silver at my feet. I'm naked beneath because fae have no concept of underwear, and his eyes burn bright as they roam my body.

I wait for his gaze to return to mine then kneel on the bed between his thighs. Zephyr sits up and I pop the first button at the top of his shirt. He stills my hand, stopping me from reaching for the next button. Rejection slices through me then disintegrates into shock, when his clothes just disappear in a glitter of purple light.

'Very handy,' I murmur.

Zephyr chuckles and cups my chin, bringing my gaze from the carved lines of his torso back to his face. He waits for me to lean forward then presses his lips to mine. His tongue dips into my mouth and I press closer. My chest meets his, skin on skin, and I moan into the sensation. I wrap my arm around his neck and curl my legs around his hips, getting as close as I can.

Zephyr leans back to study my expression. His body is hard against mine, like he's hewn from stone. My softness moulds to him and it feels decadent in a way I didn't know it could. We're opposites in so many ways. He's hard to my soft and I'm dark to his light. But we fit together and it feels so right.

'You want this?' he asks.

I trace a finger over the angular lines of his face, learning his features. I trace around the pointed curve of an ear. His purple eyes are framed by thick lashes and have an exotic tilt. Dark eyebrows. High cheekbones. Defined jawline. His lips are full and softer than they look. I smooth the pad of my thumb across the bottom one and he inhales, flashing a hint of sharp incisors.

Wild.

Untamed.

Mine.

'Yes,' I whisper.

A growl sounds from deep inside his chest. Pressed this close, I feel it reverberate through me, and it makes the tiny hairs on my body stand up. His eyes glow bright purple, like he's lighting up from the inside.

'Let me see you,' he breathes.

'I can't get anymore naked than this, Zephyr.'

'Your wings,' he clarifies.

Oh.

I release my wings and Zephyr's eyes turn molten. I glance over my shoulder in surprise. Does he...? Does Zephyr find my wings sexy? The concept is foreign to me, but I suppose fae are used to seeing them that way. I think of the look Darrack gave me when he saw my wings then push the thought away. I don't even want to go there right now.

I trace the design on Zephyr's skin. 'Now you,' I tell him.

The pattern lights up, before peeling away to form a pair of wings behind him. They're bigger and sleeker than mine – powerful – and I appreciate the appeal in seeing them. The angular design is in tandem with the rest of his body. Zephyr's tall and lean, with ropes of muscle sculpting his frame. I skim my fingers over his shoulders then down to his chest, committing the sight and feel to memory.

'Strong,' I murmur, captivated by the hard planes of his body.

Zephyr captures my hand against his chest, forcing my gaze back to his. 'Beautiful,' he tells me.

Warmth fills me at his declaration. Before I can answer, he teleports and I find myself on my back, staring up at him. My wings are fanned out against the mattress and he's situated between my thighs. I curl my fingers into his hair and pull him down for a kiss. Our tongues twine, tasting and exploring.

He breaks the kiss. 'Next time I'll spend hours worshipping your body,' he promises, aligning our centres.

My back arches off the mattress when he pushes inside me. There's no pain, just immense pleasure mixed with a sense of finding home. My fingers tighten in his hair and warmth blooms from my centre. The coiled creature in my middle uncurls, waking from a lifetime of slumber.

I open my eyes. Everything is drenched in the shadow of my darkness, except Zephyr. He gazes right back, eyes blazing violet. I trace the purple swirls in his skin and they peel away to twine with the midnight swirls on mine. I watch, entranced, as they knit together.

'Stunning,' Zephyr rasps.

I cup his face and black glitter spangles over his skin. The glitter soaks into his skin and Zephyr groans. The purple haloing his body fringes with midnight and frames his beauty with dark tones.

My tones.

Mine.

'Do it again,' he pants.

I lift my other hand and cup his face between my palms. Purple light bands my wrists, holding me to him. The cage inside cracks wide open and wildness pours out. Zephyr closes his eyes, and I suck in a breath when he opens them to gaze down at me. His eyes are black, like he's drowning in my darkness. I start to pull away but he strikes, sinking sharp incisors into my shoulder. I scream, bliss twining through the pain he's causing. My mind splinters and I'm lost to sensation.

Zephyr's right there with me. His essence weaves with mine collecting my splintered pieces then glues them back together. He gathers me from the edge of oblivion and guides me back to Earth. I'm aware of blood trickling over my shoulder then Zephyr's tongue licking at the punctures. I should be frightened that he bit me, but I can't bring myself to care. He pulls back, crimson staining his lips. I brush my fingers over the wound, except there isn't one. I peer down at my shoulder, glimpsing a silvery scar on my skin.

'I wondered why you have fangs,' I mutter.

'Perhaps one day yours will grow in and you can bite me back,' he murmurs.

I feel my eyes widen, as I lick the end of one blunt incisor. 'That's possible?'

Zephyr shrugs. 'I don't know. Halfling fae are so rare.'

I finger my neck. 'Are your kind where vampire myths come from?'

'*Our kind*,' he corrects. 'And vampires aren't real, Primrose. Most of the Archaic Races have fangs, so perhaps vampire myth spans from there.'

'Archaic Races?'

'Fae, Mer, Shifters,' he answers. 'We're all Archaic Races.'

'Right,' I murmur, letting the subject drop. There are more important things to discuss, like his onyx gaze. 'Zephyr, your eyes.'

He smiles in understanding. 'Your eyes are violet.'

I gape then wriggle from beneath him. I scramble from the bed and stare into the mirror.

'Holy crap is this permanent?'

I don't look like me without black eyes. I look more like my mother.

'I don't know,' he shrugs. 'But I like it.'

I turn to face him. 'You do?'

He climbs from the bed, a predatory gleam to his eyes. 'Everyone will know you're mine.'

I roll my eyes. 'Everyone will know you're mine, too then.'

Zephyr grins. 'Good.'

It's barbaric, but I like the concept. The wildness Zephyr released permeates my insides, no longer trapped deep in my middle. It delights in knowing other females will recognise he's taken. His grin fades and he sighs.

'What is it?'

'Your eyes are returning to black,' he says.

I study his gaze to find amethyst sparkles amid the midnight. 'Yours are changing back, too.'

Zephyr takes my hand and pulls me to him. 'Let's see what we can do about it,' he grins then presses his lips to mine.

CHAPTER 16

I'm dreaming.

The waking world sits at the periphery of my conscious mind, but I don't want to wake. Mum's sitting opposite me on the blanket, grinning at something I just said. I glance at the cake between us and match her grin, remembering this moment.

'No really, it's wonderful,' I say.

'It doesn't look anything like the picture,' Mum argues.

'I'm sure it tastes great,' I counter, holding back laughter. 'If-'

'If what?' Mum presses.

'If it doesn't fall over before I get chance to taste it.'

We both look at the cake on the plate between us. The top layer is currently sliding from the bottom, the buttercream between the uneven sponges melting. Mum never did have any patience, and she iced it before it was cool enough. Our gazes meet and we both burst out laughing.

'I should've asked Kate to make it,' Mum mutters. 'She's always been the cook in the family.' She lights the candle on top. 'Quick, make a wish before it collapses.'

I close my eyes and blow out the candle. To this day, I can't remember what I wished for, but when I open my eyes Mum's got a wistful look on her face.

'What did you wish for,' she asks.

'I can't tell you or it won't come true.'

Mum grins. 'We should cut the thing before it falls over.'

Mum plates two slices of cake and hands me one.

'Mm, chocolate,' we hum at the same time then laugh again.

'Happy birthday, baby girl,' Mum says.

'It tastes good,' I say around a mouthful of cake.

'Are you sure this is okay?' she asks for the millionth time. 'You only turn twenty-one once.'

'This is what I want, Mum. You, me, the meadow and a lopsided cake.'

Mum puts her cake down and drags me into a hug. 'I love you, Rose.'

I bury my face in her neck and inhale the calming fragrance that's uniquely hers. 'I love you.'

I glance up to see Zephyr standing a few feet away, watching us. I close my eyes, holding onto the dream for as long as I can. Mum's scent fades and I open my eyes to find myself surrounded by cotton sheets. I'm in bed, wrapped around Zephyr. His purple gaze eclipses my vision when I tilt my head to look up at his face.

'I saw you in the meadow. I whisper.

'I didn't mean to intrude,' he whispers back.

Sunlight streams through a crack between the curtains, illuminating the room in a soft glow. It feels early and the house is quiet. I can hear waves lapping nearby and realise Caleb must live by the ocean.

'You should've joined us.'

'That was your mother?' he asks.

'It was.'

'She was beautiful,' he tells me.

A tear escapes and rolls down my cheek, soaking into the pillow. 'I miss her.'

'What was she like?' he asks, brushing tears from my lashes.

'Like me, only nicer.' I smile. 'Mum lacked my prickly persona. She was filled with warmth, love and sorrow.' I chuckle when I think of the cake. 'She couldn't bake to save her life. I mean, you saw her attempt at baking a cake.'

'That was a cake?' he grins.

I laugh and Zephyr laughs with me. The laughter dies and my smile fades.

'When the doctors told her she had cancer, Mum made it sound like a little glitch,' I murmur and stare at Zephyr's chest, so I don't have to look in his eyes. 'She never told me it was terminal, until I came home early to find the funeral director sitting in our kitchen.'

I think of that day and cringe. I hadn't known who the man was at first, until I spotted the brochures on the table. Mum was picking her coffin and I'd freaked. I'd wasted three days of the life she had left barely speaking to her, and I'll regret it until my last breath.

'She was just trying to save me pain,' I whisper.

'Primrose,' Zephyr murmurs, putting a finger under my chin to tip my face back to his. He presses a kiss to my lips and his empathy soaks the air. He wants to take away my pain, and I think I love him a little bit for it.

'What happens when fae die, Zephyr?'

'We fade,' he tells me. 'Our corporeal form diminishes and our light ascends to the next place.'

'The next place?'

'A place filled with the ones who've passed before us,' he answers. 'Your mother will be there, Primrose. She'll have her ancestors and mine to look after her.'

A lump forms in my throat. 'You think so?'

He wipes my tears with his thumb. 'Yes,' he answers. 'Our ancestors watch over us until it's our time to join them. They'll be there to guide the way when we fade. Until then, I promise to take care of you.'

'Won't we fade at different times?' I argue. 'You're very old, Zephyr and there's no guarantee I'll live the millennia a full-blooded fae does.'

'Human's age quickly,' he agrees. 'But you're not human anymore.'

'So I'm going to live a long time?'

'You don't sound happy about it.'

I shrug. 'What the hell does a person do with thousands of years to live?'

Zephyr chuckles. 'You'll find out.' His laughter dies and he tucks a length of hair behind my ear, expression serious. 'If we'd bonded during the equinox, our lights would've been linked, meaning they'd fade together.'

'That's why your parents are fading at the same time?' Zephyr nods and I get the feeling I'm missing something important. 'So when we bond we'll be tied in a way that means we'll fade together?'

'The equinox has passed,' Zephyr says. 'Our window to bond is gone.'

'But-' I sit up and look around, panic setting in. If I'm not bonded to Zephyr then it means I'm still up for grabs. 'I said I'd bond with you!'

Zephyr sits up too. 'Last night you said you weren't ready, and I thought-'

'You're an idiot!' I shout. 'How can someone so old be so dense?'

'Primrose-'

A ball of purple light shoots from the mirror and smacks Zephyr in the chest. I suck in a breath, feeling Zephyr's need to open a portal. Our intimacy has increased my ability to sense his emotion. It's so powerful it's difficult to differentiate between his emotion and mine.

'What is that?' I ask.

'A summoning sprite,' Zephyr says. 'I'm being summoned by whomever I gifted this sprite.' He growls, sweat beading his brow. 'I'm not leaving you.'

I scramble from the bed, pick my dress up from the floor and tug it on. There's not a crease in it, despite being in a ball all night on the carpet.

'You don't have to,' I say then frown. 'It's not Alissa, is it?'

Zephyr smirks, clothes materialising on his body. 'It's not my mother.'

'You need to teach me that trick,' I tell him then gasp when a jacket materialises over my dress.

I finger the sliver fabric then look at Zephyr. 'You?'

He nods. 'I don't like others seeing your wing markings,' he admits.

I shake my head and admire the pretty jacket. 'You've got to teach me how to do that!'

He chuckles and pulls me close. 'Later, my rose.'

Zephyr's light burns my retinas before I realise we're teleporting. I was expecting to use the mirror, so didn't close my eyes in preparation. It takes a second of blinking for the blue-tinged room to come into focus. The blue is emanating from a woman on the bed in the centre of the room. A huge male with dark hair and burning green eyes kneels beside the bed, bending over the woman's writhing form.

'Zephyr,' the male rumbles, voice more animal than man.

I *know* he's not fae but don't know *what* he is. Zephyr pulls me into his side as we approach the bed. The male growls but it's like he can't help it.

'Lucas,' Zephyr greets, tone wary. 'Did you summon me here just to attack me?'

'Can't help it,' Lucas grits out. 'She's my mate.'

Understanding, Zephyr looks down at the woman. 'She's not lupine.'

Lucas shakes his head. 'Human. One of your kind did something to her.'

Zephyr sniffs the air and his eyes go wide. 'She's a Halfling?'

'Halfling?' Lucas snarls.

'I thought you said we were rare,' I mutter.

'It's a damn epidemic,' Zephyr grumbles then looks back to Lucas. 'Your mate is half fae.' Zephyr sniffs the air again. 'And she's been Marked by a compatible male.'

Lucas roars, 'Mine!'

'This scenario looks familiar,' I remark.

Blood drips from the woman's eyes, ears and nose, streaking her pale face. I stare at her in horror, crimson forming a growing stain on the bed below her. Neon blue lights her from the inside, adding to the surreal effect. Did I look like this when I turned fae? Flashes of remembered agony skitter through my frame and I wince, wanting to help her. But I don't think there's anything I can do. Once fae genes are triggered there's no stopping the Change. I watch her arch and writhe, knowing I could be watching her death.

'Help her!' Lucas begs.

'I can remove the Mark,' Zephyr answers, 'but can't guarantee she'll survive the transition from human to fae.'

Lucas stares down at the woman, like she owns his soul, and my heart wedges in my throat. 'If she's to die she'll die mine,' he answers. 'Remove the Mark.'

Zephyr looks at me. 'You know how a Mark is removed?' he asks.

'How do you think I got yours out of me?' I murmur.

Zephyr's face twists into a scowl. 'Who?'

I shrug. 'Darrack.'

'I'll kill him,' he snarls.

'This isn't the time or place, Zephyr' I remind him.

'This conversation isn't over,' he growls.

'Fine,' I snap, 'but can you direct your focus toward the issue of the moment?' I push around Zephyr and crawl onto the bed beside the woman. 'What's her name?' I ask Lucas.

'Amber,' he breathes then snarls when Zephyr moves closer.

'I'm a mated male, Lucas. If you can't control your beast then get out. I don't have time to remove the Mark if I'm to fight you,' Zephyr says.

Lucas closes his eyes then pushes to his feet. He breathes deep a few times then stalks to the opposite side of the room. Another male pushes from the shadows, surprising me. I've been so focussed on Amber I didn't even realise he was there. He's the same height as Lucas, with the same green eyes and sun-darkened skin. The only difference between them is the other male's blond hair to Lucas' dark mane.

'Restrain me, Mason,' Lucas orders.

Mason moves behind Lucas and wraps muscular arms around him in a criss-cross. He's pinning Lucas's arms to his sides.

'Do it,' Lucas growls.

Zephyr returns his attention to Amber. 'Breathe, little female,' he murmurs, before pressing his lips to hers.

Darkness rushes forward at the sight of Zephyr kissing another female, even though I know it's to help her. My eyes tingle the way they do when they've turned black, and I snarl. Amber's writhing increases, like whatever Zephyr's doing is causing more pain. It was uncomfortable when Zephyr's Mark was ripped from me, but not as painful as Amber makes it seem. Her back jerks from the mattress, muscle and sinew straining tight.

Zephyr pulls back and she gags, coughing out an orb of gold light.

I stare at the light and think instantly of Darrack. It's the same honey shade of his essence, but he's in the Dark Realm, isn't he? Zephyr catches the light, drawing my focus, and snarls. He throws it at the nearest mirror, and it ripples the surface on impact. The ripples smooth out, the surface of the mirror settling back into place, once the orb has passed through.

'It's done,' Zephyr growls then looks at Lucas. 'You've quarrel with the Dark Fae?'

'Hell no,' Lucas denies.

'He's stupid, not crazy,' Mason intones.

'How do you know it was Dark Fae light?' I defend, not liking where this is leading.

'Colour denotes the lineage,' Zephyr explains. 'Only castes of Dark Fae carry gold light, Primrose.'

'But if we had children and they had black light, wouldn't they be Light Fae, if they were born in the Light Realm?' I argue.

'Light and Dark Fae don't mix,' he answers, not missing a beat.

'But surely-'

'At all,' he barks.

I snap my mouth shut and stare at him in disbelief. He makes the idea sound wrong, like the thought of having children with me disgusts him. It's not that I'm desperate to have children or anything, but I'm going to live a long time. The father of any future offspring needs to love them with all his heart. If they do, indeed, inherit my light, I don't want him looking at them with distain.

'Why not?' I ask.

'We're enemies,' he states, like the answer is as simple as that.

'So *we're* enemies then,' I say, darkness crackling over my skin.

Realisation dawns on his face, as if he just realised what he's words mean to me. My disbelief punches higher. For someone so old, he's so bloody stupid.

'My Rose-'

'You've made your sentiments about me quite clear,' I cut in, hurt beyond words. I'm fighting back tears and don't want him to see.

'Please,' Amber whispers, drawing everyone's attention. Blue eyes meet mine, as she reaches a shaking hand to grip my arm. 'Make it stop.'

'Do something,' Lucas demands, pulling from Mason's hold.

Zephyr is at my side in the blink of an eye, resting his hand on Amber's forehead. There's a glare of amethyst and she slumps against the bed, out cold. Her breathing comes in ragged pants and she's getting paler by the second.

'She's dying,' Zephyr murmurs. 'She won't survive the transition.'

'No,' Lucas shouts.

'Can't you do something?' I ask Zephyr.

'I cannot,' Zephyr answers then tilts his head and looks at Lucas. 'But, perhaps you can.'

'I'll do it,' Lucas vows.

'Bite her.'

Lucas and Mason suck in a breath, shock painting their faces.

'Mate a female without her consent?' Mason snarls. 'It's forbidden!'

'Then she'll die,' Zephyr answers his gaze turning my way. 'Some things are worth breaking all the rules for, Lucas.'

My insides grow warm at his meaning. It's against the rules for Zephyr to mate a Dark Fae, but he broke them for me. I still want to punch him, but the urge is softened by his romantic words.

'Mate her or lose her, Lucas; those are your options,' Zephyr counters.

'It's against our laws,' Mason argues when Lucas stares down at Amber.

'You think I don't know that?' Lucas growls, the air growing thick with the scent of undergrowth and green places.

'Lycan only get one mate,' Zephyr intones, like he's reminding Lucas of the fact.

Lycan? I look between Lucas and Mason in awe. They're wolf shifters?

'We do,' Lucas agrees.

Amber's back bows from the bed her scream renting the air. Blood gushes from her mouth and nose, staining the bottom half of her face red. It snakes down her neck and puddles beneath her shoulders, the mattress too drenched to absorb it. How much blood does she have left? Blue light crackles over her skin, wrenching another scream from her lips.

'Help her!' Lucas demands.

Zephyr shakes his head. 'I've done all I can, Lucas. You must claim her or let her go.'

Lucas closes his eyes, like he's in pain. The smell of wild woodland and fur pulses into the air, a heavy sensation settling on my shoulders.

'She can't leave me,' he whispers and looks at Mason. 'I can't lose her.'

Mason swallows hard then nods, and Lucas doesn't hesitate. He sinks impressive fangs into the juncture between Amber's neck and shoulder. She chokes on her next scream but relaxes beneath him, a sigh escaping, as she stills in his arms. Lucas groans, closing his eyes. When they open again blue wolf eyes stare back at me, replacing Lucas's green. He releases Amber's neck and laves the bite with his tongue. I watch, fascinated, as the wound heals before my eyes. My fingers itch with the need to touch the bite Zephyr gave me. Watching Lucas bite Amber makes me feel like a voyeur.

'It's done,' Zephyr breathes.

'She'll live?' Lucas asks, voice more animal than man.

Zephyr nods. 'Congratulations on your mating.'

He pulls me close and I tuck my face against his chest. Purple light blazes bright around us and I wince. He really needs to warn me before he teleports. I swear I'll be blind if I'm not careful. When I open my eyes we're back in Caleb Harrison's home.

CHAPTER 17

'The hell!' Caleb barks.

Anima catches the plate he drops and hands it back to him in one fluid motion, before taking a casual bite of her food. Caleb shakes his head and takes his plate to the breakfast bar in the middle of the kitchen.

'Damn fae, popping in and out all over my house,' he grumbles. 'Just give me some damn warning next time. I almost had a heart attack.'

'What's a heart attack?' Navi asks from the other side of the breakfast bar.

'Mer don't have them,' Zephyr says.

'But what *is* one?' Navi persists.

'Shut up, Navi,' the brunette to his left answers.

Navi grins at her, his grey eyes soaking her in. She elbows him in the ribs and his grin widens, gaze adoring.

'You are well?' Anima asks me.

I hear her unspoken question and nod my head. 'I'm here by choice.'

She beams a dazzling smile and that strange, silvery light pulses over her skin. Anima pushes from her seat and pulls me into a hug. I hesitate for just a second, before hugging her back.

A loud crash sounds from upstairs and we break apart. Everyone looks at the ceiling, like it has the answers. The air electrifies and my darkness surfaces.

'Primrose!' Aric roars from upstairs.

'Dad?' I squeak in response.

Zephyr scoops me into his arms, as Aric appears in the kitchen doorway. His black eyes look impossibly darker, the whites drenched in ebony. Black veins stain the skin around his eyes, his light bleeding into the flesh. Midnight hair writhes around his shoulders, caught in the energy crackling over his skin. A silver tunic and black leggings hug the strips of muscle carving his frame, and he looks menacing as hell.

'Release my daughter, he snarls.

'Put me down,' I breathe, fearing for Zephyr's life.

I need to calm the situation, before someone gets killed.

'*Mine*,' Zephyr answers, ignoring my request.

Rage pours from Aric and my darkness turns frenzied. I squirm in Zephyr's hold, sensing the building energy from Aric. Zephyr tightens his grip to the point of pain and I squeak in protest.

'Put me the hell down,' I hiss.

Zephyr bares his fangs and hisses back. Though his gaze never leaves Aric, I know the threat is directed at me. My shock turns to anger, but before I can respond he teleports us to Caleb's bedroom. He opens a portal in the mirror and carries me through, finally placing me on my feet.

'Zephyr-'

He blasts an essence orb at the exit mirror, shattering any chance of Aric following. I glance around the room to get my bearing. We're in Zephyr's bedroom, in the Light Realm. He turns to face me and I stare right back.

'Primrose-'

'You hissed at me,' I say, folding my arms across my chest. '*Hissed* at me.'

'You were being unreasonable.'

Anger narrows my eyes to slits. 'Excuse me?'

'I couldn't let you go with him,' Zephyr shouts.

'I wasn't going to go with him,' I shout back. 'My intention was to calm him down, Zephyr.' I take a deep breath and let it out slowly, releasing some of the tension. 'So he wouldn't kill you.'

Zephyr's feral expression softens. 'You were worried for me.'

'Of course I was! My dad is very powerful, and it doesn't take a genius to see he wants you dead.'

Life is so cheap to the fae. They live such a long time, and they don't care if they end somebody's eternity. Maybe it's because they live so long that they don't value what they have, while they have it. Mum was stolen too soon, her light extinguished before it had a real chance to shine.

Zephyr sighs and pulls me into his arms. I rest my head against his chest, listening to the steady beating of his heart. It's a reassuring sound, one I need to hear right now.

'I'm sorry, Primrose.'

'You could've handled that so much better,' I say, not finished chastising him.

'His clothing provoked me,' he admits.

I pull away to look up at his face. 'What do you mean?'

'Aric was wearing the traditional attire for a father during a Bonding Ceremony,' he answers.

'His silver tunic,' I murmur. 'It matches my mating gown.'

Zephyr nods. 'It's tradition for fae to wear silver during a Bonding Ceremony.'

His sadness mists the air around us, and I understand why. 'We'll never have that,' I breathe, fingering a button on the front of his tunic. 'We've missed our chance.'

He takes my hand and kisses my palm. 'You're still mine, Primrose.'

Alissa pops into the room behind a flare of amethyst. 'As ever, Zephyr you've ignored my wishes to do things your way,' she hisses.

Zephyr hugs me to him as we turn to face her. She's paler than the last time I saw her, with grey lacing her black hair. Her dress is still see-through, though and I sigh at the sight of her nipples.

'I've done what's right for Primrose and myself, a factor that doesn't matter to you,' Zephyr answers. 'Primrose is my mate, and you cannot take her from me.'

'Everything I've done is for you or your sister,' Alissa scoffs. 'You brought this girl from the Realm of Man, determined to mate her even though she didn't want you. I begged you to return her, but supported your choice when you refused, despite having endured her fate myself. And you tell me I care not for your interests?' Alissa moves closer, incensed. 'You may have disliked my counsel because it opposed your wishes, but do not delude yourself into thinking I did anything for my own gain, Zephyr.'

'And yet you're here to take Primrose from me,' Zephyr argues.

'Why in the runes would I take your bonded from you?' Alissa demands.

Zephyr stiffens against me. 'Bonded?'

'I'm upset you negated the traditional ceremony during the equinox, but a Blessing Ceremony can be arranged,' she answers.

'Are you saying we're bonded?' I ask, needing to be sure I'm understanding this right. 'We didn't do the ceremony during the equinox.'

'The ceremony is for show,' Alissa answers. 'You already carried Zephyr's Mating Mark. All that's needed to complete a bond after that is the joining of flesh.'

'How do you know we, um, joined that way?' I counter.

She rolls her eyes, like it's the stupidest question. 'Your lights are woven, Primrose. Any fae with breath in their body can feel it.'

I stare at her in shock. All this fuss over bonding and I did it without even realising. I feel like such an idiot, yet warmth fills my chest. I claimed Zephyr and I don't regret it.

Something occurs to me and I look at Zephyr. 'Did you know?'

The sudden joy I'm feeling teeters on a thin ledge. Zephyr acted like we weren't bonded after last night, but is it all an act? Even if it is, does it matter? *I* initiated the horizontal mambo, so *I'm* to blame.

'No,' he answers and I *feel* his sincerity.

I shake my head in wonder, unable to deny the sense of relief I feel.

'Come, Daughter,' Alissa commands. 'We must prepare for the Blessing Ceremony.' A shiver rips down my spine at her calling me Daughter. 'We must let the Realm see it's future queen and settle any discord.'

'Queen?' I squeak.

Why does everyone insist on me being Queen?

Alissa smirks at my discomfort. 'Come,' she orders. 'I know your discomfort with our fashions. I will take you to the dressmaker and she'll make you a gown.'

Gone is the cold demeanour from before, when Alissa insisted I had no choices. I think of her little speech to Zephyr, and how she'd argued with him in my favour. The woman is the most mercurial creature I've met, and it makes me wary. But she's loyal to her children and fiercely protective.

I follow her to the door, where her entourage of women await, and turn back to Zephyr. 'I'll see you later?'

'I'll be waiting for you at moonrise, my rose.'

CHAPTER 18

I'm in another silver gown, a crown banding my forehead.
The silver metal has been braided into my hair, blonde
strands woven into a spectacular design around it. Alissa
approved of the lace I chose to make my mating gown,
before leaving me to work out the details with the
dressmaker. Once she left I added the black bodysuit
underneath. It's made from a glittery material that
shimmers when I walk, silhouetting my frame beneath the
lace. The bodysuit is backless like the dress, displaying my
wing markings.

'It's perfect,' I say.

The dressmaker smiles and bows low. I fidget,
thinking I'd escaped such things when I escaped the Dark
Realm. Mating Zephyr nixed that for me though, and I
don't like it one bit.

My gaze slides back to the dressmaker. She has
indigo hair and lilac skin, with matching violet eyes. She's
got a body built for sin and I'm itching to ask *what* she is.
She made my outfit from thin air; spinning the ideas I gave
her into existence. You'd think I'd be used to the crazy
stuff by now, but no. Things fill me with fear or
amazement here, and it's exhausting.

Her eyes widen as I step from the little plinth she had me stand on. The floor in here is organic and my feet are bare, meaning I leave a trail of flowers as I move across the room. She stares at me like she wants to say something.

'I'm a Lumen,' I tell her.

She nods. 'And Dark Fae,' she murmurs staring at my wing markings.

'I thought you knew.'

She shakes her head. 'Nobody told me.'

I hesitate, wondering whom else Zephyr hasn't told.

'Your markings are the darkest I've seen,' she says. 'Does,' she closes her eyes, like she's drumming up courage, 'does Prince Zephyr know?'

I snort at her concern. 'If he hasn't figured it out by now then he's an idiot,' I tease.

She grins, cheeks turning a darker shade of purple. 'But Queen Alissa is ignorant?'

'We haven't had chance to tell her, yet,' I murmur feeling a spike of worry.

She studies me. 'I pledge to craft beautiful garments for you, Majesty.'

'You don't need to worry about that,' I answer hoping to get away with something less formal once the ceremony is over.

Her smile falters. 'You wish to dismiss me?'

Worry creases her features and blind panic saturates the air. I curse when she starts sobbing and hurry to pull her into a hug. Her skin lights with neon freckles and she jerks away.

'I didn't mean to touch you,' she apologises.

'I touched you,' I counter. 'If you don't mind me asking, what are you? Why did you light up when I touched you?'

'I'm a sprite.'

I think of the little, purple beings wrapped in light, that keep appearing from mirrors to force Zephyr into going places. 'Like the ones that come to summon Zephyr?'

She nods. 'I used to be as they are, before I gave up my true form to be with a fae.'

'I don't understand.'

She fidgets. 'Centuries ago I made a promise to leave my home and bond with a fae male. But he never bonded to me, and now I'm stuck.'

'Stuck?'

'I'm banished from my realm for choosing a fae over the mate my parents chose. I was blinded by my feelings and didn't question the possibility of the fae rejecting me.'

'What do you mean?'

'He wouldn't bond with me, so when he faded from this life I remained.'

My heart squeezes. She's living the fate I would've suffered had I not bonded Zephyr.

'You can't go home?'

'I tried, but my parents refuse to acknowledge me as their daughter. I shamed them and they cannot see past it.' She looks away. 'It's why I got upset when I thought you were dismissing me. There aren't many realms I can blend into, and I've nowhere else to go.'

I study her lilac skin and imagine her walking around the village back home. She blends in here because it's common knowledge there's more than one realm and universe. It makes me wonder how many realms there are, and how many of them are ignorant like the Realm of Man.

'You'll always be welcome in the Light Realm,' I promise. 'But, perhaps I can speak to your family-'

'Queen Alissa has spent many decades trying to reason with my parents,' she says. 'And given the chance,

I'm unsure I'd return now. I miss my sisters, but why pine for a place that doesn't want me?'

'Alissa tried to help you?'

'Of course,' she answers. 'She's my Tether.'

'Your what?'

'I'm tethered to her, like Zephyr's sprites are to him,' she explains, though I still have no clue what she's talking about. Her expression turns sad. 'I'll miss her when she fades.'

'What's your name?' I ask.

Her violet gaze meets mine. 'Rana.'

'I know the pain of losing someone you love, Rana. Please don't hesitate to seek me out if you need someone to talk to.'

'Thank you,' she whispers then looks past me to the doorway. 'Alissa comes.'

Alissa appears in the doorway and smiles at us. The smile is the most genuine I've seen, and it lights her face. She's wearing another transparent gown, made from a material that turns dazzling in the light. There are strategically placed swirls in the fabric, hiding her most intimate parts, and I breathe a sigh of relief. Her hair hangs dark around her shoulders, with a crown of silver filigree circling her forehead. A pair of gossamer wings stretch out behind her, adding to her mythical appearance.

'I approve,' she murmurs, appraising my outfit.

I bite my tongue to hold back sarcasm. Alissa argued my corner after Zephyr abducted me, and she tried to help Rana. She's got warped ideals, but maybe she isn't as cold hearted as I originally thought.

'The moon is rising,' she says and offers me her hand.

I shut my eyes, knowing she's going to teleport us somewhere. The back of my eyelids light up and I keep them closed until the light is gone.

'A lake?' I ask, looking down at the water beneath my feet. What in the ever loving…? I wiggle my toes against the surface, which is oddly gelatinous beneath my feet. The polished surface glitters silver in response. 'At least we're not sinking,' I mutter.

Alissa chuckles. 'Your reactions to things is refreshing,' she tells me.

'So everyone keeps telling me,' I grouse then look back to my feet, where water lilies mix with a plethora of exotic flowers blooming around my bare feet.

Alissa's grip on my hand turns painful and I realise I've turned my back to her. She spins me fully then hisses at the sight of my back. I'm facing her again before I can blink and wince at the pressure of her hand on mine.

'Dark Fae,' she snarls.

Darkness floods my vision and creeps over my skin, before I'm ripped from her hold and curled into a familiar pair of arms.

'*Mine*,' Zephyr snarls at his mum.

'She's Dark Fae and a Black!' Alissa snarls back.

A Black? Am I being penalised by the colour of my light now? How freaking racist!

'Kill her and I die,' Zephyr answers.

Oh right, conditions of the bond.

Alissa stares between us, realisation dawning on her face. Zephyr's light is bound to mine now. If she kills me then he'll die too. She can either accept me or lose her son. The ramifications of what mating him means, unfurl in my brain. I look up at his defiant expression, as he glares at his mother. Zephyr knew what it meant to mate a Dark Fae, yet he chose me. He was *that* lonely.

'Do you realise what you've done?' Alissa snarls.

'You think I don't know the consequences of this choice?' he answers.

Alissa studies his face then appears to calm a little. 'If you allow one Dark Fae into the Light Realm, you present an opening to accept more,' she says.

'I'm aware of the precedent I'm setting, Mother. I'm to be the next King of this realm and I'm seeking the best future for faekind.'

Alissa regards Zephyr for a silent moment then holds her hand out to me. 'I will escort your Consort, as is tradition,' she tells him.

'No way,' I answer nursing my bruised hand. 'There's no way I'm-'

'Please,' Alissa cuts in shocking me. 'I must do this for Zephyr, before moonset.'

Zephyr stiffens. 'It's not time,' he breathes. 'Father isn't-'

'Oric faded this morning,' Alissa mutters, betrayal lacing her tone. 'He tried to remain, to pass the crown, but was too weak.'

'He's gone?' Zephyr whispers.

I wrap my arms around his waist and hug him tight, but instead of the grief I expect, I get relief from him.

'Now you understand the urgency for the Blessing Ceremony,' Alissa says. 'At moonset I'll be gone and you'll be ruler of the Light Realm.'

'Mother-'

'I wish to see your Mating Ceremony before I fade,' she interrupts then offers a sad smile. 'For it has been a long time coming.'

I squeeze Zephyr a little tighter when grief finally floods from him. Then I let go and take Alissa's offered hand. He gives me a grateful smile then disappears in a flash of light. I watch his light flare bright in the centre of the lake, where a gathering of fae waits on the silvery water.

'Thank you,' Alissa tells me.

'I'm not doing this for you.'

She presses us into a slow walk and I groan internally at the snails pace. Darkness prickles beneath my skin at her nearness, regarding her as a threat.

217

'You love him,' she whispers.

My gaze snaps to hers, ready to deny it. But…I can't. I fumble for the denial again but my mouth stays shut. Zephyr told me I'm more than a means to an end, but he's never said he loves me. We don't even really know each other, and it's too soon to spout words like love, isn't it?

A gentle smile curves Alissa's lips at my silence. 'Oric and I didn't love each other,' she says. 'We…tolerated each other.' It's silent for a few moments before she says, 'I fell in love with a Dark Fae the year I came of mating age.'

My eyebrows brush my hairline at her admission. 'What?'

'We met in another realm,' she murmurs, gaze unfocussed, like she's reliving the past. Her lips smile in a way that says she has a secret. 'I should've known he was Dark Fae the second I saw him, but I couldn't reason over the pounding of my heart. His green eyes snared mine, the call of his light drawing me like no other.' She meets my gaze. 'Harlan taught me what love was in three, short days. I didn't discover he was Dark Fae until the day we parted, and by then it didn't matter.' The smile bleeds from her lips. 'On my return to the Light Realm, my father announced I was to be Consort to the next King.'

'You had no choice,' I say remembering her words to Zephyr.

Alissa argued with him to let me go because she'd been in my situation and empathised with me.

'What happened to Harlan?'

Her gaze hardens. 'He never came for me, and then it was too late,' she answers giving me insight to where her hatred of Dark Fae comes from.

'I'll take care of Zephyr,' I promise.

Her gaze softens. 'I know.'

Murmurs from the fae gathered around Zephyr reach us, and the word Luman is gasped more than once. I glance at the flowers sprouting around my feet.

'Hold your head high, Primrose,' Alissa orders. 'The old king is dead and you're mated to the new one. You're their queen now and you bow to no one.'

'What if I'm not ready to be their queen?' I argue.

What the hell do I know about being a queen? Part of leaving the Dark Realm was tied to my need to escape this title.

'You're ready,' she answers.

'I have no clue what I'm doing,' I counter.

'You'll learn.'

'You seem so sure,' I mutter.

'You've adapted quickly to more than one stressful situation, handling each with grace and poise,' she tells me. 'You're a natural at this.'

I withhold a snort, grace and poise? Alissa didn't see me squeezing my backside through Anima's bathroom mirror then face-planting on the floor. Fear and shock are the adjectives she should be using for me since meeting Zephyr. It's been a rollercoaster and there's been nothing graceful about it.

'Release your wings,' Alissa whispers when we reach where the fae are gathered.

The gathering sucks in an accumulative breath when I do, glittering black peeling from my skin to stretch out behind me. I ignore the whispers as I make my way to where Zephyr is standing, toes touching the edge of the moon's reflection on the water.

He's dressed in the tight trousers favoured by the fae, with a long, tailored tunic in rich silver. His hair is like ink in the moonlight, eyes burning jewels amid the razor lines of his face. He looks hewn from stone, like a god carved him from alabaster, his skin bleached by moonlight. He shimmers with purple glitter when he moves to take my hands, tugging me closer, until my toes meet the edge of the moon's reflection on the water.

'Are you ready?' he whispers.

I nod. 'I-'

I gasp, looking down to see a masculine hand shackling my ankle. It drags me down before I can react, wrenching a scream from my throat. I lose my grip on Zephyr and find myself under the water. My back tingles as my wings return to tattoos and the hand releases my ankle. I try to swim up but the mating gown clings to my legs and I start to panic. My chest aches with the need to breathe. This is how I'm going to die.

A hand latches onto my wrist and pulls me against a body lean with muscle. Lips press to mine and a tongue pushes into my mouth. I try to push away but another hand snakes through my hair and anchors my head in place. Darkness prickles over my skin, as air pushes down my throat. I stop struggling and suck it down, thinking of the need to stay alive because Zephyr will die if I do.

The hand on my head lets go and I push away as far as the grip on my wrist allows. My hair has come lose from its braiding, and I stare through a flowing curtain of blonde to neon-green eyes and a body sprayed with neon freckles. Something smooth and coiled with power brushes my feet, and I look down at the shimmering outline of a tail.

I'm still staring at the tail when the merman grips my waist and pulls me against him. I start struggling again, looking back to the surface to see Zephyr frantically hammering on it. He stops when he sees me looking, lips forming my name. I reach for him but the merman drags me deeper.

I'm at the merman's mercy, a savage ache filling my flesh the further we get from Zephyr. Being in this airless vacuum is terrifying, and I don't know what my captor wants. My fingernails dig deeper into his back, and I delight at the wince that wracks his frame.

Light pierces the darkness and I turn my face to it, like a flower reaching for the sun. It grows brighter, and my heart soars when a circular opening appears. I suck in air the second we break the surface of a light pool, the merman swimming us to the edge. Hands pull me from the pool and a fluffy towel is draped around me. I'm pulled against the familiar lines of a hard body and start to sob.

Aric brushes sodden hair from my face and holds me close. 'I've rescued you,' he soothes. 'You don't have to be afraid anymore.'

I meet his gaze. 'That was horrifying.'

He chuckles. 'Not many fae like being submerged in water.'

I shove from his hold and stumble away, clutching the towel around me like a shield. 'It isn't funny!'

My voice is raspy and my nose stings from the salt water. I hurt all over, and it's difficult to catch my breath. I point at the light pool with a shaking finger.

'I thought I was going to drown,' I hiss. 'And I didn't know what he was going to do with me.'

The skin around my eyes tingles and my head pounds; vision filling with darkness. Onyx swirls snake up my arms, my light roiling in agitated waves inside me. I try to breathe but the air is too thin.

'Calm down,' Aric orders.

'Can't breathe,' I gasp and the room tilts.

Aric catches me before I hit the floor. Pain rakes clawed fingers through my insides and my spine arches, a scream ripping from my throat. My vision blurs and Aric's voice dims. Beloved darkness wraps me in a warm cocoon of night and I shut my eyes.

CHAPTER 19

'Stay where I can see you, Primrose,' Mum says as I pick up my bucket.

I dust sand from my knees. 'I will.'

The sun is hot on my shoulders as I weave between people on the beach. I glance back to see Drew digging a moat around the sandcastle we're building, his brow furrowed in concentration. It's my job to fetch water to fill the moat. Maybe I'll find some shells to stick around the keep, but I don't want Drew calling me Princess Primrose for wanting the castle to be pretty.

Waves fizz around my feet when I reach the ocean. There are too many people on the beach to see Mum, Drew or any of my family from here. I bite my lip wondering if I should go back, but I have to fill my bucket with water. I wade into the surf then crouch and dunk my bucket, filling it to the brim. Something glitters from beneath the water and I reach to pick it up. I smile when I study the shell in my palm. It's small and round, with a scalloped edge. The inside is rose pink and the outside glitters with silver and gold tones.

'Hey.'

I glance up at the man beside me. He's a stranger and I shouldn't speak to him. I stand up, the shell clutched in my hand. Water sloshes over the edge of my bucket, splashing against my leg.

'I'm looking for my daughter,' the man says, 'have you seen her? She's about your age, brown hair and brown eyes. She's wearing a pink swimming costume like yours.'

I shake my head. 'No.'

Worry creases his face and he glances around the beach before returning his gaze to me. 'Will you help me find her?'

He puts his hand on my shoulder and I flinch. His panic blasts through me, leaving a funny taste in my mouth.

I shrug him off and step back. 'I-'

'Please,' he insists.

'I need to-'

'There's no time,' he says and grabs my wrist.

He pulls me through the water and my panic rises to match his. The bucket slips from my hand and I turn my head to see it disappear beneath the waves. The water is deeper, reaching my thighs, but the man is taller and it only reaches his knees. I struggle to keep up but he drags me along at his pace. I realise we're to the left of the breakers, where rocks rise from the sand. We're cut off from the crowded beach, this side of the rocks eerily quiet of laughter.

'I-I don't see your daughter,' I say over the crashing waves.

The man looks at me as he pulls me from the water, onto the rocks that lead up to the roadside. I stumble on the slippery surface but his grip on my wrist keeps me from falling. I hiss when I scrape my shins and tears fill my vision, but he doesn't stop.

'I saw you from the beach,' he tells me. 'You've got such pretty, blonde hair.'

His voice is soft, different, and I struggle to hear him over the crash of the waves and shrieking seagulls. I can hear people laughing and squealing faintly from beyond the rocks, but they seem a million miles away. I think of shouting to them for help, but I don't think they'd hear me. Why didn't I scream when I had the chance?

'You're hurting me,' I say.

He looks back at me eyes glinting, and smiles. 'You're really pretty. Prettier than my last girl.'

'Your daughter?'

He laughs. 'I don't have a daughter, girly.'

He stops and turns to me, cupping my face in his meaty hand. He rubs his thumb over my bottom lip and I try to jerk away, but he's too strong.

'How old are you: seven, eight?'

Six.

I don't like the way he looks at me, or how his hand feels sweaty against my skin. Nobody except family ever touch me like this, and it feels strange for this man to do so.

'Please let me go.'

He shakes his head. 'I need you.'

'Why?'

'You'll find out.'

I tug against his hold, trying to twist from his grip, but he's too strong. The man laughs and my panic turns to terror. I don't understand what he wants but know it's not good. He drags me closer, until I'm plastered against his body. He smells like sweat and my stomach clenches. I smack him with my free hand but he grabs hold of my other wrist and grins down at me.

'We'll have so much fun,' he murmurs.

Something cracks inside. There's no sound, just a feeling, like a hair tie snapping in my stomach. I want to look down but the man has me pinned against him. Movement draws my attention and I gape at the dark swirls on my right forearm. My skin tingles and I look at my left arm to see the same midnight pattern creeping over my skin.

'What is that?' I squeak.

The man squeezes my wrists so tight it makes me squeal and tears bead my lashes. The pattern races up my arms and bleeds over my hands. Coal ribbons shoot from my palms and spear into his chest. His eyes go wide and his mouth opens, like he's going to scream, but no sound comes out. I scream for him, black veins webbing over his face as his eyes fill with midnight.

The darkness spreads, little rivers of night snaking from his eyes to blanket his skin, until the man looks made from shadow. Fear cramps my stomach, but it isn't all mine. He's terrified, and the more midnight covering his skin, the stronger I feel his terror. It needles my insides, making it hard to breathe, and bile creeps up my throat. My darkness remains coiled around him, slowly tightening, and pulsing in time with the rapid beating of my heart.

His grip disappears from my wrists and I fall onto my backside. My heart drums loud in my chest as I stare up at his shadowy figure looming above me. He's let me go but we're still connected. His whole body shudders and the darkness uncurls in long ribbons. Midnight tendrils return to me, sinking beneath my skin to drench me in feelings I don't want or understand.

The man is gone and crimson stains the rock where he was standing. There's so much of it, painting the rock and sinking between the crevices. I've never seen so much blood, and it takes a second to pull my gaze away. I look down at my arms to find the pattern gone. Bruises circle my wrists where the man held me and my shins are scraped.

My feelings break through the thick sludge of the man's still lingering inside me. I start to cry, desperate to escape. I've felt other people's feelings before, but never like this. They never stay once the person isn't touching me, but the man's are like a brick in my belly.

My legs are shaky when I push to my feet and stumble over the rocks to the sea. I drop into the water, shins stinging, as I wade through the waves until I'm in view of the beach. Mum appears through a crowd of people as I splash through the surf. She sees me a second after I see her and starts running in my direction.

'Primrose,' she breathes as she wraps me in a hug. 'You're trembling!'

She tries to pull away but I'm wrapped tight around her, soaking in the warmth of her relief. Her love eclipses the man's emotion, until it's gone from my belly, and I sigh in relief.

Mum pries my arms from her waist then drops to her knees in front of me. 'Darling, what's wrong? Where were you?'

'T-there was a man,' I whisper.

Mum's eyes widen and her gaze darts around us. 'Where?'

I shake my head unable to answer. All I know is he's not coming back. Mum's gaze roams my body then fixes on my wrists. She takes my hands and gently rotates them to get a good look at the bruises there. A tear slides down her face and I brush it away.

'He did this?' she rasps.

I nod and more tears bead her lashes. 'Where is he now, Primrose?'

'Gone,' I whisper, thinking of the blood painting the rocks beyond the breakers.

Relief seeps through Mum's panic and her gaze meets mine. I ache to tell her what I felt when the man touched me, so she can hug me and take the fear of feeling those things away. I want to tell her about how my darkness did something awful to save me. But she's looking at me in the same fragile way as when she's thinking of my father. And I can't do it. I think of that visit to Doctor Minting's office and how sad it made Mum. Things have been better since I stopped telling her of my darkness. I don't tell anyone anymore, and I don't draw it in pictures either. If people ask about it I tell them it went away, and I think Mum likes that lie best.

'He defiled her!' Aric roars jarring me awake. His rage saturates the air, sticking to my skin and making my head pound. 'I'll kill him.'

'Such an act will start a war,' a calm voice answers. 'Perhaps-'

A door bursts open, interrupting. 'Highness, they've breached the border,' another male shouts.

'Where?' Aric snarls.

'Evergreen Valley.'

I withhold a flinch when a warm hand brushes my forehead. The sense of rage increases on contact, mixed with an insane need to protect.

'Guard my daughter with your life, Harlan,' Aric orders.

'Of course,' the calm voice from before answers. A door slams drenching the room in silence, before Harlan says, 'You can stop pretending now.'

I sigh and open my eyes. A blond male stands over me with eyes the colour of leaves in spring. Like all fae, he's handsome as sin and looks only slightly older than me. It's difficult to be around beings that don't age, making it hard to gauge how old they really are.

'How did you know?'

He grins, flashing a hint of fang. 'I've been healing for millennia, Princess. One of my talents includes discerning when a patient is awake.'

'Great,' I mutter and push into a sitting position.

'How are you feeling?'

'I ache,' I admit.

He nods. 'I gave you something for the pain.'

I look down. 'Who changed my clothes?'

'I did,' he answers then frowns at my horrified look.

I swing my legs off the bed and look around, finding myself in my room in Aric's palace.

'Great. Just…great!' I growl and stumble onto my feet.

'You shouldn't be up yet,' Harlan cautions. 'You went into shock after being rescued and it triggered a defensive reaction in your light. Such a powerful move is unheard of in such a young fae and it knocked you out.'

'Whatever,' I mumble, staggering a little as I go to the closet and search through the racks. 'Where's all the practical clothing,' I snarl at the male as he stands concerned in the closet doorway.

'Harlan-' I start then frown, wondering why that name sounds so familiar. 'Have we met before?'

He shakes his head. 'Perhaps you should lie down, Princess.'

'Call me Primrose or don't address me at all,' I snarl then gesture to the rack behind me. 'Is there nothing but dresses in this whole damn closet?'

'If you wish for different clothing just manifest some,' he suggests.

I take a deep breath and let some of the hostility leak from me. 'I don't know how to do that yet.'

Understanding flickers in his gaze and he steps closer. 'May I?'

I take his offered hand and he smiles, green eyes lighting. Something mists over my skin, gentle pressure rising around me.

'Do you feel my light?' he asks.

'Yes.'

'Can you feel how I'm using it to blanket your form?'

'It feels like mist,' I tell him.

The pressure withdraws. 'Can you do the same with your light?'

I mimic what Harlan did, until darkness mists around me. I'm sort of impressed with how easily I'm manipulating my light, and resist the urge to give myself a pat on the back. But all the years of not being able to control it, back when I was human, makes being fae feel worth it.

'Very good,' he praises. 'Picture what you wish to wear and it will appear on your body.'

I picture a pair of skinny jeans and a long-sleeve top from my closet back home. Tingles skitter over my skin and I grin when I look down to find the items I've chosen.

'This is going to save so much time in the mornings,' I murmur.

'You did very well,' Harlan says and releases my hand.

Harlan.

My eyes snap wide with recognition. It can't be...can it? Maybe I'm wrong and Harlan is the fae equivalent to John back in my realm, but I have to be sure.

'Why didn't you go get her?' I demand.

'I don't-'

'Alissa,' I cut in. 'Why didn't you rescue her from the Light Realm?'

Harlan's face pales and I know I'm right. 'How did-?'

'She told me about you, after she discovered I'm Dark Fae.'

Harlan's grief crashes against me. 'What did she tell you?'

'That she fell in love with you, and when you didn't come for her she was forced to mate Oric.'

'She thinks I didn't fight for her?' he whispers, pain lancing his features and percolating the space around us.

I swallow hard against the agony pouring from him. 'You tried?'

'I breached the Light Realm to find my Alissa,' he murmurs. 'But Oric was waiting.' Harlan closes his eyes and when he opens them again they're burning with rage. 'He came to the dungeon on the night of their Mating Ceremony to describe how she'd fought him.'

I swallow hard. 'He forced her?'

Harlan nods. 'I'm sorry you've suffered the same fate, Primrose.'

It takes a second to register what he just said. 'What the hell are you talking about?'

'I'm a healer,' he reminds me. 'Your father tasked me with seeing if you were still-'

'Don't say it!' I shout when I realise where this conversation is going.

'There's no need to feel shamed, Primrose,' he says. 'It wasn't your doing.'

'Zephyr didn't force me! I made the decision to mate him and was the one to initiate the bonding.'

Harlan stares at me in shock. '*You* chose him?'

I nod. 'Aric had me kidnapped from my Blessing Ceremony. And that's how I know all the stuff about you and Alissa. She told me while escorting me to-'

'Alissa was escorting you?' Harlan snaps. 'Why not Oric?'

'Oric faded-'

'He left her?' he snarls, making me back up a step. His fury lessens and he stares at me in awe. 'Alissa remains?'

'Why are you so angry?'

'Mated pairs fade together because their lights are bound,' Harlan answers. 'For one to fade first is nearly unheard of, and leaves the remaining fae in pain.' He growls again, expression vicious. 'Oric loved her, yet left her to suffer?'

'Oric and Alissa tolerated each other,' I tell him. 'There was no love in their mating.'

'How can you know that?' he argues.

'Alissa's told me. Maybe Oric could fade without her because they hated each other.'

Harlan nods. 'If Alissa and Oric's mating was so disjointed there may be a window of opportunity.'

I shake my head. 'You've lost me.'

'Oric is gone from this world, their link severed. It means Alissa can claim another, before her previous bond claims her for ascension.'

'You mean she can claim you before she fades?' At Harlan's nod I ask, 'Won't that mean you'll both fade at moonset in the Light Realm?'

'Moonset?' he whispers.

'Focus,' I snap. 'I'm asking if claiming Alissa will kill you, Harlan?'

Harlan shakes his head. 'Oric was over a millennia older than Alissa. Her life span altered to match his.'

Meaning mating Zephyr knocked two millennia off of my suddenly long life.

'So, if you mate Alissa it will save her,' I say.

'I'm only a century older than Alissa. Bonding our lights will mean her lifespan will alter to match mine.'

'Then what the hell are you waiting for? We have to get you to the Light Realm before moonset, Harlan.'

He snags my wrist when I push past him to leave. 'Light Fae have breached the Dark Realm, Primrose. Zephyr is with them.'

Oh no. 'What?'

'He's here for you, but Aric won't let Zephyr leave with you,' Harlan warns.

'But we're bonded,' I argue. 'If Zephyr dies then so do I.'

'There are ways of killing Zephyr without fading you,' he informs me.

'But I chose Zephyr. Why is Aric so desperate to separate us?'

'Aric thinks you were forced into bonding, the same way Oric forced Alissa,' Harlan answers.

I remember what Aric was shouting when I woke up. 'He thinks Zephyr defiled me.'

'Zephyr is Oric's heir, and Aric believes the apple doesn't fall far from the tree.'

'He's wrong,' I snap, but I had a large part in Aric's opinion of Zephyr. I came running for help, when I should've listened to what Zephyr was saying. 'It's my fault. I made my father hate the Light Fae.'

'No,' Harlan argues, his regret weaving around us.

There's something I'm missing. 'What aren't you telling me?'

He sighs. 'Aric and I were children together, our mothers inseparable. We grew up as brothers, and when Oric imprisoned me Aric was the one who got me out. But the damage was done.'

'Damage?'

Harlan swallows hard. 'They cut off my wings.'

'Oh my god.'

'Oric wanted no female to ever find me attractive.'

'He was a monster,' I say forming new respect for Alissa.

How the hell did she survive all those years with the male? I feel blessed that I had no real interaction with him.

'Aric couldn't forgive what the King of the Light Fae did to his blood brother, and war was ignited between the Dark and Light Realms.'

'And that king's son in mated to Aric's heir,' I murmur.

'Can you understand Aric's rage?' Harlan asks.

I can understand Oric was a psychopath, and I'm lucky Zephyr is nothing like him. I thought my situation was bad, but it could've been so much worst. No wonder Alissa comes across as a Stone Cold Bitch when you meet her. That female is owed a happy ending.

'Aric's going to kill Zephyr,' I breathe.

Harlan nods and darkness rises inside me; stretched thin and boiling with rage. Harlan gasps and stares at me with wide eyes.

'You're a Lumen.'

I look down to the flowers blooming around my feet, but Harlan isn't staring at them. Onyx swirls surround me in inky tendrils, as my darkness breaches the barrier of my skin. It's frenzied, like the day of Mum's funeral, but I'm not afraid. I draw from its strength and let it take control.

'We're going to Evergreen Valley,' I tell Harlan.

I'm speaking, expressing my wishes, but there's something else driving me forward. I know what I need to do, without having the knowledge of *how* I know it. I can't explain it, other than my darkness has knowledge of things I don't.

'But-'

'The one you seek is there,' I cut in, and *know* I'm speaking of Alissa. My internal freak-out meter would be overheating, if not for the calm my darkness pushes through me. Okay then, let's do this. 'If you wish to bond her in time you'll take me there.'

He stares at me like I've grown a second head. Fear and awe taint the air, as realisation rises through his features. He knows what's happening, even if I'm not sure of it. My darkness isn't in complete control. I can take the reins back at any moment, but know it will risk Zephyr. If he is hurt in this war I'll have the reins ripped from me. What happened after Mum's funeral fills my mind. I woke surround by dead flowers, the life sucked from their crispy remains. Insidious whispers ghosts from the creature in my middle, saying I'll wake to more than dead flowers, if Zephyr is harmed.

Harlan offers his hand and I take it, skin prickling at the *taste* of his essence. My darkness is hungry, but only one fae has the nourishment it desires. The closet disappears behind a wall of green light then fades to grass so tall I have to bend my head to see the sky.

'Evergreen Valley,' Harlan murmurs then shoves me to the ground.

An essence orb wizzes over us and burns through the grass behind where I'd been standing.

'Realms!' Harlan hisses then pushes off me to hurl green orbs at our attacker.

The huge male grunts and grips his right shoulder, body crackling with turquoise light. I push to my feet and put a hand on Harlan's arm, when he puts himself between me and the other fae. Harlan meets my gaze as I step around him, and whatever he sees causes him to stand down.

Darkness reaches inky arms to wrap around the fae. Turquoise eyes widen in fear and my darkness soaks in the emotion, tightening its hold on the male. Midnight lines appear beneath his skin, the pattern of my essence lighting his insides. His eyes blaze turquoise then bleed to black. Darkness creeps over his skin, painting him in shadow. I feel the spark of life in his middle, before my darkness drains it from him.

For a moment I'm six-years-old again, standing in a pink swimsuit on the rocks, staring at blood-drenched rocks. I should be horrified at what just happened to the fae, fear tickling the fringes of my mind, but my darkness pushes the emotion away before it takes hold. The Earth is scorched where the fae was standing; nothing remaining of him, not even a crimson stain to mark his passing. Harlan's staring at me with wary eyes, but doesn't seem surprised at what I've done.

'This way,' he says.

Turquoise flowers bloom from the ground where I step, the same shade as the light of the fae I just killed. Sounds of battle reach my ears, the scent of blood and burning grass tickling my senses. We break from the long grass, onto the edge of a valley. The landscape is a mix of lush greens, blazing with flares of neon light. Hundreds of fae are fighting in varying shades of armour.

Harlan lights up in front of me, thousands of emerald scales replacing the clothes on his body. They knit together as I watch, forming skin-tight armour the shade of Harlan's light. It covers his whole body, tipping his fingers with emerald claws and his head with a vicious-looking helmet. He glances back at me, green eyes the only thing visible through the slit in his helm.

'Go,' I say when I feel his hesitation to leave me.

He turns and runs into the fray, making his way toward the opposite end of the valley. Harlan dodges essence orbs and other fae, maintaining a determined gate. I plot his course, finding his prize when lilac armour glints from the opposite end of the valley. It hugs a feminine frame, and even though I can't see her features beneath the wicked helm, I know Alissa's beneath the jewel-toned scales. She slashes lilac claws at a fae twice her size, taking him down in a graceful manoeuvre. Another fae replaces the first, but Alissa despatches him just as fast.

Amethyst flares from the centre of the valley, drawing my gaze.

Zephyr.

He's facing my father, an imposing enemy in black armour. Aric and Zephyr are the same height, though Aric is thicker with muscle. I move through the battle, essence orbs smacking into me, being absorbed by the dark smoke engulfing my frame. The attacks against me stop, fae ceasing their fighting as I pass. Silence accompanies the flowers I leave in my wake. They're no longer turquoise, but the varying shades of essence orbs I've absorbed.

CHAPTER 20

'Fight me,' Aric roars at Zephyr, throwing another orb his way.

The orb grazes Zephyr's shoulder, leaving a scorch in his indigo armour. 'I came to make peace,' Zephyr snarls.

'With an army at your back?'

'Because I knew you'd react this way,' Zephyr argues.

'You defiled my daughter,' Aric snarls.

'She's my mate!'

'She's *mine*,' Aric roars.

Zephyr grunts when Aric's next orb hits him, followed by another and another, hitting the same spot on his armoured chest. I'm so close I can see the individual scales forming the back of Aric's armour. The atmosphere prickles with static, snapping against my skin. Aric's bombardment has Zephyr on his knees, and there's an enormous charge building between them. Black light crackles over Aric, the energy intensifying, and I sprint the last few steps to stop him from releasing the blow.

'Father-'

Aric spins to me so fast he blurs. I gasp, furious midnight glaring down at me from the slit in his helm, before realisation dawns. I look between us, to the blade buried deep in my middle, and my bottom lip quivers. The numbness melts away and I'm bombarded with the emotion of everyone in the valley. It's as painful as the dagger in my flesh and a tear rolls down my face.

Aric's helm retracts, revealing his terrified expression. 'Primrose,' he whispers, releasing his grip on the blade.

Zephyr roars and pushes Aric aside. My knees buckle but Zephyr catches and lowers me to the ground. His fingers flutter around the hilt of the blade but it doesn't matter. Leave it in or pull it out, the end will be the same. The pain is unbearable, yet there's a strange, new kind of numbness creeping through my limbs.

'My Starlight,' Zephyr whispers cupping my face. His fingers are painted with blood, leaving warm streaks against my skin. 'Don't leave me.'

'You're not dying,' I mumble.

'The blade is made from iron and infused with light,' he answers, tone agonised. 'It will severe our bond as it kills you.'

So that's how Aric planned to kill Zephyr and keep me alive. My lips curve with a smile because Zephyr will live. My darkness retreats; fading with the life leaving my body. The roaring stream of power veers away, dragging me wherever it's going. It's leaving this world and taking me with it.

'I'm sorry it took so long to choose you back,' I whisper.

Something warm coats my lips, tasting like pennies. I know what it is, but can't think of the word. Everything is dimming, becoming irrelevant. There's only Zephyr, his skin lighting with neon purple. I watch in awe, as I see past his flesh to the light within. I witness the beautiful brightness and it steals my breath. The amethyst star in his centre is laced with midnight, and I watch my darkness unwinding from his light.

'Beautiful,' I whisper.

'Don't leave me,' the starlight begs.

'It only hurts for a little bit,' a beloved voice tells me.

I shift my gaze from the starlight to a face that mirrors my own. 'Mum?'

She nods, smile resplendent. 'Hello, Primrose.'

I stare at her in wonder. She's translucent and lit with silver tones; eyes like sapphires in her smiling face. Blonde hair hangs in a brilliant cloud of gold around her shoulders, curling into perfect spirals at the ends. She looks younger than when she died, no sign of the illness that killed her. She's vibrant and glowing, and I'd cry happy tears if I remembered how.

Mum cups my face with an ethereal hand and I feel it more than I feel Zephyr. She's more real to me than he is now, though there are still chords of midnight stretching between us.

'I'm dying, Mum.'

'I know, baby girl. I've come to take you home.'

Something tugs at my chest and I look away from her, staring in fascination as the blade slides out. There's no pain, just a sick sense of wonder. Shadow moves over me, eclipsing the amethyst starlight, and I look at Mum for help. But she's staring at the shadow with longing. She lifts a hand and strums her fingers through the dark mass. It curls around her fingers and up her arm like a lover, and she smiles.

'Aric,' she whispers.

I look back to the shadow in understanding, just as it pushes against where the blade was wedged. Dark starlight flares across my vision and pain lights my insides. I arch from the ground and scream. Emotion floods me: terror, determination, hope and love. I cling to the last one, using it to guide me through raging agony. The starlight reaches through me, snagging hold of the river at my centre, forcing it to change direction. Darkness pulses back into my centre, and blooms through my flesh.

Regret mists the air, as the fire inside me fades. I slump on the grass and open my eyes, meeting Aric's midnight gaze.

'Dad,' I croak.

He smiles down at me. 'I'm sorry, Primrose.'

I realise Mum's still here and she's holding his hand. I stare at Aric, studying his translucent state and understanding washes through me. His ebony hair has a glittery sheen and his skin is the same pearlescent shade as Mum's. I sit up and look around to see if anybody else is seeing what I'm seeing, but there's a wall of black light around us. We're in the middle, cut off from the rest of the valley. I look down, fingering the hole in my top, where the blade sliced through. Blood soaks the fabric, slicking my fingertips but the wound is gone.

'What the hell is going on?'

I look back to my parents – both of them together, and my heart stutters. I've never seen them together, or Mum looking so happy.

'You're dead,' I whisper. 'Both of you.'

'It was the only way to save you,' Aric answers.

'You're leaving me.'

My parents move either side of me and wrap me in a hug. Unconditional love seeps into me from both sides and I start to cry. I don't want to let this moment go, because they'll be gone with it. The loneliness will creep back and I don't know if I'll cope this time.

Something slams against the wall around us, and I look toward the sound. It comes again, harder this time, and I'm filled with the need to reach for it.

'Perhaps you should let your mate in,' Aric says.

I meet his gaze then study the wall of black light. 'I thought you made the wall,' I say.

'You don't realise yet how powerful you are, but you will,' Aric tells me. 'It took me centuries to master skills you've presented.'

'How can that be?' I argue. 'I'm only half fae and you're whole.'

His smile is sad. 'You found what I couldn't, Primrose.'

'Which is?' I snap when he doesn't elaborate. 'You can't die!' I shout. 'Who the hell is going to teach me all this stuff?'

'There's a reason I never mated, Primrose.'

'Because you loved Mum.'

He shakes his head. 'My heart belonged to Christine, but I was King of the Dark Fae. I was expected to take a mate and produce an heir. But I couldn't because I never found what you have.' He chuckles and shakes his head. 'And I tried to take it from you.'

Zephyr? 'You're talking about Zephyr?'

Aric nods. 'He's your Balance, Primrose.'

'My what?'

'Lumen Fae, like you and I, need a Balance,' he tells me.

'You're a Lumen? Why didn't you tell me?'

'I was born in a time when Lumen Fae were culled at birth,' he answers. 'As heir, I wasn't tested and my mother taught me to hide it before anyone found out. I even hid it from my father because he was the one to order the culling.'

'Why?' I whisper, horrified at what he's telling me. 'Will I be culled?'

I haven't exactly been hiding my Lumen side. Everyone that sees the flowers I leave knows what it means, so it's no secret what I am.

'The culling ended when Lumen talent was thought to have died out,' Aric soothes. 'That was ten millennia ago, and those times live only in the memories of the oldest fae, if they choose to remember.'

'If they 'choose' to remember?'

Aric shrugs. 'Some memories are buried deep and take a lot of effort to find. There are archives, of course, but you'd need to know where to look and what to look for.'

'So why the culling?'

Aric glances at my mother before answering, 'Lumen Fae need to find their Balance. Without it, our light finds other sources to feed from.'

My gaze slides to Mum and understanding trickles through me. My light fed from Mum's life force until it killed her. Then it fed off those around me, until the moment I found Zephyr.

'Zephyr's my Balance,' I murmur. 'That's why my light is blind to all others when he's around.'

'Your light will crave no other,' Aric tells me.

'Won't Zephyr die, like Mum?' I argue.

Aric shakes his head. 'He's your Balance. Zephyr's light is equal to yours and will feed from your light in return. You balance each other out, feeding each other in an unending cycle.'

'If Zephyr's light is equal to mine, how come he isn't draining everyone around him and leaving flowers all over the place?' I demand.

'He's a twin,' Aric answers. 'He and his sister balanced each other out.'

His reasoning makes sense, but if I'm Zephyr's balance now, who the hell is going to be Caligo's? I press the heel of my palms into my eyes, trying to ward off the headache forming. No wonder Zephyr struggled to find a mate. He needed someone with compatible light and Lumen Fae were almost culled from existence.

'If you knew I needed a Balance why'd you try mating me to Darrack?'

'I wanted to see you drain him,' Aric answers.

'What the hell?' I bark, dropping my hands to glare at him.

Aric rolls his eyes, like my outburst in uncalled for. 'Don't let his easy smiles and unending charm fool you, Primrose. The only thing Darrack cares about is gaining the crown. If you knew the things he's done, the females he's forced-'

'Back up! What?'

'Darrack has done more than murder and pillage to gain the power he seeks,' Aric says. 'I was considering his death when he approached me asking for your hand.'

'So you whored out your daughter for the kicks of watching Darrack get what he deserves?' I snap.

'Do you think your light would've let it get that far, Primrose? You're more powerful than I could be because you've found your Balance, and Darrack is no match for that.'

I hate that Aric's right. My darkness handled challenges without me realising I'd even been challenged. It would never let Darrack get close enough to force a mating. Zephyr was different, because my light craves him more than I need air. I huff at the wasted moaning about needing a choice, when I never really had one. I need Zephyr and he needs me, so we don't drain the life of those we love. Which begs the question of how Aric feeds his light.

'Lumen Fae weren't culled because of the danger they present if they never find their Balance,' Aric says, disrupting my train of thought. 'We were culled because of how powerful we become when we do.'

The banging on the wall stops and purple light weaves through it. Tingles shoot over my skin when Zephyr pushes through the darkness, expression furious. He stalks my way as I push to my feet then looks between my parents and me. Comprehension dawns on his face and he gapes at my mum. Then Aric. His gaze meets mine and I'd laugh at the shock on his face if I didn't feel mentally bruised.

242

'I love you, Primrose,' Mum says, drawing my attention. She's fading and my heart lodges in my throat. 'I'll be waiting for you in the next life.'

She fades away, and I stare at the space where she was standing. That's it? She tells me she loves me then expects me to just get on with the fact I've suffered losing her twice? I'm angry and ungrateful but can't help it. Most people don't get the chance I just had, but I'm really struggling to find the joy in this moment. All I feel is a yawning sense of loss.

'Take care of my daughter, Zephyr,' Aric orders. 'Your union will unite our people.' He turns to me. 'I'll watch over you from the next place, my flower,' he whispers.

Then he's gone, taking the answers I need with him.

A tear slides down my cheek, while strong arms wrap around me. Zephyr buries his face in my shoulder, body curling around mine, like he can't get close enough. I bury my face in his chest and soak in his nearness. It feels like he's the only thing holding me together.

'My mate,' he breathes.

My light wastes no time weaving tightly with his, taking greedy pulls of his essence. His armour is gone, my fingers curling into the soft fabric of his shirt. He's warm and solid, heart beating a steady rhythm in my ear. He's here. I'm here. It's going to be okay.

'Don't ever leave me again,' he orders.

'I'll try not to get killed again,' I promise then ask, 'Where's the knife?'

'What?'

'The knife,' I repeat. 'The one that-'

'Aric destroyed it,' Zephyr cuts in, understanding.

'Good,' I murmur, relieved a weapon powerful enough to kill Zephyr no longer exists.

Zephyr's arms tighten around me; his fierce need to protect me, and…love, infusing the bond between us. I look up at his face and he gazes down at me. Zephyr brushes his thumb over my lips then bends to press a kiss there. It's tender and drenched in emotion, seeping between my fractured parts.

'That was your mother?'

My breath mingles with his, hot and fragrant. 'She came to guide me home,' I say then shrug. 'But she got my father instead. Mum finally got her happy ending.'

'I think they both did,' Zephyr murmurs.

I breathe deep at his words, releasing the resentment I feel that my parents left me. Aric sacrificed himself so I'd get a second chance with Zephyr, and I'm more than grateful. I shouldn't begrudge my mum and dad the same opportunity.

'We should go out there,' I say, looking at the wall of midnight separating us from the rest of the valley.

'You know what will happen when we do?' Zephyr asks.

'I just became Queen of the Dark Realm,' I mutter, bitterness for Aric flaring because he knew this would happen.

Zephyr grins. 'You sound thrilled.'

'What the hell do I know about ruling, Zephyr? Hell, what do I even know about Dark Fae? I barely know enough about myself, let alone a whole realm of Dark Fae.'

'Dark Fae aren't that different from Light Fae,' he soothes. 'And I've been raised my whole life to rule, Primrose.'

His words are a balm to my impending panic attack. 'You're my mate.'

'You remembered?' he chuckles.

'That makes you King of the Dark Realm,' I answer.

'You've connected the dots,' he smirks.

I smack his chest at his sarcasm but I'm too relieved to put any real effort into it. Zephyr's here and I don't have to do this alone. He captures my hand against his chest, expression serious.

'You're not alone in this, Primrose,' he says, like he plucked the thought from head.

'Can you read my mind?'

'No, but I feel you in here,' he says patting the hand over mine on his chest.

I glance at my captured hand, feeling the strong beat of his heart beneath my palm. 'Okay,' I whisper.

I concentrate on the well of light in my middle. The wall melts around us, revealing a valley of fae surrounding us. Instead of fighting, they've formed a circle around where the wall used to be. Jewel-toned eyes watch Zephyr and me, the air pregnant with expectation.

'We're in the Dark Realm,' Zephyr murmurs, like I don't already know. He smirks at the death glare I give him. 'They're waiting for you to tell them Aric is dead and claim the throne.'

The words feel like ash in my mouth, as I push them through tight lips. 'My father has faded.'

Denlyr pushes to the front of the gathered fae, iridescent orange scales glinting on his body. His helm is retracted, dark hair and mocha skin matted with blood. His irises glow deep umber and his fangs seem longer than the last time we met.

'You claim your birth right, Heir?' he demands.

It's on the tip of my tongue to tell him no, but Zephyr gives me a meaningful stare and I sigh. 'I claim the throne, as is my birth right.'

Denlyr stalks up to me and drops to one knee, bowing his head with a fist to the grass. The fae behind him follow his lead, dropping onto one knee, heads bowed and fists to the ground.

'What are they doing?' I whisper to Zephyr.

'Swearing fealty to their queen,' he whispers back.

'Great,' I mutter feeling the enormity of what's happening press down on me. 'Any idea what I'm supposed to do next, Darling?'

Zephyr coughs on repressed laugher and takes my hand, lacing his fingers with mine. 'I am King of the Light Realm and mate of Queen Primrose,' he tells the gathered fae. 'Our mating joins our lives and our people. No more will there be Light and Dark Fae,' he decrees. 'From now on we're one people, and will be known simply as Fae.'

The heat of many eyes burn through me then, one by one, the fae in the valley stand. I watch in wonder, as each holds out their right arm. Orbs form in every upturned palm, drenching the valley in a rainbow of neon. As one, they lift their palms to the sky and the orbs float away. I crane my neck to watch the display then look at Zephyr when he strokes my arm. He's holding his hand out, amethyst orb sitting in his palm.

'It's our turn,' he says. 'Help me unify our people, Primrose.'

I look at my right palm, a ball of dark light forming. Zephyr smiles, before lifting his arm and I do the same. Our orbs circle each other on the way to the sky and I lean into Zephyr's side, watching them ascend.

'It's beautiful,' I murmur.

I glance to the gathering, as flashes of neon light the valley. The Dark Fae teleport away, while the Light turn back in the direction they came. A few minutes pass before I find myself alone with Zephyr.

'I didn't think I'd ever see this day,' he murmurs. 'It's difficult to believe it's real.'

'Bringing peace to the fae is kind of awesome,' I agree.

'No,' he answers looking down at me. 'I lost hope of ever finding you, Primrose.' He cups my cheek. 'You've saved me from a life of loneliness.'

Tears blur my vision and I hide my face against his shoulder. 'You're doing a good job of making me like you,' I mutter.

'Perhaps one day I'll entice you to love me,' he whispers.

My gaze snaps to his and I see vulnerability there. It's not a side he lets many see, but he's showing me, and I think I love him a little more for it.

'I've never believed it possible to fall in love in a short amount of time, Zephyr,' I say and watch the hope die in his eyes. 'But, despite the fact you kidnapped me and tried to force me to mate you, I find myself in love with your arrogant, entitled backside.'

'You – What?'

I huff a breath and smile. 'I love you.'

He gazes down at me, like he can't decipher the words I'm speaking. I suck in a breath when his lips meet mine, Zephyr moving so fast I don't see it coming. His hands are in my hair, fingers weaving through the strands. I wrap my arms around his neck and kiss him back. The love I feel is new and fragile, but has the potential to grow into something wonderful.

Light shines behind my eyelids, turning them pink. I open them to find Zephyr's teleported us to my room in the Dark Realm. He picks me up without breaking the kiss and carries me to the bed.

'My Anya,' he murmurs.

'You've called me that before, but I don't know what it means,' I say.

'It's old Fae, meaning 'most treasured star,' he answers.

'You thought I knew what it meant when you met me.'

He nods. 'And then you ran.'

A sliver of pain echoes through his words and I pull him in for another kiss. Something cracks wide open inside at his tenderness. The warmth of his love fills me, drenching my body in heat. The wild entity in my centre flows free, reaching for Zephyr, and he groans. The kiss becomes urgent and my clothes feel restrictive. I claw at his clothes in response.

'Get naked, Zephyr.'

Zephyr's laughter rumbles through our kiss, before his clothes blink away. I press my fingers to his mouth, putting a barrier between us while I concentrate on the task at hand. Tingles skitter over my body, before the heat of Zephyr's skin meets mine.

'You've learnt something important,' he mumbles against my hand, eyes sparkling with amusement.

'I learned how to fly, too,' I tell him, moving my hand from his mouth then frown. 'Well, just the basics.'

'Your father taught you?' he guesses. 'I can teach you the rest.'

'Actually, Darrack taught me,' I answer, brain veering to something very important I should be doing, like finding Darrack before he has chance to hurt somebody else.

Zephyr growls. 'Darrack touched you?'

I push against him 'Let me up, we need to find him.' He ignores my attempts to push him off, so I huff and meet his glare. 'Zephyr, Aric admitted Darrack is a monster and our mating was supposed to result in his death. Now get the hell off me so we can stop him.

'Your father used you?' The disgust in Zephyr's tone makes me smile. He's on my side, even in this. 'It's no smiling matter, Primrose.'

'I know, I'm just happy you're here,' I admit.

He smiles and tucks a length of hair behind my ear. 'I'll always be here for you.'

I sigh. 'You make me feel so stupid.'

His smile fades. 'Why?'

'Because I could've had this sooner and saved so much heartache. If I hadn't run-'

'I should've stayed with you after I marked you,' he cuts in. 'I would've seen you change from human to fae and known you had no knowledge of the fae.' He strokes my face with a fingertip. 'I would've stayed with you during your change, Primrose.'

'There was nothing you could've done.'

'I could've held your hand, so you would've known someone was with you,' he argues.

'I'll forgive you for leaving me, if you forgive me for running from you,' I say.

'It's a good place to start,' he answers then presses another kiss to my lips.

Zephyr pulls away before I turn to liquid and melt through the bed. His clothes are back as he pushes from me and groans eyes raking my nakedness. I smirk and concentrate on materialising myself something to wear. I glance down at the jeans and top as I stand, making sure everything is covered, before taking Zephyr's hand. His fingers curl around mine and it feels like home.

CHAPTER 21

'What do you mean you can't find him?' I demand, eyes bleeding to black.

Denlyr doesn't flinch at my loss of temper, for which I give him brownie points. Everybody else does and because I have a short temper, it's getting old. The male challenged me before he knew I was heir to the throne, but I don't doubt his loyalty to the crown. I *feel* it, even now in the face of my upset.

Zephyr's amusement tickles my back, from where he sits behind me on one of the ridiculous thrones. The big, ornate chairs are the most uncomfortable things, but Zephyr's lounging on one like it's made of nimbus cloud. I've come to realise he's the calm to my storm. Things that make me want to suffer a rage blackout make him laugh, but then he's had millennia to work through his anger issues. He finds my outbursts amusing, which sometimes helps calm me and at others makes me want to strangle him.

'He was last seen before the battle,' Denylr answers. 'His domicile is empty and the mirrors have been destroyed, seemingly in a fit of rage.'

'Explain,' Zephyr says sitting up.

Denlyr's gaze shifts to Zephyr. 'The mirrors are in splinters on the floor. Perhaps because the seals were still intact, rendering them useless.'

'Have you checked the light pool?' Zephyr asks. 'After all, it's how I breached this realm when the portals were sealed.'

Denlyr's eyebrow ticks and I hide a smile. That ticking eyebrow only happens when he's hiding the fury I feel building inside him. It's not aimed at Zephyr, but at Denlyr himself. He hates the fact Zephyr got past his security measures, and it's taken Zephyr's explanation to figure out how.

'I'll go there myself,' Denlyr grits out then disappears in a flash of orange light. He's back less than thirty seconds later. 'Darrack's light signature is present in the chamber housing the light pool,' he growls.

'So he's gone,' I sigh beyond frustrated.

'We'll find him,' Denlyr promises.

I study his furious gaze, soaking in the tsunami of emotion pulsing from him. 'You want the right to kill him,' I murmur.

Denlyr's eyes blaze bright orange. 'One of his crimes involved my sister,' he answers rage drenching his tone.

Midnight creeps over my skin in response, darkness swelling inside in reaction to my outrage. The wild being in my centre is baying for blood.

'If you find him, you have my permission to kill him,' I say.

The words feel thick on my tongue. I'm condemning someone to death, and Denlyr stares at me like I've gifted him the moon.

'Thank you,' he breathes then flashes from the room.

I turn back to Zephyr feeling a hundred years old. I've been queen a matter of days and already sentenced one of my subjects to death. But I've seen the list of crimes Aric compiled against Darrack. Aric had no evidence to prove Darrack guilty, until the day of our supposed mating and immediately sentenced him to death. It would've happened, if I hadn't disappeared into thin air and ruined the plan. It's my fault Darrack got away, and I'll never forgive myself if he hurts another female.

'Come on,' I tell Zephyr and hold out my hand.

He pushes from the throne. 'Where are we going?'

'I've got something to show you,' I say, pulling him into the room behind the thrones.

Malak, who is like my shadow since becoming queen, closes the doors behind us and I take Zephyr to the mirrored wall. I press my palm to the glass and open a doorway to the Light Realm. Zephyr follows without question then stumbles when he sees Alissa across the room. He opens his mouth then closes it again, as if he doesn't know what to say.

'Hello, Zephyr,' Alissa murmurs.

Zephyr drops my hand and stalks over to his mum. He gazes down at her, his confusion misting the room. Then he pulls her into a fierce hug and wonder laces his confusion.

'I don't understand,' he says then looks back to me. 'You knew she was alive?'

'Not until the Dark Realm portals opened earlier and Harlan stopped by,' I answer.

'Harlan?'

'My mate,' Alissa says.

Zephyr's gaze snaps back to her. 'Your mate?'

Alissa sighs at his incredulous tone. 'Oric faded without me, Zephyr. What does that tell you about the state of our bond?'

Zephyr's expression softens. 'You finally escaped him,' he whispers then shakes his head. 'But who in the runes is Harlan?'

'I am,' Harlan says, materialising beside Alissa in a cloud of green glitter.

He takes Alissa's hand and offers her a tender smile. Anyone with eyes can see they're in love.

'I don't understand,' Zephyr scoffs.

Alissa steps forward. 'Harlan and I were in love when your father mated me, Zephyr. Harlan came to find me when he discovered Oric faded before me.'

'Then why mate my father?' Zephyr asks, though I *feel* he already knows the answer.

'I didn't...you're father didn't like the word 'no', Zephyr,' she says in a quiet voice, her pain a heavy fog around us.

My eyes go wide at the sensation. It's the first time I've felt emotion from Alissa and it's disorientating.

'I want to hear you say it,' Zephyr growls.

'Zephyr-'

'Goddess be damned!' Zephyr barks. 'Do you think I never knew the reason you went everywhere with an entourage of human females?'

I realise for the first time Alissa is without her entourage. I glance around the room to make sure they're not huddled in a corner, but they're nowhere to be seen. I always assumed the frightened women were her prisoners, but I get the feeling the reason for their being here is worse.

'Someone had to protect them from him,' she snaps back.

'From my father,' Zephyr growls.

Bile creeps up my throat when I realise what they're saying. There were more than forty females in Alissa's entourage and it fills my stomach with ice. Humans don't live as long as fae, so how many did Oric abuse over the years? The fear on their faces plays like a sick video through my mind. Those women stuck close to Alissa for protection from Oric. I remember being curt with them, playing on their fear to get an outfit to hide my wing markings, and shame blasts through me.

'He only forced me once, on the night of our mating,' Alissa murmurs drawing my focus back to her. 'Then my light was bound to his and I was strong enough to resist him.' She swallows hard, guilt pulsing from her. 'But Oric found other ways of sating his appetites.'

'Caligo and I weren't conceived the night you bonded,' Zephyr argues.

'You think the realm would be happy without an heir?' Alissa asks. 'I did that for my people, not Oric. I mated a monster, and when you kidnapped Primrose I thought-' Alissa's gaze slides to me and her eyes brim with tears. 'You'll never know the relief I feel that you gave her the choice, Zephyr.'

'I promised I'd never force her,' Zephyr breathes and goes to Alissa, pulling her from Harlan's hold to wrap her in a hug. 'No matter if we missed the equinox, I'm not my father. I'm not like the monster you mated, Mother.'

Alissa sniffs and returns his hug. 'I know.'

'Where are they now?' I ask. 'The human women,' I clarify when three sets of eyes swing my way.

'The youngest have returned to their home realms,' Alissa answers. 'But time passes differently within different realm spaces, and it's too late for many of the older women. The lives they were stolen from no longer exist; the people and family they knew dead.' Alissa sighs. 'I've provided them with homes in the Light Realm and taken time to make sure they're settled.'

'I'd like to visit with them, if that's okay?'

Alissa smiles. 'I think they'd like that, though you're queen and can do as you wish.'

I scratch the back of my neck. I'd been delighted when Harlan turned up, telling me Alissa was still alive. I was happy for them, and assumed it meant I wouldn't have to help rule the Light Realm because he and Alissa would do it. How wrong I'd been. Alissa had already passed the crown to Zephyr and he couldn't give it back, even if he wanted to.

Yay for me.

'Right,' I mutter. 'Queen.'

Alissa chuckles and pulls away from Zephyr. She shocks the hell out of me when she pulls me into a fierce hug. I'm not a hugger, and I certainly never pegged her as one. It takes a few seconds to release the tenseness from my muscles and hug her back. Warmth washes through me and I close my eyes, soaking in the sensation.

'You'll make a wonderful queen, Primrose,' Alissa says.

I *feel* the honesty of her statement and hug her a little harder. The more I learn about her, the more I realise she's not the cold, merciless female I assumed she was. I meet Zephyr's gaze over Alissa's shoulder and he smiles at me. He's standing with Harlan, the tension from earlier gone from his shoulders.

'Mother!' Caligo squeals from the doorway.

I let Alissa go, just as Caligo teleports beside us and pulls her into a crushing hug. They cling to each other, like they can't quite believe they're getting the chance, and tears sting my eyes. Caligo asks identical questions to Zephyr, her eyes spilling tears as Alissa gives the answers.

'I'm glad he's dead,' Caligo states when Alissa is done.

'How is your mate?' Alissa asks deftly changing the subject.

Caligo's face lightens. 'He's adjusting,' she answers then grins like whatever 'adjusting' he's doing pleases the hell out of her.

'You're mated?' I ask. 'When did that happen?'

'During the equinox, silly,' she answers like it's a stupid question.

Relief floods me. Caligo has found her Balance, meaning she won't start draining the life of those around her.

'I didn't know you were here, or I would've brought him,' she adds. 'Wait here.'

She pops from the room and a few minutes pass, where Zephyr and Harlan become acquainted.

'Thank you for sending Harlan to me, Primrose,' Alissa says. 'You don't know what it means to me.'

'I only told him what you told me.' I shrug. 'It's strange how everything is happening the way it is. Harlan wouldn't have known to come if I hadn't been kidnapped by Aric. Caligo's found a mate to balance her, just as her balance with Zephyr was taken by me. A lot of coincidences seem to be happening.'

'It's the way the universe works,' Alissa agrees. 'There are many layers woven together, and we're the threads that bind it.'

Okay then.

I'm not even going to pretend to understand what she's talking about. I'm trying my best not to worry about the convenience of it all. Usually when something works out this well, something happens to even the odds. The fact Darrack escaped isn't convenient and, in a weird way, settles something inside me. Caligo pops back into the room before I can dwell on it. There's a blond male with her, and my mouth drops open when they turn our way.

'Drew?' I'm running before it registers I'm moving. 'Drew!'

My body slams into his and my arms wrap tightly around his middle. I'm almost crushing him but don't care. Tears soak his tunic as he awkwardly pats my back. I feel his confusion, as the tense lines of his body register in my brain. I pull away enough to look up at his face then grow as tense as he is. A second passes then I push away. He could be Drew's twin, but he's definitely *not* Drew.

'I'm sorry,' I sniff and wipe tears from my eyes.

Caligo is snarling, amethyst eyes ablaze as she glares at me. Zephyr's holding her wrist, and there's an essence orb gripped tight in her right hand.

'Mine,' she hisses, baring dainty fangs at me.

'You almost committed treason,' Zephyr growls in her ear.

She glances between the orb and me, as if just realising it's there. Her fingers release and the orb fizzles away. She looks at me like I'm about to rain fire on her from above and I sigh.

'My Queen,' she whispers.

I think back to when Denlyr threatened my life and Aric said it gave me the right to take his. My shoulders slump at the fact she thinks I'd do that to her. Then I remember Caligo doesn't know me yet, and she was raised around a bunch of fae. They might look refined as a people but they've all got a savage living in their middle. I can attest to that, being that I have one of my own.

'Oh, relax,' I growl in frustration. 'I'm not going to kill you for getting pissed that I hugged your mate, Caligo. For the record, I thought he was someone else, so you can rein in the fury against me.'

Caligo's fear turns to disbelief, irking me a little more, and I see Zephyr grinning from the corner of my eye. At least *he* knows me enough to know I wouldn't kill her or be interested in her mate. Zephyr's amused gaze tracks to Caligo's mate, and his eyes widen.

'I see the resemblance,' he mutters.

'Does anyone want to explain what's going on,' the blond asks in an American accent. He looks at Zephyr and says, 'hey, Zee can you let go of my mate now? She's lost the lunatic look in her eyes and the blonde chick said she's forgiven.'

Zephyr releases Caligo and she scowls at him while rubbing her wrist. 'I'm sorry I reacted that way,' she tells me. 'I just saw you hugging my mate and felt a wave of love from you.'

'You felt it?'

She nods. 'You're Lumen too, aren't you? Female Lumen can sense the emotions of those around them.'

Well that answers why Zephyr never seems to feel what I can. The fact Caligo knows about Lumen Fae sends a thrum of excitement down my spine. I wasn't looking forward to picking through the archives in Aric's palace, and hopefully I won't have to now.

'I felt it,' I answer. 'And I felt love for your mate because I thought he was my friend Drew.'

My heart clenches at the thought of Drew. The Trackers haven't found him yet, and the more time that passes the dimmer my hope of finding him alive becomes. Surely if he was alive he would've found his way back to me. He obviously knew enough about fae to open a doorway once his light was activated, so surely he'd know how to at least get a message to me.

Unless he doesn't want to be found.

The thought hits me like a slap to the face. Drew's good at running away when life gets too much, and the last time we met my life was steeped in drama.

'It doesn't upset you that your mate loves another?' Caligo asks Zephyr, drawing my focus.

'Blake Frost looks almost identical to Primrose's best human friend,' Zephyr answers. 'What she feels for him is akin to the love I feel for you, as my sister.'

'Blake Frost?' I whisper.

The American – Blake, holds his hand out to me in greeting. 'Blake Frost, Caligo's Halfling mate.'

I take his offered hand, while the fae watch us shake in fascination. I don't think they've seen a handshake because they all stare at our joined hands with unabashed curiosity.

'Primrose Finley,' I grin. 'Zephyr's Halfling mate and Queen of the Fae.' I release his hand. 'Sorry for crying all over you like that. Drew is my best friend and when I saw you I thought-' I cut myself off and look at Zephyr. 'Drew's last name is Frost, and he looks like Blake's long lost twin. You don't think Drew could be-?'

'His brother?' Zephyr murmurs, finishing my thought.

His expression is as incredulous as mine, before his gaze slides to Caligo.

'Uncle Jack,' she whispers.

Zephyr nods. 'It's got to be him. He carries the sapphire light and has a thing for human females.'

'Uncle Jack?' I butt in then it hits me and I start laughing. 'Are you kidding?'

'What?' Blake asks still not getting it.

I take pity on him. 'They're saying your fae father's name is Jack!'

'Why is that funny?' he demands.

I stop laughing and wipe a tear from my eye. 'Your surname is Frost and so is Drew's,' I spell out. 'Your dad is Jack Frost.' My grin fades and I scrunch my nose up, looking at Zephyr. 'If Jack's your uncle and Caligo has mated Blake-'

'He's not actually our uncle,' Caligo says in understanding. 'He's just very old and has no heirs, so everyone calls him Uncle Jack.'

'No heirs that he knows of,' I correct. 'I'm counting two and-' my gaze whips back to Blake and the sapphire glow of his irises. 'Make that a possible three,' I mutter.

Zephyr's eyes are full of intrigue and I supress a snort. 'Who?'

'Amber was glowing sapphire,' I say.

'Amber?' Caligo asks.

'Lucas found his mate and she's half fae,' Zephyr answers.

'Lucas, Alpha of-'

'The very same,' Zephyr says then mumbles something about a Halfling epidemic.

'Jack always was one for flouting the rules,' Alissa mumbles.

'I've got a sister?' Blake asks, excited.

Everyone looks his way and I remind him about Drew. 'And a brother.'

'I already have a brother,' he says then shakes his head, answering my question before I can ask it. 'We have different dads.'

'Well, now you have two,' I tell him, feeling defensive of Drew. I shake my head still looking at Blake. 'There might even be more of you.'

'That's likely,' Zephyr agrees, 'though, Halflings remain human unless their light is activated.'

I think of Zephyr's essence orb hitting Drew in the shoulder. Aric said something like that would kill a human, but Drew wasn't dead when the doorway shut between us. And he'd *opened* a doorway, meaning he had light inside of him.

'You must've activated Drew's light when you hit him with that orb, Zephyr. He could still be alive,' I murmur not knowing how to feel about it.

Is he dead, or alive and avoiding me? Why would he let me grieve him if he's still alive? My chest aches at both possibilities and it's difficult to breathe. I blink fast to hold back tears and focus on Zephyr.

He gives a reluctant nod. 'If Drew survived the transformation into fae,' he says, like he hates to be the one to remind me how low the odds are.

My heart squeezes in my chest and I close my eyes to hide the tears I can't hold back. The conversation dies around me and I feel the concern of everyone in the room turn my way. The weight of their stares lay heavy on my shoulders, and I wish for just a few minutes alone.

Like a miracle their emotions disappear, and I open my eyes to find myself in Zephyr's domicile. Holy crap, did I just teleport? I haven't been in Zephyr's home since the night of the equinox, and I stare at the ransacked space. It's obvious he was frantic when he returned to find me gone, and guilt slashes my insides. The guilt builds when I think of Aunt Katherine and Uncle David. I've been gone a long time, leaving nothing but a scribbled note for them to find.

I go the mirror in the corner of the bedroom, which is miraculously whole again, even after Zephyr blasted it to escape my father. I think of the mended mirror in Anima's bedroom and wonder if Zephyr fixed that one too. I press my palm to the glass and open a portal. Mum's bedroom in the Realm of Man comes into view and I step inside. I glance over my shoulder to watch the doorway close then inhale the familiar scents of Mum and home. It doesn't make me sad anymore, not since seeing how happy Mum is. And she has Aric, so they have each other.

I go downstairs and turn on the TV. The menu bar tells me the date and time, and I just stare. I know time passes faster here compared to the fae realms, but I've been gone longer than I thought and it's hard to wrap my head around. I leave the TV running and go make coffee, the mindless task centring my focus. Hands shaking, I lift the steaming mug to my lips. The bitter taste helps soothe me and I close my eyes to appreciate the flavour. Coffee isn't something the fae have embraced. In fact, not many of them know what it is, which I think contributed to some of my mood swings in the Dark Realm.

I sigh and sit at the table. It feels surreal to be back in the cottage. It's been my home for as long as I can remember. My mum inherited it from her parents and I inherited it from her, so I've lived here my whole life. But it doesn't feel like home anymore. There's something missing and it isn't Mum. There's a niggling sensation in my stomach, a yearning for something I can't identify.

'Primrose?'

I turn in my chair to see Zephyr standing in the kitchen doorway. His uncertainty permeates the space between us, so I offer him a smile. Relief floods me that he's here, and the hollow in my chest closes. The itch niggling my insides settles, like he's rubbing a balm over my soul.

'How'd you find me?'

He shrugs. 'There are few places you've been to in the Light Realm. Your fragrance was strongest in my domicile and I reopened the last doorway in the mirror,' he tells me then steps closer. 'Why did you leave?'

Something occurs to me. 'I thought that mirror only went where you wanted it to go.'

He shrugs. 'Our lights are tied now, Primrose. We're one.'

Okay then.

'I came to see my aunt.' I drop my gaze and trace the grain in the wooden table. 'I guess I just needed a few minutes alone, before I go to find her.'

'I can leave,' he offers.

I shake my head and meet his gaze. 'I don't want you to go.'

Zephyr closes the space between us then crouches at my feet to look up into my face. 'You're worried,' he murmurs.

'What do I tell her?'

'Your aunt?'

I nod. 'I can't be the queen of two realms and live in this realm, Zephyr. And I can't tell Katherine the reasons I'm leaving.'

'Why not?' he asks.

'I, well-' I shake my head. 'Isn't telling her against the rules?'

'You're Queen of the Fae, Primrose. You can do as you wish.'

'Oh,' I murmur thinking of Katherine's reaction if I tell her the truth. The way she worries about me has always been borderline obsessive. I'm not sure she'd cope learning everything I've been through recently. 'I'm not sure telling Katherine is a good idea, Zephyr.'

'You're not sure telling me *what* is a good idea?' Katherine asks from the kitchen doorway.

David is standing right behind her, his hands on her waist, like he's holding her upright. She's got a few silver hairs she didn't have the last time I saw her, and hurt radiates from her in waves. Zephyr and I were so focused on each other that neither of us heard them come in. Some king and queen we are, when two humans can sneak up on us unawares. Saying that, my darkness knows they're not a threat, and I rely on it to warn me of danger.

'Tell me what?' she repeats. 'And who the hell is that?' she asks gesturing to Zephyr.

Zephyr has his back to them, still crouching on the floor before me. I look down to meet his gaze and my eyebrows inch toward my hairline. He looks decidedly less fae. His ears are rounded, like mine, and his irises are a rich shade of brown. He's still inhumanly handsome, but he'd fit into human society with ease. He squeezes my hand and gives me a reassuring smile, before pushing to his feet and turning to face my aunt and uncle. Katherine sucks in a quiet breath and her cheeks turn pink. She might be married but she's not blind to his beauty.

'I'm Zephyr,' he says surprising me by holding his hand out for a handshake.

Seems he's been paying more attention than I realised. Fae don't shake hands because it's considered rude to physically touch another's mate, probably because it aggravates the wild creature in our middle. But I was raised in a different culture, and my wildness accepts simple contacts like this for what they are.

'Hello,' Katherine murmurs tone wary.

'Nice to meet you?' David says, confusion drenching his features.

Katherine looks at me. 'Primrose, what the hell is going on?'

'I got married,' I blurt, saying the first thing that comes to mind.

It's not a lie. Bonding with Zephyr is the fae version of getting married. Katherine's mouth drops open and she stares at me in utter shock. I feel her panic attack building to a crescendo, before she manages to rein it in. If hearing I got married has her teetering on the edge of a breakdown then there's no way I'm telling her any of the fae stuff.

'To him?' she breathes in disbelief, pointing at Zephyr.

'Is that so hard to believe?' I ask sounding as offended as I feel. 'I know he's out of my league, but you don't have to be so obvious.'

She snaps from her daze and shakes her head. 'I didn't mean it like that, Prim. I just…You disappear and come back married? It's only been six weeks.'

I shrug and give her what she needs to hear. 'He's my soul mate.'

I don't know if Zephyr's my soul mate. We need each other to balance, and my insides light up when I see him, but our love is new. I know anything less than him being my soul mate won't be good enough for Katherine though, so I roll with it.

'And you know that, after a month?' she scoffs.

I sigh and soften my tone, knowing her defensive attitude is born of love. 'I love him and he makes me happy. What more could I want from life, Aunt Kat?'

Katherine turns her gaze back to Zephyr. 'And you? Do you love her?' she demands.

'Primrose is my everything,' he answers sending threads of warmth through my heart.

'But do you love her?' Katherine presses.

'I love her very much,' he answers then meets my gaze. 'I know our love is new and fragile,' he murmurs, like he's been stealing my thoughts and feels the need to reassure me. 'It can be terrifying to stand on the precipice of something wonderful, with the knowledge it can grow into something unbreakable,' he tells me. 'But a terrifying moment can be the start of something beautiful, and I want to be the one to create it with you.'

Katherine's lips curve into a wobbly smile. She wipes a tear from her cheek and nods her head. She takes a deep breath then lets it go, before coming to wrap me in a hug.

'I love you, Primrose,' she whispers. 'Don't ever scare me like that again,' she chastises.

'I love you too,' I whisper back then, 'How'd you know I was here?'

'Jenny saw your light on and phoned me.'

I roll my eyes at one of the pitfalls of village life. Everybody knows everybody else's business.

I sigh and let Katherine go. 'I came back because I was coming to see you,' I say. 'It's not my fault the nosey neighbours beat me to it.'

Her smile falters as she studies my expression. 'You're leaving, aren't you?'

How does she do that? Katherine has always been too good at reading me and it can be down right annoying. Anyone would think she was the Lumen Fae in the room with how accurate she can be. Emotion floods around me: fear and hurt and a little bit of grief. When Katherine loves it's with a fierceness that steals my breath. It's why she worries about her family to the point of suffocation.

'This village isn't my home anymore, Aunt Kat,' I murmur sliding a look to Zephyr. 'There are things I need to do and places I want to see.'

'Are you selling the cottage?' she asks.

'Of course not! This place is mine and I'll come stay sometimes, but I don't belong here anymore.' *I belong with Zephyr.* I take her hand. 'You've been there for me since the day Mum checked out to pine over my father. You were the mum I needed when she struggled to cope, and I love you more than I have words to say. But you have to let me go, Katherine. You have to let me live my life.'

She sniffs back tears and nods her head, unable to speak for a moment. Uncle David comes to stand behind her and puts his hands on her shoulders in a show of support. He gives me an encouraging smile and I feel his approval wash through me.

'You'll definitely come back to visit?' Katherine sniffs.

'I'll even bring you the tacky souvenirs you love so much,' I promise.

She laughs through her tears and pulls me into a rib-crushing hug. 'I've missed you.'

I rub soothing circles into her back. 'I'm sorry I caused you so much stress,' I say as she lets go. 'And I promise I'll phone all the time and pop in to visit when I can.'

'Okay,' she sighs and blows out a breath, 'enough tears. Let's order Chinese and open the wine in your fridge. We can get to know Zephyr before you leave, which will be when?' she murmurs.

'First, how the hell do you know I have wine in my fridge?' I ask.

'Somebody had to clean the spoiled food from your fridge,' Katherine chastises. 'You're just lucky the wine is still there. I nearly passed out from the stench the first time I opened the fridge door.'

I cringe at the thought glad Katherine was here to deal with it. 'Did I mention how much I love you?'

She smirks. 'It's never a hardship to hear, but you didn't answer my question. How long are you staying?'

'Until tomorrow morning,' I answer. 'But I'll be back in a few weeks,' I add when her eyes well with tears.

She nods. 'I can deal with that.'

I turn to the house phone before she can see my eyes roll. If only she knew the crap I had to deal with as Queen of the Fae. I dread to think what Katherine would've been like in my situation. She probably would've exploded into a cloud of terrified glitter the moment

Zephyr appeared in the garden. I snort and fish a takeout menu from the kitchen draw, while Katherine takes the wine from the fridge and collects four glasses. Zephyr stands at my side, watching while I dial the phone. I've had takeout with Katherine and David so many times I don't need to ask what they want, and the normalcy of the situation soothes me in a way I desperately needed.

Zephyr puts an arm around my shoulder and leans in close, until his lips rest close to my ear. 'You can order a Chinese person to eat?' he murmurs.

I choke on my laugher and shake my head when David looks my way. Katherine is busy pulling dishes from the cupboard in the corner and cutlery from the draw. I meet Zephyr's gaze and he's grinning down at me. He strokes a finger down my face then uses it to tuck a length of hair behind my ear. My heart skips a beat and for the first time in my life I feel complete. Violet light flashes in a corona around his pupils, before fading back to rich brown, betraying the heat I feel building between us.

'Alright you two, break it up or Katherine will be drunk before the Chinese food gets here,' David says, pulling us from our moment.

I chuckle, when understanding that we're not eating a Chinese *person* registers on Zephyr's face. Our life together is going to be fun.

CHAPTER 22

'Will you shut up?' I whisper-hiss.

Zephyr's amused gaze meets mine, burning bright violet in the darkened room. My heart beats a little faster. I don't think I'll ever get used to how beautiful he is, or the fact he's mine. His scent perfumes the air around us and I inhale a deep breath. My gums tingle and I wince, licking across my front teeth where the pain is most intense.

'I just don't understand it,' he says, drawing my attention back to him. 'Why would you want to watch something that isn't real?'

I sigh and pause the film. We're in the front room of the cottage, snuggled together on the sofa, trying to watch a movie. Except, Zephyr doesn't understand the concept, so we haven't made it past the first fifteen minutes. I can't decide if I want to strangle him or just turn the film off and go see Katherine. This week's Date Night isn't going well. We get one night a week (Realm of Man Time) to spend in the cottage away from the politics of running two fae kingdoms. We're not gone long in fae terms because time passes so quickly here compared to there, so it works out.

'It's like reading a story,' I tell Zephyr. 'Except, instead of reading a book, you watch the events play out on screen.'

'And what's this story about?' Zephyr asks.

'You're supposed to watch it and find out,' I answer.

'But how do you know you want to watch it if you have no idea of the genre?'

'It's a romance,' I snap, temper flaring. 'One I've been dying to see and you're ruining.'

Zephyr chuckles at my anger and his desire mists around us. I roll my eyes and start the movie playing again, mystified at why he finds my outbursts so sexy. I frown when my gums twinge with pain again, wondering if there's a fae version of the dentist.

'Now I'm more confused,' Zephyr says.

I huff and pause the film, slapping the remote onto the arm of the sofa, before turning my attention to him. 'Why?'

'I can't understand why you'd rather watch a pretend romance, when we're alone and able to act out our own.'

My frustration turns to lava-hot need, and my eyes tingle in a way that tells me they're completely black. Zephyr growls in appreciation, but I grow distracted by the pain in my gums. Worry pushes the desire from Zephyr's gaze and he sits up, alert.

'What's wrong?'

'It's-' I hiss as pain radiates through my jaw and I grit my teeth.

'Primrose!' Zephyr shouts and is suddenly bent over me, cradling my face between his palms. 'My Starlight,' he breathes, panic drenching his tone.

I'm in agony for what feels like hours but must only be minutes. The coppery taste of blood fills my mouth, coating my tongue. Then the agony fades to a bearable ache and I suck in a few breaths.

'I'm okay,' I pant, rubbing my hand against Zephyr's arm to soothe the raw panic swirling around us.

Onyx filigree creeps over Zephyr's hands and up over his wrists, like it's holding him to me. It leeches some of his panic and the hard lines of worry ease from his face.

'Stop that,' he chastises when he realises what I'm doing.

'No.'

He smirks at my sass and I smirk back. My panting fades and my heart returns to a steady rhythm. My gums are a little sore but the ache has gone, and I swipe my tongue over my teeth to reassure myself they're still intact.

'Holy crap,' I hiss when I reach the first incisor on my top row of teeth.

'What?' Zephyr demands panic roaring back. 'What is it?'

I ignore him, exploring the elongated razor edge of my incisor with my tongue. I move along to its twin on my upper teeth, before poking at the two, shorter but equally sharp incisors along my bottom teeth. I stare at Zephyr in disbelief then close my eyes and teleport upstairs to the bathroom. I hear his shout of annoyance but I'm too busy staring into the bathroom mirror. My incisors have grown longer and sharper, becoming more fae-like and giving me the feral appearance I associate with fae. Blood stains my lips, adding to the effect.

'You've got to be kidding me,' I growl, wondering how the hell I'm going to hide this from Katherine and David.

Maybe if I don't grin ever again-

Zephyr pops into the bathroom behind a flash of purple light. 'Primrose, what in the runes is-' He stops speaking when he sees my grimacing reflection.

Zephyr grabs my shoulder and spins me to face him. He bends to bring his face level with mine, and stares avidly at my teeth. His breathing grows heavy and his eyes burn an electric shade of purple. I squeak when he grabs me and crushes his lips to mine. Our teeth clash and I wince at the dull ache still present in my gums. Zephyr's fingers weave into my hair, holding me in place while he devours my mouth.

The room lights with amethyst and I find myself naked on my bed, looking up at Zephyr's hungry gaze. It's another thing I'm learning about fae. Wings are sexy and apparently so are fangs. It's a standard of beauty I'm yet to appreciate. When I think about it less, and let the wild entity inside me take control, I can see the appeal in the feral aspects of the fae. But I was raised with human ideals and it's difficult to let my fae side out.

'You like me with sharp teeth,' I murmur.

Zephyr grins, displaying an impressive set of incisors both top and bottom. His teeth have lengthened and grown sharper, something I've seen happen when he's angry and must be a form of defence. But he's not angry now, and I think back to the time he bit me during the first time we were intimate. My gaze drops to where his shoulder meets his neck and I swallow against the strong urge to bite him back. I meet his gaze and his grin tips higher, like he knows my thoughts. His grin is wolfish, and the wild thing in my centre snarls in satisfaction. I stroke my fingers through the silky mass of his dark hair. Zephyr turns his face into my wrist and inhales the scent at my pulse point, a growl sounding in his throat.

'I *love* your sharper teeth,' he murmurs then kisses my lips.

I frown, insecurities flaring. 'Do you like me better, now I look more fae?'

He matches my frown. 'You're beautiful, Primrose.'

I look away. 'Not as beautiful as you,' I say. 'Even with sharp teeth, I'll never look like if I'd been born a full-blooded fae,' I tell him admitting one of my main hang-ups about our relationship. 'I'll always be shorter with a few more curves, and I haven't got pointy ears. I can't say I even want them. They suit fae, with their elongated, noble features. But I look more like my mother than my father, so they'd probably just look stupid on me.'

Zephyr cups my cheek and guides my face back to his. 'Do you find me less attractive because my ears are pointed?' he asks.

'I just told you you're beautiful,' I scoff.

'Then why would you think such a thing of me?' he counters. He presses a tender kiss to my lips. 'I love your smile,' he whispers then kisses my neck. I moan, goose bumps breaking out over my skin. 'I love the sound of your laugh and your explosive temper,' he breathes, moving lower, trailing kisses down my body. 'I adore the curves of your body. He traces the curve of my hip with a fingertip and I light up from the inside. 'Yes, you're smaller than most fae females, but we fit together, do we not?'

He fits himself against me, punctuating his point by joining us together. My toes curl at the sensation and I grip the bedspread.

'You make a good point,' I moan.

Delicious heat shivers over my skin, while midnight flames lick at Zephyr. They curl around him, caressing the lines of his body and drawing him close. His bronze skin glitters with amethyst light, contrasting to the dark lines I've wrapped around him. The light pulses with the rhythm he sets and a delectable ache starts building in my centre.

Zephyr chuckles and gazes at me with an intensity that makes my heart squeeze. 'I'll never stop being dazzled by your dark starlight.' He cups my face. 'My Anya.'

'You make me believe in soul mates,' I whisper.

His eyes blaze brighter. 'You finally accept you're my soul mate?'

I curl my leg around his hip, forcing him closer still. 'Sorry it took me so long.'

I love the way we can talk this way, when making love. I've never felt more comfortable with anyone in my life, and if that doesn't scream 'soul mate' then I don't know what does. Forget the fact we need each other to balance. Zephyr makes me feel like a better person. He makes me feel whole.

'You *are* slow when it comes to this kind of thing,' he tells me.

'Hey!' I grumble and dodge his next kiss, turning my face to stare at the wall.

'We've plenty of time for me to educate you on such things,' he says, amusement drenching his tone.

'Because you're the expert on love?' I mutter.

'I know I love you,' he answers, 'what else is there?'

Warm, honeyed emotion wraps around me from Zephyr, and I turn my face back to his. His love seeps through my flesh and collides with the increasing ache in my centre. I sink my teeth into his shoulder and intense pleasure slams into me, his blood painting my tongue, as his rhythm grows erratic. It tastes like hot joy and I groan in fresh ecstasy. Zephyr's pleasure at my bite is bright and intoxicating. It coils around my insides and drenches me in bliss.

Instinct grips me as I come back from a realm of bliss, and lick at the wound on his shoulder, sealing it. A small part of my brain tells me I should feel sick over what I just did, but the beast in my middle is purring with delight. Each day I learn something new about my fae self, and it either creeps me out or fills me with wonder.

'Mine,' I whisper as I stare at the bite.

'Finally,' Zephyr whispers back.

The end of book 1.

SNEAK PREVIEW

COMING SOON

ARCHAIC RACES BOOK 2

PROLOGUE

My head breaks the surface, exposing me to air, and the next wave beaches me. It takes a moment to remember how to breathe this way, as I cough ocean from my lungs. Saltwater streams from my mouth and nose, body purging it with each inhale. Each breath is dizzying; the sensation of inhaling something so light unnerving.

I claw my way up the beach, not stopping until I reach dry sand. Grains scratch at my skin, feeling itchy and uncomfortable. I flop onto my back to stare up at the sky, sand moulding to my body like a lover. The moon is a skinny slice of white, allowing the stars to show their glory. They add to the dizzying sense of freedom.

Freedom.

My insides clench and I close my eyes, breathing briny air, as I summon the shift. Pain slices my insides so intense my spine arches from the sand. I suck in a breath and curl up on my side. It's been so long I forgot how agonising shifting is. I slump onto the sand when it's over, panting hard. Breathing air is getting easier, even though my body feels wrong now. I open my eyes and blink up at the stars. Nothing about this place feels *right*. If I was visiting it would be an adventure, but this isn't an excursion.

It's escape.

I sit up and look down at my legs. They're long and toned, the skin smooth and pale in the starlight. I wriggle my toes and cringe at the feel of sand between them. It coats my skin, sticking to my hair and the raw skin around my wrists. I prod at the mangled flesh, wondering if it will scar.

No more cuffs.

No more torture.

Freedom.

Coughing snaps my attention to the ocean and my heart skips a beat. Noami drags herself from the surf, shifting as she goes. She pushes to her feet, seeming unaffected by the shift, white hair sticking in wet ribbons to her caramel skin. She stumbles in my direction then looks down at the sand with distain, before fixing her turquoise gaze on me.

I push to my feet, legs unsteady. 'Why are you here?'

'To bring you home,' Noami answers.

'Then you've wasted a journey. I'm not going back.'

'Orcas demands your return,' she says and beckons me to her. 'Come, I will escort you.'

I finger the raised pattern on my nape at the mention of Orcas, my body forever marred by his obsession. Images of his torture play on repeat in my nightmares, and fear uncoils in my stomach.

I'm not going back.

I can't.

'I don't answer to Orcas,' I tell her, proud fear doesn't leak into my voice.

Somewhere during the endless abuse I became a coward, and I hate myself for it. Years of wearing a façade have paid off, though. I've become an expert at hiding pain and fear from those around me.

'You must return with me to safety,' Noami insists.

I snort, the sound a reminder of Navi and everything I'll miss. 'I'm safer amid rock and sun than I'll ever be with Orcas.'

'Your mind is sick,' Noami argues. 'You've imagined Orcas cruel in place of his devotion. But he can fix you, Anima. Return with me,' she orders.

I bare my teeth at the lie, fangs descending. Neon freckles shiver over my skin in a warning display and I snarl at Noami. She dares to issue orders to me, her lack of respect astounding, even if she buys into Orcas' lies.

'You risk addressing a Harbinger so informally? Disrespecting a Vessel invites the wrath of the Goddess,' I warn.

'You're sick-'

'I'm not sick, and won't return with you,' I snarl.

Noami's gaze hardens. 'Then I'll take you by force.'

I smirk to hide the panic at her threat, and pull a dagger from the harness banding my torso. Noami is a Meridian Warrior and a formidable force, but desperation infuses my anger. Death is more attractive than returning home to Orcas.

My eyes sting as they bleed from navy to silver. 'I *will* kill you, Noami.'

She huffs like I'm an inconvenience then runs at me. Noami dwarfs me by at least three feet and she's twice my weight. She's bred from warrior parents, her body flexing with muscle as she powers in my direction. I don't flinch from her advance, but my insides clench at what I must do. She's younger than me, and an asset to our race. She could have a magnificent future, if I wasn't about to take it from her.

I raise my right hand, power blasting from my palm. It hits Noami in the solar plexus and sends her flying backwards. She smacks onto the sand, sending a cloud of grains into the air. She's on her feet a second later, eyes burning turquoise with anger. Turquoise freckles flash over her skin in a display of agitation and I smirk.

'Using elementals will only save you for so long,' she hisses.

Her fangs have descended, another sign of her annoyance, and it pleases me to see I'm not the only one ruled by my emotions in this moment.

'I'm giving you a chance to save yourself, Noami.'

She laughs. 'You believe you can best me?'

'You forget what I am,' I remind her. 'You cannot win.'

Everyone forgets that I'm a Harbinger because I don't act like one. I've become a pretty, delicate thing they associate with Orcas, rather than a chosen Vessel of the Goddess. The lies Orcas spreads paint me as weak and I've done nothing to refute them. I've spent so long trying to hide the power I've been gifted, doing my best to bury it deep enough so Orcas can't find it, that I forget it's there.

'This is your last warning, Noami. Leave and I'll spare your life.'

Noami runs at me in response. I slide my dagger back into its harness and hold both hands out, palms facing Noami. Static fills the air and she slams into a wall of power, trapped in its thrall, unable to move beyond it. White hair writhes around her shoulders, caught in the static. I move forward, until I'm standing before her. Noami snarls, baring her fangs in a show of aggression. She pushes against the invisible wall then growls when she can't move through it.

'Release me!' she says – another order.

'Swear fealty to me and I will,' I tell her.

'You're mind is broken,' she snarls. 'I'll never swear fealty to you.'

I sigh. 'Then you've sealed your fate.'

I breathe deep and connect with the hidden well of energy in my centre. Power surges forward the moment I create a pathway for it, lighting the silver glyphs on my skin. They're always there, spelling out the purpose bestowed upon me by the Goddess.

'Harbinger,' Noami whispers, eyes wide. 'Life Blood.'

She meets my gaze and realisation creases her features. Panic flares in her turquoise eyes and she starts to struggle. I step through the wall of power, hair rising in midnight swirls around me, as I cup Noami's face in my hands.

'You chose this fate,' I remind her.

'No,' she growls.

The snick of metal registers a second before the pain. I look down to see Noami gripping the hilt of my blade, which is sticking at an odd angle from my side. A stupid mistake on my part, but I can't stop now.

'You think I don't know pain worse than this?' I say, even as the tang of blood paints my tongue.

Noami screams, as the power I harbour blasts from me into her. I feel it filling her, seeping into the corners of her being and infusing her essence. Turquoise swirls weave over her caramel skin, sketching the pathway of her life, as my power draws it from her. Noami's essence bleeds into mine, as life leaves her body and pours into me.

Then she's gone, her body nothing more than shimmering foam dispersing on the coastal breeze.

The glyphs on my skin fade, as I force the power back into the safe place in my centre. It's like cramming a whale through its own blowhole, and my insides feel stretched thin. I grip the hilt of the blade in my side and yank it free, snarling as I collapse onto the sand. Breathing gets difficult, so I shed my harness, abandoning it with the dagger. Blood gushes from my side in hot pulses, streaking my pale skin. I feel so weak in this form it scares me.

I scrub a tear from my face, disgusted with myself and push to my feet. I stagger across the sand, clutching my side, and search for shelter. Cars travel along the road that skirts the beach and I watch them pass, headlights luminous in the night. I've seen images of what to expect, but never imagined seeing them this close. I move to the cover of the rocks, hissing when my side starts burning, even though I know the sensation is a good thing. The burning means I'm healing, but I'm unsure how long it will take in this form.

I collapse on a patch of sand between the rocks, listening to the waves rolling onto the beach. It's a soothing sound, as my vision blurs and dims around the edges. The realisation that I'm losing consciousness is sluggish and I try to sit up, but my body feels weighted. I stare at the blurred slice of moon, wondering if this is my end, and finger the pendant around my neck. Perhaps a human will find it once my flesh has turned to foam, and think it a pretty trinket.

Pain lances my wound when I start laughing. Decades of torture and I'm dying by my own blade. Navi will be furious. My laughter fades and I clench my right hand around the pendant, thinking of the silvery scar in my palm. Navi will know through our connection that I'm dying. But we said our goodbyes. He promised he'd do anything for my freedom, and death is the ultimate escape.

Don't panic! Book 2 is almost finished and won't be too far behind. Keep going for a note from the author and places to find updates for the Archaic Races Series.

MORE BOOKS BY HANNAH WEST

FIND THEM ON AMAZON.

Siren (The Siren Series Book 1)

Siren Burn (The Siren Series Book 2)

Siren Fire (The Siren Series Book 3)

NOTE FROM THE AUTHOR

I really hope you enjoyed the start of my new series. It's different to the Siren Series, that's for sure, so I'm praying you'll like it.

There are more books in the Archaic Races Series and I'm aiming for no cliffhanger endings. But it depends on how sadistic I'm feeling at the time, so sorry in advance.

If you enjoyed Dark Starlight please take a minute to leave a review. Even if it's just to say you liked it. I love to hear from my readers, so come find me in the places below to let me know what you think.

WHERE TO FIND ME:

www.hannahwestauthor.net
https://twitter.com/Hannah_E_West
www.facebook.com/HannahWestAuthor/
www.Goodreads.com

40773253R00166

Printed in Poland
by Amazon Fulfillment
Poland Sp. z o.o., Wrocław